ELECTRIC
COUNTRY
ROULETTE

ALSO BY W. L. RIPLEY

Dreamsicle
Storme Front

ELECTRIC
COUNTRY
ROULETTE

W. L. RIPLEY

Henry Holt and Company
New York

Henry Holt and Company, Inc.
Publishers since 1866
115 West 18th Street
New York, New York 10011

Henry Holt® is a registered
trademark of Henry Holt and Company, Inc.

Published in Canada by Fitzhenry & Whiteside Ltd.,
195 Allstate Parkway, Markham, Ontario L3R 4T8.

Library of Congress Cataloging-in-Publication Data
Ripley, W. L. (Warren L.)
Electric country roulette / W. L. Ripley.—1st ed.
          p.   cm.
          I. Title.
PS3568.I64E43   1996   96-7310
813'.54—dc20   CIP

ISBN 0-8050-3792-6

Henry Holt books are available for special promotions
and premiums. For details contact: Director, Special Markets.

First Edition—1996

Designed by Betty Lew

Printed in the United States of America
All first editions are printed on acid-free paper.

1   3   5   7   9   10   8   6   4   2

For Marvin and Bill. They loved
corny jokes and Sunday afternoons.
And, they left us too soon.

ACKNOWLEDGMENTS

The idea for the setting of *Electric Country Roulette* came from conversations with Jim Purifoy and Gerald Jenkins who are as good as there is at what they do.

Thanks to Robynn and Mason who proofed the copy and who have provided years of enjoyment (and moments of vexation which they blame on genetics) for their mother and myself.

Also, thanks to Ray and Ben for believing in Wyatt Storme.

ELECTRIC
COUNTRY
ROULETTE

"One does not sell the earth upon which the people walk."

—*Crazy Horse*

PROLOGUE

I was minding my own business when they came in. Minding my own business is what I'm best at since I don't get out much. When I do, I'm often reminded why I don't.

There were three of them. A trio of postteenage mutant reptiles with loud voices, earrings in weird orifices, and the herd mentality of the MTV generation. The last thing I needed on a quiet morning in October.

I was in Frank's Trading Post, a combination grocery/hardware/sporting goods store, buying supplies—coffee, sugar, .30-30 shells, and a box of Macanudo cigars Frank had ordered for me. Frank's prices were high, but he wasn't Wal-Mart, which was a plus, and he kept fresh coffee beans on hand. In the rear was a little café where you could drink black coffee from stoneware mugs and sit at round wooden tables, scarred and nicked from use, while you listened to the farmers and retired schoolteachers discuss deer hunting, the weather, or playfully harass each other. It was a slice of Americana that was disappearing like the fading photograph of an old friend.

The Camaro squealed into the parking lot, vibrating with the bass of its overpowered stereo, skidded to a halt, and spat them out onto the concrete. They swaggered toward the store as if conquering new territory for the socially retarded. One of them tossed a beer bottle, which missed the trash barrel and broke into jagged brown shards on the pavement.

The only people in the place besides myself were Frank's cashier, Mrs. Campbell, a seventy-five-year-old widow; a retired couple buying milk and bread; and a pair of farmers drinking coffee in the café. Frank was in his office in the back room.

They brushed by the retired couple in one of the narrow aisles. "You getting any of that, old dude?" one of them asked. The old couple tried to shrink in upon themselves, conspicuous in their discomfort.

Let it go, Storme.

One of the group, a blond manchild with a fuzz-smudged chin and upper lip, grabbed a bag of potato chips from a rack and tossed it like a football to one of his friends, who swatted the bag with double fists as if hitting a fastball back through the box.

"Whoa, man," said the chip basher, a kid wearing a Nirvana T-shirt under his too-large flannel shirt. "We entered a fucking time warp. Like, it's an Alzheimer's convention." I saw Mrs. Campbell flinch at the *f*-word. I picked up the bag of chips they had left on the floor.

"Hey, Grandma," yelled one of the trio, a tall, slender man with shoulder-length hair and a long, hooked nose. "You got any smokes?"

"Yes," said Mrs. Campbell. Her mouth worked involuntarily.

"Got any beer?" asked the blond kid.

"We don't sell to minors."

The two coffee drinkers in the back kept their heads down, studiously avoiding the interruption. I walked to the counter with my purchases and the bag of chips. I put my purchases on the counter.

"Got any crack?" asked the tallest one.

Patience, Storme. They'll be gone in a few minutes.

"Yeah," said Blondie. "Got any crack? Besides the one in your butt?" He and his buddies chuckled like mental patients. Mrs. Campbell reddened.

Oh, well.

I turned and faced them.

"That's enough," I said.

Nirvana looked at me, his mouth turned down in a sneer. "Who're you, man?"

"I'm a member of the militant wing of the Emily Post Foundation."

"The who?"

"Hey," said the tall one. "What're you looking at, man?"

"Not much," I said.

"What'd he say, Parrot?" asked Blondie, yelling from another aisle.

"Modulate your voices," I said.

"Whad you say, man? Do what?" said Nirvana.

"Your voices," I said. "They're too loud. It's impolite. These people don't like it." I looked at each of them. "I don't like it."

"Hey check this out. We're pissing this guy off." He looked at me. "Tough shit, man."

I took a step toward him and said, "Another thing. I don't like the bad language, so I'm going to ask you to knock it off. Also"—I tossed the potato chips up on the counter—"you pay for these."

They looked at each other. It wasn't what they had expected.

Nirvana T-shirt said, "What if we don't?" There was a sneer in his voice, and one corner of his mouth turned up, baring bad teeth.

"I haven't decided," I said.

"This is bullshit, man," he said, stepping closer. "There's three of us and we're not paying for shit, man, so don't—"

I interrupted him by grabbing his T-shirt and with a hard jerk—like a magician pulling the tablecloth from under the table setting—tore it away from his body, revealing his bony white chest. It made that ripping sound only torn cloth makes. He staggered back like a drunk and looked down at his torso, mouth open.

"Guess we'll just have to work out a trade, then," I said. The ruined shirt hung from my hand like a tattered flag. "Now we're even."

He looked at me, wide-eyed, disbelieving. "That ain't right, man. You can't—"

"Sure I can. I did." I moved closer, inside his comfort zone. I felt something click behind my eyes, and there was a distant red roaring in my ears. "And that's just the start if you don't leave."

"There's three of us," said Parrot, without much conviction.

I shook my head slowly. "Won't be enough."

They looked at each other. Each not wanting to appear scared but scared nonetheless. They had been counting on intimidation. It had worked so many times before. Nobody said anything. Their moment had passed.

"Say good night, kids," I said.

They mumbled under their breath as they left, trying to slam the door as they did, but the pneumatic shock absorber held it up. They left the lot in a squeal of rubber.

Frank had come in from the back. "What's going on here?" He looked at the torn T-shirt in my hand. "What's that?"

"We were playing capture the flag," I said. "Our side won."

"Doing what?" Frank asked. He looked out the window at the departing Camaro. "You running off customers, Storme?"

"Trying to."

He looked away from the window and walked back to his office. "Good," he said.

After paying for my purchases I drove the eleven miles back to my cabin, the last mile of which was uphill and narrow and rocky. I put away the groceries, started a pot of coffee, turned on the stereo, and the Allman Brothers Band started singing "Please Call Home."

The phone rang. An unusual occurrence since only about a half-dozen people knew the number.

It was a long-distance call from my long-distance love, Sandy Collingsworth.

A call that would change my whole day.

1

Few things frighten Sandy Collingsworth.

She is a strong, confident person and had taken on difficult things before, rising from anchorperson of Denver's top-rated news program to her present dual occupation as a staff writer and the host of a weekly segment of the *Today* show, rising above petty jealousies and bitter infighting that was part of that world.

This time she'd gotten hold of something dark and savage; something outside the realm of her experience. The fact she'd called upon me proved that. Not that I hadn't helped her out before. That wasn't it.

There are only three things I'm really good at. I can catch a football, a talent for which there is little market at my age, and I love Sandy Collingsworth like no one else can. She didn't need me to run a flag pattern, and my love was constant.

Her need was for the third talent, a talent she would rather not see utilized. But it was the third one she was interested in this time.

It takes a lot to get me out of my Missouri retreat, a log cabin built back in the thick woods of the Missouri Ozarks. Even more to get me back into the city. I don't have much use for society and even less for civilization in the nineties. But this was Sandy, and I was willing to endure it for her. And only for her.

"Where are you staying?" I said into the phone. She told me the Best Western in North Branson, Missouri. She wanted to know how soon I could be there.

"Three hours," I said.

"That will be fine," she said.

"Do you have the gun I gave you?" I asked.

"Yes."

"How is the girl doing?"

"She's frightened."

"Who does she say did it?"

"Travis Conrad."

I whistled. "Have you called the police?"

"This is the new Nashville, and they are protective of their local treasures. Besides, date rape is an elusive thing. I believe her. Their spin is she asked for it. Just another snuff queen."

"Nobody asks for that. At least nobody asks me."

"This isn't funny, Wyatt."

"Sorry. I'll be there. Soon as I hang up."

"Wyatt?"

"Yeah."

"One more thing. Could you call Chick and have him come, too?"

"Yeah. I can do that."

"I love you, Wyatt."

I admitted to loving her also and hung up. Then I dialed Chick Easton in Colorado. He answered on the third ring.

"Live and in color, this is Chick Easton."

"This is Storme. Sandy's got trouble in a place called North Branson, Missouri. You ever hear of it?"

"Fastest-growing community in America? A spur of Branson,

the new Nashville? Roy Clark, Andy Williams, Glen Campbell, Bobby Vinton, Silver Dollar City, two-mile-an-hour traffic, and the highest property values in the Midwest?"

"That's it."

"I vaguely remember it being mentioned somewhere."

"How soon can you be here?"

"I'll call you back," said Chick. He broke the connection. Five minutes later my phone rang.

"I'll be there this evening. I arrive at Springfield airport, flight 351, at 7:07 P.M. Can you fix me up with what I need? Won't be able to bring it through the metal detectors."

"I'll have it," I said.

"What kind of trouble does Sandy have?"

"She was doing a piece about North Branson when she met a coed who said she was picked up by Travis Conrad and they had sex. But she tried to tell him no. It was a date rape thing."

"Travis Conrad? You mean the guy sings "The Lies in Her Eyes?" The by-God CMA country singer of the year?"

"That's the guy," I said.

Chick whistled lowly.

I said, "When the girl went to the locals they weren't interested, so she told Sandy. Sandy asked the police why there was no follow-up, and they stonewalled her. Then Sandy was stopped for failing to indicate a lane change, and her car was searched. She says while one cop was talking to her, the other took a videotape from her vehicle. When she reported it, she was told no tape was removed from her car. The police explained the search by claiming her car matched the description of a car that had been stolen. Now she's getting threatening phone calls and is being followed. She thinks the police are watching her room."

"We can certainly put a stop to that. Be there soon as I find my cape and bodysuit." He hung up. I threw some clothes into a duffel bag and loaded up the items Chick requested, left the cabin, bounded down the dusty back roads until I hit concrete, and headed for North Branson.

When I exited State Highway 65, I saw the sign saying, WELCOME TO NORTH BRANSON—BIRTHPLACE OF MISSOURI LIEUTENANT GOVERNOR JUSTIN YORK. I hadn't voted for him, which was no big deal. I hadn't voted for anybody else either. The city-limits sign listed the population at 15,796. Of course, that didn't count the millions of tourists who passed through each year.

Twenty years ago North Branson had been two bait shops, a gas station, and an "Authentic Ozark Souvenir Shop," but while the Branson–Table Rock area grew rapidly, North Branson had burst forth like a ripening melon, growing at a velocity even greater than that of its big sister. Nestled in the Ozark Mountains between Table Rock and Taneycomo Lakes south of Springfield, the two Bransons boasted nightclubs to rival anything in Las Vegas and a real estate boom unprecedented in Missouri history. Local realtors boasted that if you laid a thousand-dollar bill on the ground, it wouldn't pay for the area it covered.

America had found a new paradise to pave over. Which was fine. Let them move around all they want from one concrete playground to another. Just stay off my mountain.

In the backseat of my Bronco was a Browning Hi-Power nine-millimeter pistol, a Smith & Wesson Chief's Special .38, and a Remington pump shotgun. Also a Walther PPK I'd removed from the condominium of a dead drug dealer last year. The dealer didn't have any use for it anymore, and Chick preferred a gun with a compact frame and had expressed an interest in buying the Walther from me. I wouldn't sell it but might give it to him. The drug dealer had removed the serial numbers.

I arrived at the Best Western Executive Center and asked for Sandra Collingsworth's room number. The desk clerk wouldn't give me the number but rang her room for me. She wasn't there. "We're very sorry, sir. Would you care to wait?"

Where would she be? I thought. It wasn't like her. I decided to wait. I sat on the lobby's pit furniture and read a tourist pamphlet on the wonder and attraction of North Branson, Missouri—only five minutes from the Branson strip. Less traffic, more fun. It was the kind of place you brought Aunt Martha and the kids. Or even your girlfriend.

Originally named Stoney Ridge, the town changed its name to Enterprise in 1864 after the Battle of Taylor Heights, when a family of slaves was liberated from the Confederate encampment. The name was changed again in the 1970s to take advantage of the growing popularity of its big sister. North Branson was the home of the North Branson High School Patriots 1985 State 3A basketball champions and Table Rock Methodist College, the 1988 NCAA Division II National Football runner-up. There was a winery listed as a Missouri Historical Landmark, as well as a distillery that produced Judge's Choice, a limited distribution whiskey. Both advertised tours and tastings. I made a mental note to steer Chick clear of these places.

I was reading about Table Rock Methodist College when two uniformed police officers entered the lobby, walked to the desk, and asked for Sandra Collingsworth. The clerk said she wasn't in and indicated that the gentleman sitting "over there," meaning me, had also asked about Miss Collingsworth. Such indiscretion. Bet this wouldn't happen at the Hyatt.

The two uniforms turned their attention to me. They walked over to where I sat soaking up comfort and local propaganda and stood in front of me. They were both wearing Glock autos and, oddly, sheathed nunchakus, the kind Bruce Lee whipped around. The older of the pair—his name tag said BREDWELL—was a dark-haired man with a heavy five o'clock shadow and thick eyebrows. He asked if I knew Miss Collingsworth.

I looked at him and nodded. Inscrutable. Enigmatic.

"What is your business with Miss Collingsworth?" he asked, trying another tack.

I looked at him some more. The mysterious stranger. How could he know I knew the secret of Judge's Choice whiskey or that T.R.M.C. had finished second in 1988? He was to be pitied.

"Sir," he said, with a little more force, "I asked what your business with Miss Collingsworth was."

"None of yours."

He knitted the thick brows and gave me a practiced cop glare. I was ticking him off. "Usually," said the cop, controlling himself, "when a police officer asks a reasonable question, he gets a civil answer."

"You asked what my business was with Miss Collingsworth. Without preamble. I don't know you, you don't know me. That seems to fit more into the realm of presumption or prying than reasonable."

He hooked a thumb in his belt and rested a forearm on the butt of his gun. "What's your name?"

"Benjamin Franklin."

"Do you have any identification?"

"There's a pretty good likeness of me on the hundred-dollar bill."

"Sir," said the officer, "I've had about enough of your surly attitude. Now, I'm going to ask that you produce some identification. Right now."

I shook my head. "Don't believe I will."

"You're getting yourself in trouble here."

"You know better," I said. "You have no probable cause. Without that, this is just a roust. And not even a very good one. Why?"

"Are you a friend of Miss Collingsworth's?"

"Maybe."

"She is butting in where she's not wanted."

I nodded.

"She's hardheaded."

I nodded again.

"We've asked her to share information with us, but she refuses to cooperate."

"Sounds like her. What information? Has there been a crime committed?"

The policeman chewed the corner of his lower lip. He had said more than he wanted and knew it. He looked at his partner and nodded in the direction of the exit. His partner walked in that direction, and Bredwell said, "You enjoy yourself, Mister. Don't stay long, and be sure to drive safely and observe the speed limit." They left.

First day in town and already making friends. Good to know I hadn't lost the knack.

2

Ten minutes after the policemen left, the phone rang and the desk clerk asked if I was Wyatt Storme. I confessed I was, and he indicated the call was for me. It was Sandy.

"Where are you?" I asked.

"The Holiday Inn. I changed motels. They're watching the Best Western."

"I know. I met the Welcome Wagon." The desk clerk was hovering nearby. I looked at him. His face flushed, and he backed away. "They don't like you much. Said you were stubborn."

"Which you agreed with?"

I smiled. "I told them just give you a good smack, and you'd straighten right up. What do you want me to do?"

"Get the rest of my things out of my room." She gave me a list. I turned to the clerk and said, "Miss Collingsworth is checking out. I'll need her room key and her bill, please."

"I'm afraid I can't do that."

Speaking to Sandy again, I said, "He says he can't do that."

"Put him on the phone," she said.

I held the phone out to him and said, "She wants to talk to you."

"Hello, this is Marvin Fieldmeyer . . . yes, of course, Miss Collingsworth . . . yes. . . . But this is highly irregular. You will have to come in personally and . . . well, yes, I did tell the police what room you . . . I didn't see the harm. . . . There is no need for that tone of voice, Miss—" He let out a sigh of resignation. I gave him a sympathetic male smile. He thumbed through an up-right file and pulled up an invoice.

"Here it is," he said into the phone. "Yes, ma'am. I'll give him the key. Yes, ma'am. Thank you for staying at—" He took the phone from his ear and looked at me with surprise on his face. "She hung up."

He handed me the key. "Women are inexplicable," I said.

Thirty minutes later, after making sure I wasn't followed, I was in the lobby of the North Branson Holiday Inn. I gave my name to the desk clerk, and he directed me to Sandy's room.

I knocked on the door, and Sandy asked who it was.

"It's me," I said. "Charles Manson."

"Good," she said, opening the door. "Just as long as it isn't some washed-up football player." She stood in the door, and I looked at her. Same golden hair. Same perpetual tan and snow-white teeth. Same faint sprinkle of freckles across the small nose. "Thanks for coming, Wyatt."

She pulled me into her room by my jacket and kissed me, long and hard, her tiny mouth opening. Her perfume swirled around my head, then into my head. I kicked the door shut, and half pulling each other we fell onto the large bed. I pulled her close and felt her body, lithe and taut and warm, against mine. As always, the closeness of her, the lightness of her being, relaxed and comforted me. Goethe says we are shaped and fashioned by what we love. The shape of my love for Sandy Collingsworth is round and smooth and complete. It is a necessity, not a chosen luxury, though it carries with it the weight and wonder of luxury.

Let me die here, Lord, if it doesn't matter where.

After I unpacked, we drove to the airport to pick up Chick. Sandy explained more of what was transpiring in North Branson. The girl's name was Francine Wilson. "She said she'd had an argument with a boyfriend," Sandy said, "and he made her get out of the car downtown. As she was walking back to the dorm, she accepted a ride from a man who turned out to be a member of Travis Conrad's entourage. He was nice to her, she said, then he asked if she'd like to meet the great man, in person. She's young and a fan, so she accepted the offer, and he took her to his club to meet him. She was impressed even though he was drunk. He took her back to his office and offered her a line of coke. She declined the offer but allowed him to kiss her a few times. Then he asked if she wanted to go back to his place and spend the night. At this point she was getting nervous. She wanted to leave. Then he forced himself on her."

"Still, she willingly went into his club and office," I said, getting a nasty glare in return. "I'm not excusing it, but that's the angle the cops are taking. That correct?"

She nodded. "She's only nineteen. A beautiful young girl, Wyatt. She's bright and has a lot going for her, and now her life's been turned upside down. She couldn't stop him. It isn't right."

"I don't know what we can do about it, though."

"That's not all," Sandy said. "The other night an off-duty policeman tried to put the move on her. When she refused, he threatened her with a soliciting charge and jail. She was given a song and dance about how this would look after the incident with Conrad, and perhaps she would be kicked out of school, and what would her father think if he found out? She was able to get away from the cop, but now the incident with Conrad is killing her inside. She's afraid to say anything because of her parents and because she's ashamed."

"She know the cop's name?"

"No. But she's seen him around."

"Anything else?"

"I talked with a working girl named Chastity. A call girl. She was picked up the night Francine had her problem with the cop. I think it may be the same cop. She admits that she was soliciting when she was picked up. She gave a freebie to the cop to get out of the arrest. She won't give me his name, either."

"Scared?"

"Terrified. She says you don't mess with this guy. Says he has too much juice. Says a year ago he beat up a friend of hers for refusing him, then raped her anyway."

"Sounds like a nice guy."

"Mr. Wonderful. Wyatt, it makes me angry that they're getting away with this. I want to expose these creeps. I want this cop and Travis Conrad." Her cheeks were flushed, and her breathing was agitated. "You know I'm not the type who thinks every time a man makes advances or shows interest that it is some sort of rape scenario. But this . . . this is repugnant. I want them to burn."

"You say they're threatening you. With what?"

"With arrest. With litigation. And I received a phone call, just before I called you." She looked down at her hands. "It frightened me. Threatened me with the same thing that happened to the two girls. He was graphic."

"The same thing? Is that what he said?" She nodded. "What did he sound like? Did you recognize the voice?"

"No. I think he was disguising it. It was all . . . guttural."

"But he knew about the two girls?"

"Yes."

"Had you told anyone about them?"

"No. But I've been seen with the girls, and they know I'm asking around."

My heart sank a little with the realization that Sandy had kicked over a rock and uncovered something slimy. "You realize the caller is either the cop or—"

"Or it's Travis Conrad. Yes. I've thought about that."

It was quiet for a few minutes while I pondered the situation. I didn't want her in this, but she would pursue it regardless. As if reading my mind, she said, "You think I shouldn't be involved in this?"

"Didn't say that."

"But you're thinking it."

"Yes."

"Too dangerous for a woman?"

"Dangerous for anyone." I kept my eyes on the road. I could feel the force of her eyes on the side of my neck.

"What could a man do that I can't?"

"He wouldn't get raped."

"That's not fair."

"No. But it's relevant."

"I can shoot a gun almost as well as you."

"As well, in fact. But you've never shot anyone."

"There's something to be proud of."

"It's a matter of experience and will, not pride. I don't want to argue with you, Sandy. You're intelligent and resourceful and have great inner courage. Courage isn't enough. This could explode into something bigger than you're ready for. You're not Hulk Hogan."

"Size isn't everything," she said.

"Sometimes it is the deciding factor. Female platitudes and stubborness won't be much help if these guys get hold of you."

"You're not so tough," she said, playing with me now.

"Two yards and a quarter foot of angle iron. I don't bend, and I don't break."

She smiled. "I won't back off from this."

"I know. I wish you would, but know you won't. And wishing it won't make it so. I'll have to settle for backing your play and hoping I'm there in time."

"You always are," she said. "I know it's hard for you, Wyatt. I appreciate having you here. You still love me?"

"Only more than anything," I said. But love would stop no bullets.

The sky looked like rain when I parked Sandy's rented Taurus on the parking area of Springfield Regional Airport. It was a small facility that no longer attracted much large commercial traffic. Chick had to fly from Denver to Tulsa, then hop over to Springfield.

As we started to get out of the car it began to rain. Sandy said, "If this were Kansas City or Denver, we could've parked underground and walked into the terminal without having to go outside."

"You mean you can park under tons of cement and walk inside a concrete cave through an air-conditioned hallway and never have to risk breathing fresh air? Boy-howdy. What'll they think of next?"

She frowned and shook her head. "All the men in the world, and I get Jeremiah Johnson."

"You're right," I said, being agreeable. "You are in heaven."

We walked across the parking lot, into the terminal building, and made our way to gate 36. It was 7:00. At 7:05 Chick Easton walked into the building. An unlit cigarette dangled from his lips. He was wearing a blue poplin L.L. Bean travel blazer over a white-collared rugby shirt, with jeans and the usual smile as if inwardly amused at life. He walked with the self-assured gait of a man who had grown into himself.

"Chick Easton, bodyguard extraordinary, no job too tough, no fee too high," he said. Sandy hugged him, and I thanked him for coming on short notice. He stopped at the terminal bar and bought a bottle of Heineken, then with the other pilgrims we stood around the baggage belt so we could worship the luggage as it swept by.

Within an hour of retrieving Chick's luggage we were on the outskirts of North Branson. En route Sandy and I explained the situation to Chick. He listened without interrupting.

"So where do we start?" he asked.

"Probably talk to the girls again," I said. "Sandy says the coed will be reluctant to talk to us. Afraid the episode will get back to her parents. The hooker might be more help, if she feels like talking. Mostly, Sandy needs us to clear a path for her so she can finish her story."

"Or at least get it started," Sandy said. "The police took what I had videotaped, so I may have to backtrack. So far, what I have I can't print without leaving the company open to litigation. I need something with teeth in it."

"So that's the situation," I said. A strange reflection struck the rearview mirror. I looked into the mirror and saw the police unit just as Chick said, "Looks like we got company."

"Yeah." I pulled the Taurus to the side of the road, and the cop car pulled in behind, blue lights twirling. Uniformed officers got out of either side of the vehicle. One stayed near the police car, while the other one walked toward us. I recognized them. "I know these guys. They're the cops I met at the Best Western."

"What a coincidence," Sandy said.

In the rearview I could see Chick smiling. He said, "Try not to get us thrown in jail, Storme. Be cooperative. Cheerful."

Officer Bredwell looked in at Chick before he stepped up to my window. Then, with a big smile to let me know he would soon have my identification, after all, he said, "May I have your operator's license, sir."

I already had it out and handed it to him.

"Wyatt Storme?" he said. "The football player?"

"Not anymore," I said.

"Why'd you quit playing so suddenlike?"

"Wanted to pursue my dream of becoming a traffic cop."

The phony smile left Bredwell's face. "The reason I stopped you, Mr. Storme, is that a car matching this description was on our hot sheet. Stolen."

"Did it have a rental sticker on it, too?" Chick asked from the back seat.

"This is the second time," said Sandy. "For the same lame reason."

Bredwell leaned his face into my window to get a better look at

Chick. Spotting the green beer bottle, he said, "We have an open container law in this city."

"Is it an empty open container law?" Chick asked, holding the bottle upside down.

"Who are you?"

Chick told him.

"May I see some identification, please?"

"You think I'd make up a name like that?"

"Step out of the car, sir."

"What is all this about?" asked Sandy.

"Just doing my job, ma'am," said Bredwell. "Now, if all of you would please step outside your vehicle."

"This is ridiculous," said Sandy.

"Let it go, Sandy," I said. While we stood outside the car, Bredwell searched the car while his partner kept an eye on us in case we decided to make a break for it. Cars hissed past us. The passengers looked at us. Chick waved at a few of them.

"Cut that out," said the other officer. Officer Pethmore by his name tag. His face and arms were covered with pale, pink freckles, and he spoke with a heavy southwest Missouri accent. "What do you think you're doing?"

"Sign language," Chick said. "I'm signaling them to get help."

"Well, knock it off."

"He's onto us," Chick said to me.

After fifteen minutes of feckless searching of the Taurus, Bredwell allowed us to return to the car. "I apologize for the inconvenience," he said facetiously. "A lot of drug dealers rent cars to transport drugs. It's an epidemic. Sure do hope you people understand." With that he returned to his unit, got inside, and pulled back onto the highway.

"Can you believe this?" said Sandy.

"Miss Collingsworth," said Chick, "I believe you have pissed these people off."

3

We rented a block of rooms at the motel whereby Chick and I would be on either side of Sandy. My room was connected to Sandy's by a suite door.

Chick was pleased with the Walther and the Smith & Wesson .38 I'd brought him. I kept the shotgun in the Bronco. "You can keep the Walther," I said. "Payment for riding to the rescue."

"Almost like real employment," he said. "You actually paying something in return."

The next afternoon Sandy left to drive to Springfield to make an appearance at the local affiliate, which carried her weekly broadcast news show, *Morning Coffee Break*. Chick and I went uptown to see if we could shake anything loose. Sandy had given us some leads such as the names of possible places we might find the girls.

We drove up the tree-lined avenues to the campus of Table Rock Methodist College. Like North Branson, it was shiny and new. We drove to Halsey-Cotes dormitory and parked in the visitors' lot, which was delightfully littered with gold and orange maple leaves shaken loose by the gentle autumn breeze.

Sweatered coeds with washed faces, books in arms, walked past us as we entered Halsey-Cotes. The sense of being an alien was pronounced. We didn't know the codes or the rhythms. We were very much the intruders here—chronological trespassers who smelled of aftershave and experience. The spark of campus life is bright and painfully brief, and once its moment passes it cannot be rekindled.

The young female student working the desk gave us a once-over when we asked about Francine. We were adult males and not to be immediately trusted. I told her that we were there on behalf of Sandra Collingsworth, and her disposition brightened.

"You mean the lady on television?" she asked. "The one on *Morning Coffee Break?*" I nodded. "Oh, I love her. She's so beautiful. And intelligent. Just last week she was interviewing one of the president's advisers—what is his name? Anyway, she cornered him on the president's . . . what'd she call it? Oh yeah. She cornered him on the president's 'elusive' position on foreign policy, and he was sweating it." Her expression changed, and she asked, "Do you work for Mrs. Collingsworth?"

"Yes," I said, wishing to avoid the prolonged explanation if I said no. "And she's not married."

"Yet," said Chick. "But she's engaged."

"To who?" the desk girl asked, leaning forward.

"To some semiliterate ex-jock who used to play for the Dallas Cowboys," said Chick, enjoying himself. I said nothing.

"A football player?" said the girl, as if it were distasteful to think it. "What's his name?"

Chick told her.

Her face bunched in thought, she said, "I don't think I've heard of him."

"Few people have," I said. I tried to put her back on track. "Francine Wilson?"

"Oh yeah," said the girl. "I'll call her." I watched her punch 312. Probably Francine's room number. After several seconds had passed, the girl put the phone back on the hook and said, "She's not in her room."

"Could you leave her a note to call Miss Collingsworth?" I said. I gave her the Holiday Inn number and Sandy's room number.

As we turned to leave, the desk girl asked, "Who will I say you are? What's your name?"

"Wyatt Storme."

She started to write, then looked up and said, "Hey, you're the guy who's engaged to Sandy Collingsworth."

We made the descent down the hill from the manicured grounds of Table Rock Methodist College to the hard streets of the North Branson strip—a river of neon and wood and pastel stucco buildings. North Branson's traffic was a crawl during this time of day, though it was nearing the end of the tourist season. Soon, with weekends the exception, North Branson's people would reclaim it. But only briefly and only during the winter months.

We pulled into the freshly surfaced parking lot of Travis Conrad's Hickory Wind Nightclub and walked inside. The Hickory Wind had a dance floor and bandstand and was also set up for a disc jockey to spin CDs and roll tapes. The days of the live band were over in most places, replaced by programmers with smoke machines and a wide selection of prerecorded music. The fact that live music was still king in the Branson area was part of its charm, a charm I couldn't deny.

The afternoon study group was there—a handful of college students drinking draft beer, which they poured from frosty glass pitchers emblazoned with beer manufacturer's names—as well as some late season tourist types wearing Ripley's Believe It or Not! sweatshirts and carrying Silver Dollar City tote bags, their shirt collars open, their bellies spilling over "relaxed-fit" jeans.

There was a wraparound bar in the middle of the room. The bartender was in his mid-twenties with bored eyes, droopy mustache, and wearing a rugby shirt. He was sluggishly wiping the mahogany bar with a white tea towel. Chick and I sat down on two stools. The bartender sauntered over and set two cardboard Budweiser coasters in front of us and asked, "What'll you have?"

"We're looking for a girl named Chastity," I said. "Working girl? Heard she comes in here. You know her?"

He considered us from under fleshy eyelids. Pursed his lips, said nothing.

"We're not the heat," Chick said. "We just want to know where we can find Chastity. God, what a name. We're not looking for a massage either. You know the girl?"

"You guys drinking?" the man asked. "It's a cash business, you know?"

"Give me a Jack Daniel's, neat, and two bottles of Budweiser. Bottles, not cans."

The bartender nodded and with an economy of movement filled our orders. He placed a shot glass in front of Chick and filled it with bourbon and pulled two long-necked Budweisers from a cooler under the bar. He set one of them in front of me. I looked at it.

"Eight fifty," he said, his palms on the bar top.

I laid a twenty on the counter and told him it was his to keep if he answered a few questions.

"How about another twenty on top of it?"

"I'm trying to save myself some time, not send you to college. You know her or not?"

He thought a moment, then palmed the twenty. "Yeah, I know her. She hangs out here some. Usually later, though. Sleeps during the day. Doesn't live here, you know."

"She hustle?"

He shrugged. "Hey, I don't care what she does. She pays her bill."

"Didn't ask that. I asked if she does business here. I'm not interested in what you allow or how she pays the rent. I just want to know who she does business with."

"What do you want to know for?"

"Naturally inquisitive, I guess. Besides, you took the money."

He acknowledged that by nodding his head slowly. "You guys aren't dressed like cops. Not any I've seen, anyway. You look like an Eddie Bauer catalog."

"We've been looking for one of those great cowboy hats with the feathers in them," said Chick.

"Anyway, the girl, Chastity, she comes in about two, three nights a week. Got a messed-up ear, keeps it covered with her hair, but a good-looking bitch. Clean, too. Orders gin and cherry cola—there's a nasty drink for you—smokes cigarettes, dances with some of the customers. I see her leave with some of them."

"Does she leave and come back?"

"Sometimes. Yeah."

Chick said, "Old Travis Conrad sure is an understanding superstar. He know about it?"

"I don't know what he knows," said the bartender.

"You ever get any police in here on their off-hours? Maybe they come by for a drink or to pick up girls?"

"Sure. Some of the younger guys."

"Any of them ever pick up Chastity?"

"Why you want to know that?"

"They pick her up or not?"

"I don't know. Can't remember. Doubt it, though."

"Why do you doubt it?" I asked.

"Cop would be shit in this town if he picked up a girl like Chastity. We may have a lot of celebrities, but this is still southern Missouri. He'd have to move out, he did that."

"But they know who she is and what she does?"

"Probably. They're cops, aren't they? They gotta know, I figure."

"They ever arrest her?"

"They never busted her in this place." He looked up. A student at a table was gesturing with an empty pitcher. The bartender filled a new one from a tapper and said, "Back in a minute."

After the bartender left with the pitcher, Chick said, "The cops know about her, they know she frequents this place, but they've never busted her for hooking?" He grinned. "Now that's what I call progressive police work. Kinda makes me want to move here and get my own string of girls."

"In a town where the cops know better than to dance with her for fear of losing their jobs," I said.

"Maybe they're too busy rousting visiting media personalities to mess with vice," Chick said. "Or?"

"Or maybe they're giving her a pass for some reason. Like the fact the place is owned by Travis Conrad."

The bartender returned. I asked, "Did Chastity have any regular customers?"

He leaned back and looked at me.

I rephrased the question. "Does she have any friends who dance with her regularly?"

"Not really. The college kids love her. About a different one every night. I heard she's been at a couple of frat parties. Does some dancing at them. Some striptease stuff. Wouldn't mind seeing her myself."

"She ever get any calls here?"

"A few times, yeah."

"Same person?"

"Most of the time it's the same guy."

" 'Most of the time' meaning what?"

He thought about it for a moment, then said, "Once she got a call here wasn't from the guy who usually calls. When I asked who I should say's calling, he told me to 'just put her on the phone.' Like that. Real pissed off–like. Usually it's a guy named Robby Blue who calls. Calls himself her agent. He's an asshole."

I thanked him for the information and put down an additional five for his cooperation.

"What's your name?" I asked.

"Bob."

"You think of anything else, let us know."

Bob shrugged in response. "Aren't you going to drink your beer?" he asked me. "You haven't touched it."

"Never said it was mine," I said.

Chick picked it up. "Needed one for takeout," he said.

"Not supposed to leave with an open bottle," protested the bartender. "It's against the law."

Chick smiled. "Be all right. A police force that overlooks prostitution's not likely to bust me for walking out with a beer. Besides, I'm a famous country singer in my own right. At least I would've been if my high school music teacher had been on the ball."

We returned to the motel and I called Francine Wilson's dorm, but she still wasn't in. Sandy hadn't returned. I waited an hour and tried to call Francine again. Wasn't there. I ordered coffee and a sandwich from room service. Turned on the television. No messages in the sandwich, no clues on the television. Curious. The phone rang, and I picked it up. It was Sandy. I reported. Told her I was unable to make connections with either Chastity or Francine Wilson.

Sandy's voice was agitated.

Francine Wilson was dead.

4

Francine Wilson had died accidentally—or committed suicide. That was the police's preliminary assessment. Sandy picked up the information on the newsroom scanner at the Springfield television station. She had come in as a Jane Doe, but Sandy was worried when she heard she was a Table Rock student and hurried back to North Branson. She drove to the police station, and, since no one had identified the body, Sandy did it herself.

"I called you first thing after identifying the—" She stopped herself, then continued, "After identifying Francine."

"Why do the police think accident or suicide?"

"No marks on the body."

"Did you see the body?" I asked.

"No. Just her face. It's a big deal down here. They don't get many suicides. I don't buy the suicide thing. Accident either."

I asked why not.

"I talked with Francine. On more than one occasion. The rape bothered her because it would hurt her parents so much. She loved her parents. Had a good relationship with them. She wouldn't do anything to hurt them. Especially kill herself."

"People get depressed."

"She didn't kill herself," Sandy said. "I just know she didn't. And the accident thing is too convenient. The police chief, Alec York, has been in to check on things."

"York? He related to the lieutenant governor?"

"Yes. He's a big man around here."

"So why's he interested in the death of a college girl?"

"I asked the same thing. The cops said it's because they don't get many suicides around here."

"Probably not many murders either."

"Besides, York started out in the morgue. Used to be in charge of it."

"Odd work for a future police chief."

"He was good at it, though," Sandy said. "In fact, he's a good police chief. At least that's what I'm hearing. Highly thought of statewide. Being the lieutenant governor's brother doesn't hurt him. He's being touted as the top man in a new state drug enforcement agency being formed."

"Can you find out anything else about Francine's death?"

"No. They're treating me like a nosy reporter."

"You are a nosy reporter."

She ignored me. "They're keeping a tight lid on things. My producer can't allow me much more time on this. I have some local color stuff on tape for the network. As for the thing with Travis Conrad . . . so far I don't have enough to put on the air. With Francine gone . . . she was a nice young woman, Wyatt. I hate this. She wouldn't kill herself." She chewed on her lower lip, then said, "I won't let go of this, Wyatt."

"I understand. But be careful. The people in question know who you are, but you don't know who they are."

"I've got to hang up," Sandy said. "I see Chief York. I want to ask him some questions. Good-bye."

She broke the connection. I dialed Chick's room number, but he had left to get some cigarettes and wasn't back yet.

I placed the phone on the hook and lay back on the bed. Thought about what she had told me. Sandy talks to two locals. Following that, Sandy is hassled by the cops, and now one of the girls is dead. The police are calling it a suicide or an accident, but Sandy says no. But why kill Francine? Was the cop afraid Francine would reveal his name? Why wait this long if he was afraid of that? Sandy said Chastity was afraid to talk. Said this cop was bad medicine. Was it a uniformed cop? Or someone else? A detective? Or someone higher?

Sitting here in my room wasn't doing anything for me. It was hard to imagine Francine not telling someone. People aren't very good at keeping secrets. Sooner or later nearly everyone will tell another person, who will swear they'll never tell another soul. Then that person will tell another person, of whom they will require the same oath. Francine had to have told someone. I was going to find that person.

I had just got up off the bed to get my jacket when a knock came at the door. Probably Chick. I opened the door to find a heavy man in a rumpled brown suit, tie askew. He had heavy jowls and friendly blue eyes.

"Wyatt Storme?" said the heavy man. "I'm Detective Fred Merrill, North Branson Police." He showed me his shield as he said this. Flipped it back into his jacket. "There has been a death of a local student under unusual circumstances, and I'd like to ask you some questions. May I come in?"

I nodded and opened the door wider. Much wider. He was a big man. The kind of big that doesn't look like fat, though he was overweight by several pounds. He was my height, about six-foot-three, but close to three hundred pounds. He thanked me and entered. He sat down on a room chair with some difficulty. He was able to situate himself in it with a twisting motion.

"Never fit these chairs," he said. "My wife's after me to lose some weight. Been after me to do it for twenty-five years. I say to her, 'What weight? I'm like a butterfly.'" He gestured with his arms as if he was spreading his wings. "She'll say, 'A really big butterfly.'" He smiled. His face and eyes smiled along with his mouth. "So tell me. Why's a former football superstar spending time in our little town?"

"Visiting a friend," I said.

"Oh." He nodded his head. "Telling the truth without telling all of it. Browne said you'd do that."

"You know Sam Browne?" I asked.

"Yeah. I know Sam. Good friend of mine. Told me quite a bit about you. Knew some things already. I'm a big football fan. Played at Branson High and later on the first Table Rock College team. Offensive line, though you'd never know it by looking at me. Got the body of a wide receiver, don't you think?"

I smiled. While he had been smiling and gesturing, he had produced a notepad like pulling a rabbit out of a hat. I would need to watch myself with this guy. He was sharp and disarming.

"Anyway," he continued, "like I said, I know quite a bit about you. You've led an interesting life. Vietnam hero. Super Bowl MVP. Two touchdowns in the final quarter against the Raiders. Gave the Cowboys a comeback win. Then you just walked away from it all. Nobody could find you anywhere. Why'd you do that?"

"Seemed like the thing to do," I said.

"But that's nothing compared to some of the things you've done since. Browne says you smoked two mob mechanics and broke up some kind of drug ring in Paradise County." I said nothing. If he knew about this, he also knew they had come to kill me. "And there's more." He patted his pockets. "You mind if I smoke?"

I told him I didn't.

"Thanks," he said, lighting a cigarette. "Not supposed to smoke on duty anymore. Chief York's new policy. He's a very progressive guy."

"But you do it anyway?"

He gave me the big smile. "Yeah."

"Sandy, that's the friend I'm visiting, says York's a good police chief."

"That's the rumor."

"What do you say?"

"He knows his way around the station. Good administrator. The press loves him. Got all these new cop techniques, nunchakus instead of nightsticks, stun guns like it was *Star Trek* or something. No smoking on duty. Some of it seems to work."

"Some not."

He nodded. "But back to business. Why's a guy like you trying to talk to Francine Wilson, a girl who turns up dead the same day?"

"Thought it was an accident."

The jolly eyes narrowed to cop's eyes. "Now, why do you say accident?"

"My friend, who is a reporter, called me from the police station. Said they told her an accident or suicide."

Merrill put both hands on his knees, his cigarette between two meaty fingers. His mouth twisted to one side in thought. "They told her it might be a suicide?"

I nodded. "You're a homicide detective?"

He nodded slowly. "I was just out at the college, checking the girl's dorm room. Girl at the desk said you and another guy came by and that you'd called twice since to talk with Francine. Why were you attempting to contact Francine Wilson?"

"Sandy is doing a story on small colleges, and she sent me to set up an appointment with Miss Wilson."

"That's bullshit. You aren't the gofer type."

I shrugged.

"You know something I don't? What've you got, Storme?"

"A suspicious nature about the North Branson police department."

"Why?"

I told him about Sandy being stopped. About being rousted in the Best Western my first hour in town.

"Bredwell and Pethmore?" asked Merrill. "I'll check into that. Those SOBs think they're Batman and Robin. Couple of real storm troopers. They're the chief's boys. I'll see what I can do about getting them to back off. Don't judge the whole force by those guys. We've got some good people working here. This is a good town."

I watched him. He didn't want me to have a low opinion of his community, a community where he had grown up and played football. Where he was raising his family. His colleagues had him on the outside of things for some reason, yet hadn't removed him entirely. An honest cop on the outside of things. An honest cop who was a local hero and probably well thought of by the community. They couldn't remove him or bust him down. It would cause too much trouble. So they gave him the mushroom treatment. Kept him in the dark and fed him crap. But that wouldn't work with this guy.

I didn't know him that well, though knowing Trooper Sam Browne was to his credit. Still I couldn't give him too much of what I knew or thought. He was an honest cop. A good cop who might feel compelled to share any information I gave him with his department, and there was no guarantee the info wouldn't be shared, accidentally or otherwise, with the wrong person. I couldn't chance it.

"What's the real reason you went to talk to Francine Wilson?" asked Merrill. "I gotta know."

"Can't tell you. Sorry."

"I'm going to find out anyway. I'll serve you if I have too. Waltz you around down at the station. You don't want that, do you?"

"Sorry, partner."

"Why?"

"Can't tell you that, either. Besides, you've got nothing to investigate. Suicide, remember?"

He considered me for a moment, chewing his lip. "It has to do with somebody on the force, doesn't it? You've got something you don't want me to know. You don't trust somebody on the force. That it?"

"Maybe. How did Francine die?"

He shook his head slowly. "Not going to go that way, Storme. You know better."

"Always worth a try."

"Talk to me."

"I'll tell you this much. Francine Wilson had something on a local policeman."

"What was it?"

"I'm not sure. Ask her friends. They might know something," I said. "All I can give you right now. Let it sit for a day or two. If the information doesn't come back on me in the form of threats or being rousted, I'll give you more."

"You don't trust me?"

"It isn't about trusting you," I said. "It's about not trusting someone you work with whose identity I don't know."

"It's an honest force."

"That calls murder an accident."

"I never said it was murder."

"Never said it wasn't, either," I said.

He stood up from his chair. He had to push on the chair arms to keep the chair from sticking to him. "Well, I'm not getting anywhere with this. Wish we could've met under different circumstances." He put out his hand. I accepted it. He said, "I'll be back, you know."

"Yeah."

"Browne said you could be a pain in the ass."

"Browne was right."

5

Chick returned after Detective Merrill left. He had with him a bottle of Canadian Club and a six-pack of Labatt's Blue with him. I updated him, telling him about Francine Wilson's "suicide." Detective Merrill's visit had made me more worried about Sandy. Whoever it was—if Sandy was right about the Wilson girl not killing herself, and Merrill had confirmed her hunch by his presence—had demonstrated a willingness to kill to keep his secret.

"Sounds like it's getting more important to talk with the hooker," Chick said. "Before we run out of people to ask. Found out some interesting stuff myself. About the local fuzz. You know why these guys carry nunchakus instead of nightsticks?"

"They're more fun?" I said.

"If the bad guys take away a baton, they use it on you. But if the bad guys take away a nunchaku, they don't know how to use it."

It made sense. "So how do you know this?"

"It's never been a secret that I am the bullgoose of bodyguards. Or that I am constantly researching new methods of law enforcement and weaponry. Also, I overheard some guys talking about it down at the grocery store."

"What else did you hear?"

"That the cops are initiating a neighborhood program. The cops are going to walk a beat rather than ride around in their cars all the time. They also sponsor touch football and recreation basketball leagues to keep the young rowdies off the streets."

"Very progressive."

"Also found out the chief of police is up for a new state position."

"Head of drug investigation. His brother's the lieutenant governor." Chick raised his apostrophe eyebrow, the one he only half brought back from Southeast Asia. "He serves also who sits and waits."

"So what now?"

"Let's wait for Sandy, then take another shot at locating Chastity."

"You won't mind, then," Chick said, cracking the seal on the Canadian whiskey, "if I spend the time in heavy genuflection."

Sandy returned, and we decided to take in the Jim Stafford show on the Branson strip. Sandy wanted to see Andy Williams, but we vetoed that by virtue of our superior numbers.

"Facist male porkers," said Sandy.

The Stafford show was good. Laughter is great therapy. Mark Twain says against the assault of laughter nothing can stand.

We left the theater and returned to North Branson. I drove, while Chick repeated Stafford's best bits, and Sandy complained of being bored twice, the second time by Chick.

By 9:30 we were sitting in the smoking section of the motel restaurant. Curved glass on the windows, plastic plants. Wasn't bad. But I'd never met a steak I didn't like. Chick was dining on veal parmigiana and washing it down with cabernet. Sandy was eating some kind of dietary martyr's meal consisting of lettuce and vegetables and half a grilled chicken sandwich. There were few people in the restaurant. To our left was a table of women, lip-synching the latest topics and fighting off middle age with cigarettes, wine, and Maybelline cosmetics. They looked like the audience on the *Oprah Winfrey Show*.

"You need to cut back on the cholesterol," Sandy said, chiding me.

"Why?" I said. "So I can be in good health when I die?"

"As your dietician," Chick said, "I would advise you to pass me the rest of your steak and order yourself a nice fruit cup. You need your vitamin C."

She shook her head, smiling. "Don't know why I bother."

"What did you find out at the police station?" I asked her.

"Not much. But more than they wanted to tell me."

"You are resourceful. It amplifies your beauty."

"I got a glimpse at the coroner's report before I got yelled at to get away from it by a rude cop."

"Name the scum," Chick said. "And we'll cut his liver out with a Ginsu knife and eat it. Though it may be saturated with cholesterol, we're willing to chance it to avenge you."

"Thank you, Chick," she said. "Have you been drinking?"

"Only this fine low-cholesterol cabernet," he said.

"It's full of calories."

"Dammit," he said, "I specifically ordered the no-calorie wine. Is there no professionalism among waiters?"

She ignored him. "What did the coroner's report say?" I asked.

"That she'd had sexual contact just before she died. They have a semen sample."

"She have a boyfriend?"

"Yes. But he's on the football team, and they're in Cape Girardeau playing Southeast Missouri State University. A good three- to four-hour trip from here."

"What about the possibility of another boyfriend, one the football player doesn't know about?"

"She's not the type," said Sandy.

"What was the cause of death?"

"I didn't have time to find out for sure. But I saw something about 'electrical shock.' "

"The cops think she had sex with someone and then committed suicide by giving herself an electric shock?"

"I don't know what they think for sure," Sandy said. "Not even sure that's what the cause was."

"Where did they find the body?"

"They won't say. Said they wanted to contact the family before they released details."

I took a Macanudo Hyde Park from my pocket and lighted it. Unlike most, Sandy enjoyed the aroma of cigars if it wasn't in too close quarters. The restaurant was large and open, and we were sitting in the smoking section. I took a nice languid draw. I told Sandy about my visit from homicide detective Merrill.

"Is he a heavy man with nice eyes?" asked Sandy. "Brown suit?"

"Yeah."

"He came into the station right before I left," she said. "He was agitated and demanded to see York. He went into the captain's office, and that was the last I saw of him."

"So how do you know he had nice eyes if he was mad?" I asked.

"He smiled at me and said hello when he came in."

"Leave you alone for a minute."

The waiter arrived at our table. He was nervously rolling a serving cart. "Sir," he said. "I hate to bring this up, but the ladies at the next table wanted me to . . . that is, they wanted me to ask if you would . . . ah . . . extinguish your cigar. If you don't mind."

"You mean those women over there?" Sandy said. "The ones who have been smoking cigarettes ever since we've been in here?" The color was rising in Sandy's face.

"Pardon me, young man," said Chick. "I'm this man's dietician. Dr. Salvatore Manilla's the name. This man has a digestive disorder. I *prescribed* that cigar. He risks strangular dystrophy of the lower intestine if he does not smoke after every meal."

"I'm sorry," said the waiter. "But, they're . . . well, one of them is the mayor's wife, and another is the police chief's wife."

"Tut, tut," said Chick, lighting a cigarette. "How could you know of his condition? You were just doing your job."

"It's all right," I said. "I'll put it out. No problem."

"Give it to me," said Sandy, holding her hand out for the cigar. I did so. She had that look in her eyes, the one like a butane flame at the back of her ice-blue eyes. She took the cigar, leaned back and tossed her head, causing her honey-blond mane to flip and swirl around her shoulders. She put the cigar to her lips, made the end glow, removed the cigar from her mouth, and released a magnificent cloud of smoke in the direction of the table where the women were sitting. The women now had indignant looks on their talk-show faces. Sandy smiled back at them and in a low voice said, "Protocol Nazis give me a pain."

We left soon after. I gave the besieged waiter a hefty tip. As we were leaving I said to Chick, "Sal Manilla? Strangular dystrophy?"

"Dr. Manilla to you," he said. "Culinary adviser and drinker of low-cal beverages."

Sandy's cheeks were a high reddish color as if a low flame glowed beneath them. Emotional swings made her more lovely. And she was already the fairest in the land. "Thanks for coming to my rescue," I said.

"Nobody messes with my man," she said with a conspiratorial smile. "Except me."

We walked her back to her room. The night air was cool and smelled of engine exhaust and faint snatches of Ozark woods borne in on puffs of a western breeze. The low hum of vehicle tires and fading radio sounds came from the highway. The pulse of automobiles and night activity thrummed around us like the purring of a large animal.

We were at her room now. "Chick and I are going to try again to get hold of Chastity," I said. "You going with us?"

"No," she said. "I think I'm going to go back down to the police station and ask some more questions. If I get anything, I'm going to bring in a camera and shoot some footage. You go ahead, but don't buy any genuine Ozark souvenir T-shirts. Okay?"

"I was eyeing one that says, 'I'm with Stupid,' " I said.

"Give it to Chick."

"You carrying the gun I gave you?"

"Yes. But *I* feel stupid carrying it." She kissed me, and I smelled her perfume and tasted the warmth of her mouth. She pressed herself against me briefly, then pushed me away. "That'll have to hold you." She placed a hand alongside my face, cupping my jaw. "You be careful, too. Okay?"

"Sure. I'm taking Dr. Manilla with me. In case I'm attacked by wives of important locals."

She closed the door, and I walked to Chick's room and knocked on the door. Chick opened it. "She's going to the police station," I said. "Take the Bronco and follow her. Keep an eye on her. Weather's pretty nice. Think I'll walk uptown and find Chastity. Don't let her know you're following her."

"Got it," said Chick. "Anything else?"

"Yeah," I said. "Anybody looks funny, anybody comes near her, I want you to put them in the trauma ward, okay?"

"Got it. Dr. Sal Manilla, dietician by day, leg-breaker by night."

He knew what I wanted. I turned down the hallway, pushed open the glass door, and stepped into the vibrations of the night.

6

⁓⁓⁓

I walked nine blocks south from the motel, turned east, and walked four more. Fortunately I wasn't superstitious. The cool air on my face and the low burn of exercise in my legs felt good. I was wearing a Royals warm-up jacket Sandy had given me, along with jeans and a pair of Adidas Superstars. I arrived at the Hickory Wind at 11:15 and was greeted by the stale breath of enclosed space and human activity and by a doorman who didn't even bother to check my ID. For all he knew, I could be a very mature-looking freshman. No tip for him.

The evening shows were over, and the inside of the place was alive with college students and tourists; drinking, clinking glasses, talking loudly to be heard over the pseudomusic that belched and coughed from the speakers. Frat brothers crowded the bar, order-ing beer and ogling the short-skirted waitresses. No talk of the degradation of women as sex objects was to be heard. I made a mental note to report them to the local NOW chapter at the first opportunity. I found a table and sat down. When the waitress came around, I ordered an O'Doul's and scanned the crowd for

Chastity. Sandy had given me a good description: "Copper-colored hair, cut short and flipped under. Five-foot-five, slender waist, green eyes, nice heart-shaped face, delicate cheekbones. The only flaws are her legs, which have underdeveloped calves, a misshapen left ear, and a crooked eyetooth on the left side. Looks a little like an undernourished Jill St. John. Smokes Virginia Slims."

I didn't see anyone fitting that description in the room at the present, and I decided against checking the ladies' room. They might not be that enlightened here. Prostitution is one thing, invading the ladies' powder room is quite another. I felt like an outsider again, just as I had when I visited the girls' dormitory. The wave of isolation was more sentient than overt, as if I existed on another dimensional plane from the dancers, the vacationers, and the beer-guzzling frat boys. Ordering a nonalcoholic beverage added to the distance between us.

But distance from the watering herd was the direction I'd chosen. Civilization in the last decade of this fading century is a feeding frenzy of lust, power, and PC vengeance for the sins of John Wayne and Mickey Mantle. There were few havens in this last arena. Time for the dissenters to head for high ground, build a fire, and watch the waters rise. The mob wanted blood and low entertainment, and there could be no peace between us.

After several more songs not by Bob Dylan, she walked into the place. No mistaking the burnt-red hair or the provocative clothing, which consisted of a form-fitting shell that stopped millimeters south of the rental property. Stiletto heels. One didn't see stiletto heels all that much anymore. Not a faddish item on campus. Prostitution on college campuses was nearly killed off in the late sixties and seventies by amateurism. The working girls couldn't compete with the hippie chicks and had to retreat to the truck stops and the inner city. The double whammy of herpes and AIDS had shut down the free stores, and the profession was making a comeback using prophylactics, hand jobs in the backseats, and updated lab tests to calm clients' fears and sate swollen libidos.

Chastity made her way across the room, moving through the

crowd like a sleek fish cutting the water. She received glassy-eyed appraisal from the boys and malevolent feline looks from the females. I stood as she neared my table and pantomimed the offer of a seat across from me. She stopped and eyed me appraisingly, having to raise her chin to look up at my face. She cocked her head, gave a look around the room like a rancher appraising cattle, and sat down.

She leaned forward and placed her elbows on the table, then rested her chin on the backs of her hands. It was a pose. Practiced. Coquettish. "I'm Chastity," she said.

"And I'm chaste," I said.

She laughed. I was a wonderful man. Funny. Fun to be with.

"We'll see if we can do something about that," she said.

"There's nothing to be done about it. I'm that way intentionally. Balzac says the motto of chivalry is the motto of wisdom: to serve all, but love only one."

"And yet you're here all alone," she purred. A waiter set a frothy caramel-colored drink in front of her. Gin and cherry cola. She took a sip, wetting her lips, then tilted her head and considered me. She traced my forearm with her fingers. "What's your name, good-looking?" She slid her hand into mine.

"Name's Wyatt. I came to see you," I said. "I'm Sandy Collingsworth's friend."

That stopped her. The vampish pose disappeared. She took a big swallow of her drink, then said, "What do you want?"

"Ask a few questions."

"Well, fuck that," she said. She started to stand up, but I still had her hand in mine. As she started to push her chair back, I tightened my grip on her hand.

"A girl's been killed, Chastity," I said. "I have questions to ask, and I don't have the patience to make an appointment. So sit down and relax."

Her eyes flashed for a moment, then she relented, as if she could see in my face or manner that it would not be other than the way I wanted. Almost a resignation on her part; the latest in the series of small capitulations that went with her profession. There is a theory that whores are self-loathing man haters who give themselves for money because it gives them power, however briefly, over their customers. I think it's less complicated than that.

"My time costs," she said.

"Love gives itself, it is not bought," I said. "Besides, I'm not in the market, so turn the meter off."

"You smug son of a bitch," she said, baring her teeth as she said it. "You probably can't even get it up."

"The ultimate barometer of manhood. Sandy said a cop gave you a free pass in exchange for your charming services."

"Maybe," she said. "That surprise you?"

"Not really. You're very attractive."

Her shoulders relaxed. "You think so?"

"Prettiest girl in the place."

She smiled, and I saw the crooked eyetooth, which enhanced rather than marred her beauty. Perfect teeth would have made her look too porcelain, too fragile. Reflexively, she patted the hair covering her bad ear. "You engaged to the reporter?"

I nodded.

"You love her?"

"More than anything."

She nodded, absently, then said, "Yeah. I boffed a cop for free. So what?"

"I think he killed the college girl, Francine Wilson. You know her? She shook her head. I continued. "And he's now threatening my fiancée. I don't like it and want to turn him. Who is he?"

"I can't tell you."

"You afraid of him?"

"No."

"What're you afraid of, then?"

"Robby Blue."

"Your pimp?"

She nodded.

"Why?" I asked.

"He don't like it when I make trouble for the cops. Couple of them are 'friends' of his like he wasn't a noxious asshole or something."

"They're on the pad?"

Her eyes searched the room. "I've gotta make a call. Can you excuse me a minute?" I gave her a questioning look. "Don't worry," she said, reading my mistrust, "I'll come right back. Promise."

I let her go, and she slipped through the crowd, making her way to the pay phone near the entrance. I considered following her and listening in on the conversation. She was calling Robby Blue, I figured. Be glad to meet him. If she tried to run, I was confident she wouldn't be able to run very fast on stiletto heels. So I waited at my table and watched her. She looked at me once as she was talking, and smiled at me. Make the client feel special. Wanted. Loved. She hung up the phone and walked back to my table. Sat down.

"I've got to go," she said.

"What is the policeman's name?"

"Robby Blue is coming. I gotta get to work."

"First, the name."

"You gotta pay me something before he gets here."

"Why?"

"Robby Blue doesn't like it when I waste time on dry humps."

"Tough for Robby Blue."

"He'll be pissed."

"I don't care."

She swallowed. "Why should you? You aren't the one's going to get the shit beat out of them."

"He beats you?"

"Boy, you are a rube," she said. "That's the way it's done."

"So quit."

"Yeah," she said, laughing as she did so. It was more like a bleat; half laugh, half whimper. "That's a great idea. Then we can both move into your castle in Disneyland and live happily ever after."

"Life isn't an even bet."

"Shit," she said. "Look, I have money, nice clothes, nice car, an apartment. All I have to do for it is look pretty and boff the college boys and the tourists, most of whom last about five minutes and some who are even cute."

"Then, once in a while you have to perform a similar function for one of Robby Blue's buddies, maybe some fat politician out of the city, one of his cop buddies, the odd drug dealer. It's a dream come true, isn't it?"

"You're kind of a shit for a guy looks as good as you do. Everything probably looks simple from your side of the street, doesn't it?"

"I need the cop's name."

She frowned. "I . . . let me think about it. But you have to pay me something now, so Robby Blue don't beat me up."

"Robby sounds like a real he-man. Perhaps I'll hang around and meet him. Maybe pick up a couple of pointers about slapping women around. Never know when that may come in handy." I pulled out my wallet, took out a twenty, and offered it to her.

"Fifty," she said.

"You've been here maybe fifteen minutes. I wouldn't pay Cindy Crawford fifty bucks to accompany me to my high school reunion. Twenty's all you get unless you tell me the cop's name."

She shook her head. "Not tonight. But if I tell you later, you can give me a hundred."

"Done. But it'd better be the guy and not some fish you throw me to get me off your back."

"Wouldn't mind having you on my back," she said, biting her lower lip. "Or on my front, for that matter."

"Very flattering," I said.

"I'll see you later, then," she said. She gave my arm a gentle squeeze as she stood, then she walked off to work the college boys. I sat and looked at the green O'Doul's bottle and wished I'd ordered a Dr Pepper. Appearances. So important.

While I watched the crowd and Chastity, an attractive middle-aged woman wearing too much makeup entered the bar. I recognized her from the restaurant. Was she the mayor's wife? Or was she Chief York's wife? Neither?

She moved through the crowd like a pinball, bouncing off dancers and chairs. She was wearing heels, a dark evening dress, and diamond earrings the size of Mercury dimes. If I was out of place, her presence was as jarring as if the disc jockey suddenly decided to play a Barbra Streisand tune. She made her way to the bar and squeezed between boys young enough to be her sons but old enough to gaze in voyeuristic appreciation at her backside. One of them cupped a slender hip and pulled her against him. He said something to her, and his buddies laughed raucously. She seemed oblivious to the attention.

Gaining the bartender's attention, she ordered a drink which I would've laid good money was a martini. She turned around and shrugged off the young man's arm and searched the room's interior. Then she set off across the room again, hairdo unraveling, bumping revelers, and sloshing liquid over the cusp of her glass.

She approached a table to my rear where a group of college females sat, drinking wine coolers and Zima. As she neared, they became aware of her and looked up from their conversations. I turned in my chair, sensing, as did the coeds, that this was trouble. The woman stopped at the table and pointed at one of the girls, a lovely dust-blonde wearing a patterned vest, and began yelling something at her, which I couldn't hear, but from the body language knew wasn't a compliment on her attire.

People in the bar turned to see what was happening, as I rose from my chair and made my way toward them. I was within two steps of the older woman when I heard her say, "Little whore," then watched helplessly as she flung the contents of her glass into the girl's face. Her companions squealed and knocked chairs back as they jumped up to avoid being drenched. By this time a bouncer had noted the commotion and was muscling through the crowd. The doused coed stood and whipped her hands downward to shed the liquid. The older woman started around the table, but by that time I was near enough to step in her path.

I started to say something comforting when she aimed a clumsy roundhouse at me, which I easily avoided by leaning away Muhammad Ali–style. The force of the miss caused her to lose her balance, and she spun and toppled onto the floor. She sat down hard, a heap of pearls and Chanel perfume.

A bouncer helped me lift her to her feet. Her purse and one of her shoes had come off, and I reached down to pick them up. Some of the purse's contents had spilled, and I scooped them back into the purse. I felt her small fist fall against my back, then lay there momentarily as if it were a bird that had fallen, exhausted, from its perch. I straightened and offered her the fallen items, which she accepted and clutched against her chest, her eyes heavy lidded and opaque. In a voice thick with booze she said, "Thanks, you lousy bastards. You're all . . . lousy bastards here." Her head drooped, and we helped her to the door, the assembled crowd parting and following us with dull expressions and liquid smiles.

Once outside, the bouncer asked if she was with me.

"No," I said, "but I'll watch her if you'll call her a cab."

"You know who she is, don't you?"

"Not really."

He laughed. "She's the chief of police's wife." He shook his large head slowly. "Shame, ain't it."

"Fug you, you bassards," she said, slurring the words.

"Good night, Mrs. York," said the bouncer. "I'm going to get you a cab."

"I have . . . a car."

"You want to drive her home?" he asked me.

"No. Call the cab."

"Okay," he said and went back inside the bar.

"Drive myself," she said, leaning against me. "Where's my martini?"

"You baptized some girl with it."

"That little bitch. She's fugging my . . . hubzand. Husband. Fugging Alec. He's bassard, too, jus' like you." She lifted her eyes and looked at me. "I know you. You're that asshole with . . .

with the cigar." She shook a limp finger in my face. "Not nice to smoke in public." Then she smiled. "You're cute. You want to screw me?"

"No."

"Whassa matter? Don't you like what you see?" She stood back and presented herself, stumbling slightly as she did. "Still looks pretty . . . good. You think?"

"You're drunk."

"Oh, my cutey pie don't like drunks. Screw you better than those college sluts. Betcha. Fuck Alec. You know my husband? He fugs the college sluts. Gonna . . . get them all . . . Alec, too. He's a bassard . . . like you." Her head lolled, and I caught her around the waist as she slumped against me, her head against my chest.

The bouncer stuck his head out the door and told me that someone was coming for her. I thanked him, and he went back inside. Within two minutes a police unit pulled up, and Officer Pethmore got out.

"You here for her?" I asked.

"What are you doing with her?" he said sharply.

"We're going to run off together, and she got all excited and celebrated too much. Help me get her in the car."

He opened the back door of his car and then helped me lift her inside. Holly Golightly sleeping it off on Desolation Row.

Leaving the door open, Pethmore turned to face me. "Not a good idea to be hanging around with the chief's wife," he said. "I'll just tell you this the one time. Don't make me tell you again."

"You know," I said. "I've had about enough crappy treatment from you and your Gestapo buddy. You make a move on me sometime without the badge, junior, and I'll help you claim some workman's comp."

"That sounds like a threat to me. Not good to threaten a police officer in this town." He placed a hand on the nunchaku sheath on his belt.

I felt heat rising on the back of my neck. At that moment Mrs.

York made a wet, gurgling sound and vomited onto the floorboard of Pethmore's police unit.

The color drained out of Pethmore's face. "Aw, shit," he said, letting the words escape from his lips like steam hissing out of a boiling teapot.

I smiled, reinforced in the knowledge that God was paying attention and that, for whatever reason, He loved broken-down wide receivers.

7

When I returned to the interior of the bar, Chastity was nowhere to be found. Whether she'd slipped out the back door with a john or whether she'd merely slipped out to avoid me, I didn't know. I returned to the table and waited. I was a world-class waiter. Twenty minutes later I gave up and left. Outside I saw her walking through the parking lot with a tall white man dressed in an electric blue Italian suit, no tie, collarless black shirt, his hair pulled back in a ponytail. She was pointing in my direction. Looked like I was going to meet good old Robby Blue.

He moved toward me, spinning a key chain around his index finger. The flickering neon reflected off his suit, giving him a flat, cartoonish quality. The music swelled from inside the bar like the breathing of a dinosaur. Chastity stood behind him, her hands clasped together in front of her, as if pleading with me. He stood in my path, arms crossed at his chest and glaring at me; his rings and bracelets twinkled in the shifting lights. The glaring thing was supposed to be scary, I guess. When I didn't melt into a helpless puddle of sweat and fear, he leaned forward and said, "What do you want with my girl?"

"Who's your girl? A snappy dresser like you probably has to beat them off with a stick."

"You know who I'm talking about."

"Who're you?"

"I'm asking the fucking questions here."

"And doing a swell job of it, too."

"What do you want with her?"

"None of your business," I said.

It stopped him for a heartbeat. He turned his head a quarter inch to one side and said, "People know better than to talk to me like that."

"It's amazing anyone talks to you at all. You dress like a Bourbon Street strip-joint barker. Where do you buy that stuff? Pimps R Us?"

A car parked two rows away, and a group of college kids in sweatshirts and windbreakers got out and walked into the bar. Chastity leaned against a car and smoked, her fingernails clicking rapidly as she did. I saw Robby Blue's fingers tighten around the key chain. I don't think he liked me. Happens every time I meet a pimp. He stuck the key chain inside his pocket, letting me know he was serious now.

He said, "You got anything you want to ask her, you gotta ask me first. She don't speak unless I say she can speak."

"That doesn't sound very enlightened. Did you miss the entire twentieth century? Maybe I can get you into therapy."

"That's some mouth you got on you."

"Goes with the soulful gray eyes and the nineteen-inch biceps."

"You don't know who you're coming at with that shit, do you?"

"Sure I do. Some lightweight mouth-breather looks like he buys his clothes blindfolded."

"I had enough of your shit," he said, reaching inside his jacket. As he did, I chopped his forearm. He flinched, and I jabbed three fingers into his throat, twisting my hand as I did so. Then I dropped my hand down and pulled his arm from his jacket. He made a choking sound, put his hands to his throat, and leaned a shoulder against a Buick for support.

Quickly, I spun him around, and grabbing his ponytail, I

wrenched his head to one side while he gagged and gasped for air. I jerked the collar of his jacket downward over his arms, and reaching inside the liner pocket, I found a .25 Beretta auto.

"Now, Robby, old buddy," I said. "What were you going to do with this nasty little implement of destruction?"

"Fuck you," he rasped from his damaged throat.

I kicked him behind the knee, and as he collapsed I jerked up on the ponytail. He yelped, and I pulled him up on his toes as if holding up a largemouth bass for a picture. I dug the point of the gun against his kidneys and pulled back on the ponytail. He was off-balance and helpless, unless he wanted to pitch the back of his head against the cement. I leaned close to his ear and said, "Now, let me give you the ground rules, partner. First, no more dirty talk. It offends me. Second, I even hear you're in town, I'm going to feed this gun to you one bullet at a time. We together on that?"

He didn't answer, so I banged his head off the Buick. He groaned and sputtered. I heard Chastity suck in her breath.

"Okay, okay," he said. "I got it."

"Good. Now, the last requirement. You'll notice these are requirements, not suggestions. I find out you hurt the girl, even talk bad to her, I'm going to look you up and cramp your lifestyle. Does that connect for you?"

"You're fucking dead meat," he said. With the gun I cracked him hard on top of the hipbone, and he screamed out.

"What'd you do to me?" he said, leaning sideways to take his weight off the damaged hip.

"Hip pointer," I said. "Free of charge. It'll quit hurting in a week or two. But until then it will bring tears to your eyes even to put your underwear on."

"Who are you?"

"Roy Rogers. King of the cowboys. Don't make me ride you around the corral again; it gets my choler up."

8

I pocketed the little auto pistol, left Robby Blue to contemplate a career change, and headed back to the motel. When I arrived, I noticed my Bronco and Sandy's rental car were in their parking slots.

I knocked on Chick's door, and he let me in. I sat down in a chair and related my evening at the Hickory Wind while he drank Canadian whiskey from an icy motel glass. When I was finished, he said, "How is it everywhere you go people try to stick a finger in your eye?"

I shrugged. "Naturally amicable, I guess." I asked him how it went with Sandy.

"I didn't get to subdue or shoot anyone," he said. "She was in the police station for about an hour and then returned here. No incidents en route. I waited back in the parking lot before I came inside. A police car rolled past the parking lot twice. Same unit. Number thirteen eleven. Bredwell's car."

"Checking on her."

"Looks like it."

"She's stirred up something. She see you following her?"

"Naw. Shadows are invisible after the sun goes down. You think she'll be mad we're covering her back?"

"Maybe. But I feel better. It's her deal and she needs to do it on her own, but it makes me nervous when she exposes herself. She won't let us watch over her all the time, so we'll have to do some of it on the sly."

"You're saying we can't let her know we're watching her all the time or she'll feel like we're patronizing her, but we've got to do it in a way she won't know we're doing it because you don't want her to be pissed at you. That it?"

"Close."

"You guys are funny."

"The ways of love are tangled," I said.

The sky was lavender and gray the next morning and by noon had turned a hard slate color. A cold wind blew down the upscale hillside of Taylor Heights, and the slate-colored clouds boiled and shifted and released marble-sized raindrops, which slapped the pavement like rapping a pan with wooden spoons.

Sandy had arisen at 4:00 A.M. and driven through the predawn darkness and worked six hours for her fifteen-minute segment. Who says television journalism isn't glamorous? Chick shadowed her.

I ate breakfast at Perkins, then I called Halsey-Cotes dormitory and talked with Francine Wilson's roommate, Sharon Keltner. Sharon had last seen Francine the day before her body was found. Had she noticed anything unusual about Francine's behavior? No, she'd been a little depressed after the incident with the police, but since Sandy had been in town she had been doing better; it seemed to help that she was doing something about her problem. Had there been any unusual calls or visitors? Not any she could remember. I thanked her and gave her the motel phone number and told her what rooms Sandy and I were staying in; I asked her to call if she thought of anything else. Before I hung up, she added one more thing.

"Mr. Storme, Francine wouldn't kill herself," she said.

"What makes you say that?"

"She had too much to live for. Oh, I know that makes me sound like a dumb kid, but she had plans. She was always looking ahead. She had all next week planned out on her desk calendar. A person wouldn't do that if they were going to kill themselves, would they?"

"What plans?"

"Hang on a minute, and I'll look." I heard her put down the phone and then heard movement echoing through the phone line. "Here it is," she said. "Monday, Bio test, see Kenneth. That's her boyfriend. Tuesday, meet with Mr. James, her adviser. Sig Tau, five thirty. Wednesday, she's got a funny note here. Says V. Cavalerri, two o'clock, I don't know anyone by that name." I heard her flip a page. "Here it is on last week's calendar, also. Velonne Cavalerri, two thirty."

She read the notations for the rest of the week, and it was more of the same. Meetings, movies, tests, appointments, the kind of thing someone preoccupied with death might not bother to do. I thanked her again and hung up. I pulled out the phone book and thumbed through the C's until I found Cavalerri. There were three listings: Frank at 1306 South Liberty, V. L. at 606 Jefferson Avenue, and Velonne L. Cavalerri, attorney-at-law. Bingo. I called her office and asked to speak with her, but her secretary said she was in court at present but might be back in her office in the afternoon. I asked where the office was located, and she told me the address. "It's right across the street from the city courthouse," she said.

I called the police station and asked for Detective Merrill. He came on the line. I shared my conversation with Sharon Keltner and told him about Mrs. York and my conversation with Pethmore. I left out the part about Chastity and her pimp. I asked for a description of Velonne Cavalerri, which he supplied. "Cavalerri is hot," said Merrill. "Supposedly, she and York got something going."

"Corroborates what his wife said about his extracurricular activities."

"Pethmore and Bredwell are like on permanent patrol to keep their boss's wife out of trouble. Sychophant and toady, wife-watchers."

"Is she a juicer?"

"Yeah. Pathetic, isn't it? She's an attractive, intelligent woman. Some days she starts hitting it with her cornflakes and doesn't come up for air until she passes out."

"How does the community feel about it?"

"The community? They think Alec York can do no wrong. He's their boy."

"I'm surprised they stay married."

"Felicia Taylor York is the daughter of the wealthiest family in North Branson, one of the wealthiest families in the Branson area. Big financial supporters of the lieutenant governor."

"You mean Taylor like Taylor Heights?"

"Yeah. Also like Taylor Cadillac and Taylor Manufacturing and Taylor Industries," he said. "Well, thanks for the information. They're still calling it an accidental death or possible suicide down here. The chief and I had a heart-to-heart, and it was even money whether he was going to fire me or we were going to dance the knuckle boogaloo. Another thing. There was a disturbance last night, outside the Hickory Wind. Somebody bounced a pimp named Robby Blue around the sidewalk. The description said it was a big, rangy guy did it. Somebody from out of town. That bring anybody to mind?"

"Can't say it does," I said.

"Which is okay, because Robby Blue is your regulation dirtbag. Whenever he comes to town, the cockroach population goes into heat."

"How does a guy like that operate in a nice tourist town like North Branson?"

"Ask the guys in charge of vice and pest control. I'm just

a guy doesn't know the difference between murder and suicide."

North Branson proper lay across the dual-lane highway from the
North Branson strip. At 2:00 P.M. I was sitting in the Bronco,
radio tuned to a classical music station, listening to Bach's Bran-
denburg Concerto No. 3, watching the rain pelt down, wrapping
the streets in a translucent sheet that reflected the lights and buildings of North Branson's city square. The rain pinged off the roof
of the Bronco in a staccato patter and ran in narrow rivulets down
the windshield. Rhythmic. Soothing.

By 2:20, the rain had ceased, as if catching its breath. It was
then I saw a woman matching the description Merrill had given
me. She walked down the steps of the courthouse as if she had
personally stopped the rain, crossed the street with brisk steps,
checking the traffic only once before crossing. She passed in front
of my vehicle without looking in my direction. Once she entered
the brick-front office of Hopkins, Hopkins, and Cavalerri, I
stepped out of the Bronco and walked to the office. I opened the
door as Cavalerri was walking down the hall to her office. I followed her, skipping the formality of speaking to the secretary,
who raised a hand and opened her mouth to speak as I walked
by.

Cavalerri was removing the belt of her raincoat as I walked in.
She looked up at me as she continued to unwrap the coat. She
removed the coat, hanging it on a white-knobbed walnut coat
tree, turned, and, fixing me with black eyes, said, "May I help
you?"

"I'd like to ask you some questions," I said.

"Mildred makes the appointments."

"I'm impetuous, though. A couple of questions, and I'll be out
of your hair."

"Are you in need of legal advice?" Her raven-black hair flipped
forward as she sat in her executive chair and swung her dark-
hosed legs under the desk. The desk itself was a deeply lacquered

cherrywood. It was organized and neat. Everything in its place. A wall-mounted diploma said she'd graduated from Drury College in 1978, and another one said she'd received her law degree from the University of Missouri in 1981.

"No. I just wanted to ask about Francine Wilson."

Her olive cheeks paled at the mention of the name, and her hand reached for the penholder mounted on a plaque that announced her as the American Business Women's Association woman of the year, 1993. She plucked the black pen from the holder and leaned back in her chair. She was composed now, but I could see the knuckles, clutching the pen, were pale and rimmed with pink blotches. "You won't be offended if I ask who you are?"

"No," I said. "I won't be offended at all."

She crossed her arms. "Your name?"

"Wyatt Storme. Why did Francine Wilson seek your services?"

She gave me a smug smile. "What makes you think she had sought to engage me?"

"Your name was on her planning calendar. Twice."

She held the pen between both hands and looked up at me. "Do you have any official capacity to ask these questions?"

"I'm doing some background for a reporter."

"And his interest?"

I didn't correct her gender error. "She thinks somebody in the police department has wires crossed in his psychological makeup."

"Are you a private investigator?"

"No."

She pushed the chair back and crossed her legs. "Well, I'm afraid I am unable to share client information with you. It would be unethical to do so."

"This client is dead."

"So I understand. A pity."

"It'll give you something to talk about at cocktail parties," I said, "so your relationship with her won't be a total waste."

She set her white teeth in a line. "I don't think I like your condescending tone."

"You thought it was condescending? Darn. I was going for disgusted."

"She committed suicide, didn't she? That's her choice, not mine."

"Is your compassion always this intense, or do you just throw in the warmth free of charge? The police are calling it an accident or possibly suicide, but her roommate and others think differently."

"I'm sure the police know what they're doing. Now, if you have nothing else, I need to get to work."

"What kind of guy is Chief York?" I asked.

Her throat colored, and she said, "Why do you ask that?"

"Word is you know him." I let it hang.

Her eyes blazed up, like sliding back a panel on a woodstove. "What is that supposed to mean?"

"Just want to know what kind of guy he is."

"Mildred makes the appointments, Mr. Storme. And I don't give a damn what some television personality with more sex appeal than brains thinks about what happens in North Branson."

"Actually, she is more intelligent than sexy, but her sex appeal is of such high octane that it's hard to imagine it being rivaled by her intellect," I said. "And, Ms. Cavalerri, I don't remember mentioning she was a television personality. Interesting you mentioned it. Would you care to expand upon that, counselor?"

"Good day, Mr. Storme."

"I was in the Hickory Wind last night when Mrs. York came in and accused a coed of having sex with her husband."

"That means little to me," she said, but her ebony eyes were hot and her cheeks had colored again.

"Is Chief York a breather? You know, gives it the theatrical heavy breathing when you're with him, or is he more workmanlike? You know the type. Like it was putting together a bicycle on Christmas morning. Tab A fits into—"

"That is enough!" she said, jumping from her chair. "Leave

now, Mr. Storme, or I'll call the police." She picked up the phone.

"Might be interesting to let you do that to see who shows up. Go ahead."

She squeezed her eyes shut, and her jaw worked. "Would you please leave, Mr. Storme."

"*Please* is a good word," I said. "See you around, Ms. Cavalerri." As I left her office, I could feel her eyes burning into my neck.

It was raining again.

9

The message light was flashing on my room phone when I returned to the motel. I called the desk and was told I was to call Chick Easton. I rang Chick's room, and he answered.

"We're in trouble, bro," he said.

"What's up?"

"First, I'm out of cigarettes, but the more immediate problem is that Sandy's onto me riding shotgun. I followed her back from the studio, then she got out of her car and went into the motel, so I waited to see if she was going to stay inside. Five minutes later she comes back out and walks straight to where I'm sitting at the back of the lot, tells me that while she appreciates our concern she's a big girl and that if I want to do something useful why don't I protect the fathead football player since he's the one getting into street fights with pimps."

"Fathead?"

"What she said," Chick said, a little too gleefully, I thought. "Anyway, she told me she was going back to talk with Chief York and that if I followed her she was going to hit me with a tire iron. My position is I'd prefer that didn't happen."

"I thought you were invisible."

"Told you I ran out of cigarettes. They're the source of my magical powers."

"Well, let her have her head for a while," I said. "She'll get over it. You can pick her back up later."

"Easy for you to say. She's not threatening you with a tire tool. Why don't you follow her around and protect her, and I'll fight the pimps."

"The lowlifes I can handle. You're supposed to handle the heavy work. What do I keep you around for, anyway?"

"I'm charging double for this."

"I'll pick up a bottle of Chivas for you. How's that?"

"Not enough. This is a single-malt job. I want Glenfiddich, or I'm calling my union steward. What'd you find out today?"

I related my conversations with Sharon Keltner and Velonne Cavalerri. Also my call to Merrill.

He said, "You think York's got something to do with this?"

"He's a busy guy," I said. "Maybe he just likes to talk after he jumps Cavalerri. A postcoital loosening of the tongue."

"What does she look like?"

"That's irrelevant."

"To you maybe. My suite door doesn't open into a beautiful media babe's room. Besides, everything I ask doesn't have to do with sexual desire. Might be interesting to know what kind of woman is attracted to York and what kind of woman attracts him."

"She looks good. Dark eyes, dark hair, Mediterranean features. She looks like the real item." Something clicked in my head. "There was a Frank Cavalerri in the book. Make yourself useful and find out if he's related to her. They have separate addresses. May be an ex-husband."

"Be interesting to find out why they divorced if that's true, wouldn't it?" Chick said. "Anything else?"

"Not at the moment. Tonight, we'll go back to the Hickory Wind and see if Chastity is ready to talk about her cop friend."

"Okay, I'll check on Frank Cavalerri while you get the Scotch."

"Right," I said. "Let's see, what kind was it? Passport? Or Crawford's?"

The air smelled of damp pavement and scorched engine oil as I walked through the parking lot of Osco Drugs with a fifth of Glenfiddich single malt in a paper sack. An unmarked police car pulled up, and Detective Fred Merrill got out, leaving the door open. He had a strange look on his face.

"Shit," he said. "What'd you kick up Cavalerri's butt? She's been down at the station lighting up the chief like a pinball machine."

"Just asked her about Francine Wilson, and I may have let it slip about her relationship with Chief York."

"How did Francine Wilson die?"

"Electrical shock. Found her in a motel bathtub. Hair drier in the tub with her."

"Makes an accident or suicide more plausible," I said. "But I still don't like York."

He let out a big puff of wind, causing his lips to flutter, and smiled. "It's about time somebody blew up that bag of air besides me."

"There seems to be more than the standard brand of enmity between you two."

He leaned against the open door. His tie was askew and trailing down the massive chest like a campaign banner the day after the election. The bottom shirt button was unbuttoned, and I could see the white-ribbed undershirt peeking through.

"Well," he said, "year ago, one of my guys busted the mayor's kid. Possession with intent and resisting arrest. He and a uniform caught the kid with a bag of coke. The good stuff. About fifty G's worth. Threw a rock size of a grapefruit at the uniformed cop. Kid's a douche bag. The kind that every time he hears a toilet flush he attends a funeral. Anyway, my guy wants to push for the whole fall, but by this time the mayor's bending York's ear and

York tells the dick to reduce the charge to possession, like the kid carries around fifty thousand dollars' worth of blow for recreational purposes. Meanwhile, the arresting officer is on medical leave because it took ten stitches to sew up his ear where the rock hit him.

"My guy sticks to his guns, and the mayor hires Cavalerri to defend his kid. York steps in and has my detective busted on a set-up DWI charge with Bredwell and Pethmore stopping the detective. Then the mayor pays off the arresting cop. My guy's in the unemployment line for doing his job, which pisses me off so I front York and threaten to whip his ass. He charges me with insubordination, says I'm not a team player, and I catch a suspension."

His expansive face had reddened as he spoke, and his breathing was faster. His anger was deep-seated and established. "I went to school with York. He was a sneaky chickenshit then, too. I was going with Felicia Taylor until I found out she was banging him behind my back. I was crazy in love with her, too." He looked across the parking lot and shook his heavy head. Laughed. "I was a grade-A dumbass back then."

"Why don't you try somewhere else? Seems a cop with your experience could catch on anywhere."

"Thought about it." He shook his pack of Marlboros, then removed one with his teeth. He lighted it with a chrome Zippo lighter. Snapped the lid shut. "Wanda's mentioned it before. But, hell, lived here all my life. My boy's a junior in high school. Tailback. Lighter-framed like his mom, hardheaded like his old man. Got too much invested in this town to pull out now. How's that song go? 'Too late to run. Too tired to hide.' "

I could identify with that.

I left Fred Merrill and drove back to the motel. Along the way I was thinking about Francine Wilson and Fred Merrill and didn't see the two men in tailored suits get out of a maroon Cadillac Seville and walk around my Bronco.

"You Storme?" asked one of them, a bullnecked man with lips like a carp.

"Who wants to know?"

"Just answer the question, huh?" said his friend, a beefy blond with a black patch over one eye which made him look menacing; as if he needed it. They were not insurance salesman. They had cut off any avenue of escape, and the parking lot was at the rear of the motel. The only people who would see us would be looking out a window and unable to give a clear description. And I was caught between them with the Bronco behind me and an Oldsmobile in front of me. The Browning was in my room.

"Mr. Storme," said the big-lipped man, "we work for people who want you to quit stirring the water around here. We are here to communicate those wishes to you."

"How long you have to work on that speech?" I said, looking around for help or a way out. "*Communicate* has more than two syllables in it, and you didn't stumble once."

"We heard you was a smartass, Storme. Our people said to ignore it. They also said you're smart, so show some of that. The smart thing here is to disengage. You're pissing on the wrong people."

"What people are you talking about?" I asked.

"You don't need to know that," said the blond with the bad eye. "You just need to understand that this is real life and the people we represent are serious."

"Serious enough to send you two poet laureates out to speak to me."

The words were barely out of my mouth when Fish Lips punched me in the kidneys. It felt as if I had been hit with a frozen ham. Pain like icy spiders shot through my side, and my knees buckled. I placed a forearm against the Bronco for support.

"Don't step on your dick, Storme," said the blond guy. He reached out and straightened the line of my jacket. "Nobody's mad at you, yet. You're a nice guy. Just pack your shit and go back to the woods. Go fishing or whatever it is you Mayberry guys do. Y'know? All we got here is concrete and bad endings."

"Get your country ass out of town, cowboy," said the hood who'd punched me. I had recovered from the punch but was trying to buy some time. Maybe somebody would see what was going on, or maybe Chick would return. Maybe Itzhak Perlman would play center field for the Yankees. "Go home, and take the cunt with you."

"Don't talk about her like that," I said.

"Hey Joe," said Fish Lips, "guy's touchy about the gash."

"A sensitive nineties guy," said the blond.

Using the Bronco for leverage, I kicked back, and my heel caught Fish Lips below the knee. It made a nice solid sound, though I'd been aiming for the kneecap, which would have taken him out and simplified things, but it wasn't my day. I followed that with a left jab at the other guy, but his reactions were good and he managed to roll a shoulder in the way of the punch and deflect it enough that when it bounced off the side of his head most of the steam was gone. That was pretty much the extent of my uprising. Fish Lips recovered and kicked me behind the right knee, and I fell against the Oldsmobile. Taking advantage of the moment, they battered me with well-aimed shots to my torso and back. I hit back in the desperate style of a scared third-grader flailing away at the school bully, occasionally finding my target while they took the strength out of me with their heavy-handed blows.

Finally, my arms felt like sacks of wet cement, and my body slumped between them. The blond-headed man with the bad eye grabbed a handful of my hair and jerked my head up to look at him. The other thug was standing on the back of my ankles, causing electric signals to burst along lines from leg to backbone. With the satisfaction of a demented man, I noted the trickle of blood at the corner of the blond man's mouth. His eye patch was askew, and his teeth were pinkish with blood.

"We just came to talk, asshole," he said. "Remember that. You caused the rest of it. Now, we're going to check back in a couple of days to make sure you're being a good boy. Until then, get your shit packed up and point this truck any direction and drive until you're out of gas. You got that?"

I said nothing.

He let go of my hair, and I fell sideways against the Bronco. The other guy kicked me in the rear, and they walked away. I heard car doors open and shut, an engine start, and the whoosh of car leaving the lot. I sat up and hugged my sides with both arms. It felt like I had broken shards of glass under my skin, and every breath brought an involuntary shudder. My jaw tightened with pain, and anger coursed through my head like a flame-headed demon lashing a horse with a barbed-wire whip.

Yet I sat on the hard pavement realizing I'd been beaten like a dog and fought the sick shame I felt at being glad they had not done more.

10

I sat upright in the motel chair, the nine-millimeter Browning on the table next to me, and watched Tom Brokaw talk about inner-city violence. Country violence was not much better.

It was difficult to get comfortable, and each movement or shift brought pain; a throbbing and pulsing of internal wounds like bad meat under my skin. I had eaten a handful of ibuprofen and filled a plastic laundry bag with ice, covering the bag with a towel and placing it over my torso to reduce the swelling in my muscles. Ten years ago I would have shrugged off similar injuries, but age takes its toll in sinister ways. Probably needed to become more calculating in my choices.

I tried to call Detective Merrill, but he wasn't in. I didn't leave my name. I thought about who had sent the thugs. Robby Blue was the first person who came to mind, but he didn't strike me as the type with that much juice. Difficult to imagine he was connected, and these guys were pros. Who then? What had Sandy brushed up against that brought in that kind of talent? It didn't jibe with the amount of information we'd uncovered. What did

Francine Wilson's death have to do with leg-breakers who drove thirty-thousand-dollar automobiles?

At six o'clock the national news went off, and the local news took over. The lead story was about a drug bust in North Branson. The police led by Chief Alec York had arrested three Springfield men and confiscated $750,000 worth of drugs, including crack cocaine, uncut crack, and some exotics like ice and scopolamine. Alec York was dark-haired and movie-star handsome as required of those we place in the highest positions of power. The drug bust was followed by a human-interest piece on Alec York and his possible appointment as the head of a statewide drug and major-crimes enforcement bureau. File film of York rolled on the screen while the voice-over spoke of his accomplishments. He smiled into the camera with dazzling capped teeth, while the narrator spoke of his brother, Lieutenant Governor Justin York. The narrator compared the Yorks to the Kennedy brothers and called them favorite sons of North Branson and southwest Missouri. Felicia Taylor York was also mentioned along with her connection to Taylor Heights and Taylor Industries.

The station didn't show any film of her.

Sitting there, an ice bag on my ribs, a nine-millimeter pistol within arm's reach, I wondered at my self-deceptions and delusions. The mighty backwoods recluse who was going to ride into town, shove a few people around until I set things right. It was naïve. Stupid. Dangerous. I'd misjudged something along the way and had paid large for the mistake.

There was a knock at my door. I reached for the Browning and slipped it under the towel and asked who it was.

"Sandy."

"Be right there." As quickly as the soreness would allow I placed towel, ice bag, and gun under the bed. I stood and began putting my shirt on as I walked, erect and gingerly, to the door. Grunting in pain, I shrugged the shirt on with small tugs, covering my wounds by the time I reached the door. I opened it, and Sandy brushed past me and walked into the room. She smelled of perfume and female.

"I want to talk to you about something," she said, her back to me. She turned around in front of the television and fixed me with fire-blue eyes. "When I asked you to come up here, it was to help me; not for you to protect me, and not to have Chick follow me around."

"Just making sure nothing happens to you. I feel better knowing he's watching your back."

"And I feel better knowing he is with you," she said. "Did you ever think of that? You're the one encountering pimps in bars. And why are you standing like that?"

"Like what?"

"Stiff, like you had a board up your back."

"I took a nap. When I woke up my neck was stiff. Must've slept on it wrong."

I saw her look at the bed, hospital neat and unwrinkled, and knew she wasn't buying it. She looked up from the bed, and her eyes softened. "What did you do?"

"It's nothing. Be fine in a day or so."

She walked toward me. Standing in front of me, she lifted the flap of my unbuttoned shirt and touched me below the ribs on my left side, and I sucked in a shallow breath.

"You're hurt," she said. Her voice had a catch in it, a tiny lilt of fear like a child discovering a kitten run over by a car. "What happened to you?"

"Two guys objected to my conversation."

"You got beat up."

"You should see the other guys," I said. "I managed to wrinkle a shirt on one of them while they were beating the crap out of me." I told her about the altercation in the parking lot.

"In broad daylight?" she asked.

"They were highly efficient. But I still didn't buy any encyclopedias from them."

She looked up at my face, blinked twice, and I saw her lovely eyes filling. "Are you all right?" she asked, reaching up with a hand to brush the hair off my forehead.

"Sure," I said. "Ronnie Lott hits harder."

"What have I gotten you into?"

"Nothing I can't handle. Did I ever tell you about the time I held off the entire Dallas Cowboy Cheerleaders squad with only a bath towel and a crucifix?"

"Don't be evasive."

"There I was," I said, "surrounded by a swarm of vicious females with pearl-white teeth and hungry eyes. Closer and closer they came. My back against the wall. Holding the crucifix out, I raised the towel . . ."

"Oh, shut up," she said, fighting the smile tugging at the corners of her expressive mouth. She gave me a light whack on the stomach, which caused me to wince.

"Hey!" I said. "That's not nice. You're supposed to feel sorry for me. I thought women loved vulnerable men. Besides, this is the point where the heroine succors the wounded hero."

She cocked her head and eyed me. "What?"

"You know, succor. Aid, support, comfort," I said, slipping my arms around her.

She looked up at me and said, "Don't you want to know about my interview with Alec York?"

I looked up at the ceiling and made a pretense of giving it some thought. "All right. You tell me about your interview, but then we go right to the succoring."

"Alec York is a very assured and astute police administrator," said Sandy. We had ordered a pot of coffee from room service and drank it from handsome china cups. Sandy and I sat at the table as she talked. "He is self-assured to the point of smugness and is a clever and perceptive police administrator. You get the impression that Mr. York, while gracious, does not consider anyone to be quite as talented or as intelligent as he considers himself. It is more a feeling than anything else. Call it woman's intuition if you will, but there is more to Alec York than he reveals in conversation."

"What do you mean?" I asked.

She sipped her coffee and looked over the edge of the cup at me. Sandy was the whole package: intelligent, articulate, and visually stunning. There were times when I was struck by my good fortune at being loved by Sandra Castillon Collingsworth. We had met after I'd retired from playing in the NFL—actually, I had walked away and disappeared from public view. Would not grant interviews. Did not return calls. Left no return address. There was a big flap at the time. Bigger than it deserved. I was just a football player who no longer wanted to exist as a Sunday afternoon hero on the twenty-seven-inch screens of the American consciousness; a guy who loved football and the locker-room camaraderie of men trying to realize a shared dream. A dream better left off the evening news and the morning paper.

I met Sandra Collingsworth at a party put on by mutual friends. She didn't know who I was or who I had been; whoever that was. I told her I was a retired football player, but it was several weeks before she found out that I was a news item and that no one knew where I was or why I had quit. She didn't care. She had no particular passion for professional athletes. She dated me because she wanted to. She was the only person to interview me after my sudden retirement and then only to hear me say I'd quit and that there was life after, even in spite of, football.

And she began to fill the cold hole I'd felt since I'd shipped away to Vietnam.

"What I mean," she said, "is that Alec York gives off signals that are largely imperceptible and particularly so to men."

"Sounds a little sexist to me," I said.

She smiled. "No offense intended. He doesn't speak or look at men the way he does women."

"Meaning?"

"There are signals he reserves for women. A smile, a gesture, a quick glance at parts of your anatomy that are not on your face. Men do not do these things to other men. He invites with his eyes, comforts, gives the impression that you and what you are saying are the most important things in the world. Women love that. I love that. When are you going to start doing that?"

"I thought you loved muscular troglodytes who grunted and only wanted you for your body."

"Anyway, it doesn't surprise me he has other women, nor that despite this his wife stays with him."

"Does it surprise you he stays with her?" I asked.

"You mean the alcoholism? Not really. Her connections and family name are important here in North Branson. Besides, it allows him to appear tragic, the strong male who endures the pathetic wife. The male martyr. Some men love that. It also helps people to overlook his liaisons. He is a powerful man on the brink of becoming nearly omnipotent in the state of Missouri. With his brother a heartbeat from the governor's office, his possible appointment as the head of a state drug enforcement bureau will make him one of the most powerful law enforcement officials in the state."

"If not the most powerful."

"Right."

"Politics," I said.

"Yes, I know you hate politics, and if you have a weakness it is your lack of political acumen and respect for the power it creates. Political power is the reality in our society, and your aversion to it does not change that. It's not 1885, Wyatt."

"A pity it's not, isn't it?" I said, not allowing myself to be drawn into that argument. "Did you tell him that you suspect Travis Conrad of date rape and one of his officers of coercing a prostitute to have sex with him?"

"There is nothing I suspect or you suspect that Alec York is not aware of. There is nothing hidden from York in this town. He doesn't just feel the pulse of North Branson; he is the pulse. In fact, he brought up the subject, which he referred to as 'improbable' and 'inelegant.'"

"Inelegant?"

"That's what he said."

"I bet I don't know three people who would use *inelegant* in a sentence. Do you think he's covering for Conrad and the policeman?"

"Yes."

"Even rape and murder?"

She nodded.

"So how does a guy like this get so close to power?"

"Honey," she said, reaching across the table and brushing my cheek, "you'll hurt your poor little troglodyte brain trying to fathom the depths of political reality in the nineties."

I took her hand in mine. "Are you patronizing me?"

"Of course I am. You are so perceptive."

"It compensates for my underdeveloped political acumen."

"Thanks for sending Chick," she said. "But no more, okay?"

I didn't answer.

"Nothing's going to happen to me. Give Chick a couple of days off from following me around."

"I'll think about it. Meanwhile, I'm ready to be succored."

She leaned her face against the back of her hand. A dimple like a wink formed at the corner of her cheek as she looked at me with a drowsy, bemused smile. "Why did I allow myself to fall in love with someone like you?"

"Even troglodytes need love," I said.

11

We waited until half past midnight. Sandy and I sat at a table drinking coffee and hot tea while Chick leaned against the door across the room, but Chastity didn't show at Travis Conrad's Hickory Wind. Neither did Travis Conrad, though his picture was everywhere. Finally, we gave up and headed for the parking lot.

An autumn storm was building, and heat lightning pulsed like a damaged heart in the purple-black clouds. Dry leaves skittered down the oil-smudged pavement like the scratching of brittle fingernails.

"Maybe we scared her off," said Sandy as we drove back to the motel. The first drops of rain splattered against the windshield, blurring the neon of the North Branson strip and smearing the glow of the river of headlights.

"She'll be back," I said. "Robby Blue won't allow himself to be run off that easily."

After a sleepless night due to the damoclean thud and crack of thunder, my bruises, and too much thought about too many things, I awoke and decided to get some roadwork in. I rang

Sandy's room and asked if she wanted to go with me. She did. Sandy kept herself in top shape, not with aerobics and health club memberships, but with skiing, swimming, hunting, and hiking the slopes of the Colorado Rockies.

We ran by the quaint, quasi-rustic resort motels, the streets strewn with branches twisted from trees and washed down the pavement by the rain. The rain-scrubbed Ozark Mountains smelled clean. The oak and walnut and hickory trees were a panorama of vivid green, blazing orange, and butter-soft harvest gold, vivid against a morning sky the color of a newborn's eyes. Nature claimed the sunlight while the neon slept.

We started off walking, stepping over the sticks and branches, increasing the pace until my muscles warmed to the point I didn't grind my teeth each time I took a deep breath. "Are you okay?" Sandy asked, stopping to check on me.

"You go ahead," I said. "I'll get loose and catch up."

She turned her head to the side and looked at me. "This is an excuse to watch my backside."

"Motivation is the key to enhanced performance."

Finally, I was able to accelerate to a quick rhythm punctuated by the occasional ripple of pain through my ribs. Probably wasn't going to take on Roy Jones, Jr., for a couple of days yet. There is a near delight in enduring pain and playing through the pain; a masochistic holdover from my NFL days. If you could continue to play, or exercise, then the injury lost its reality. It was a form of self-deception. A mastery of sorts. The delusions of grown men playing a kid's game.

Two miles out, the road began to rise upward onto a bluff overlooking North Branson. A historic marker told me that this was where the Battle of Taylor Heights was fought in 1864. We kept running past it and through a resort development. We ran by city maintenance employees, who fed branches into a tree shredder as if the branches were corpses and the machine a mass grave. The branches popped, crackled, and shuddered as the auger chewed the wood into sawdust.

We got in three more miles before we returned to the motel and slipped into the blessed relief of the motel's whirlpool spa, allowing the warm, healing waters to swirl and soothe my injuries while I held Sandy close and dreamed of a return bout with Heckle and Jeckle on better terms.

I showered, shaved, and ate blueberry waffles with Chick at Perkins. Sandy left to drive to Springfield again. Not much time left. Day after tomorrow she would have to return to Denver. Tonight might be our last shot at Chastity.

After breakfast Chick and I drove to the city courthouse to examine land documents. Real estate was the gold that had brought the speculator and the hucksters to these hills, and I wanted to see who owned it. A look at local deeds and licenses revealed an interesting string of purchases running east to west between Highways 65 and 158, purchases which bore the names of York, Cavalerri, Taylor, and, interestingly, my good friend Officer Bredwell. The names lay like a string of pearls between two large plots of land, one at the east end and another at the west end, which were owned by the So-Mo Holding Company. I asked the recorder if she knew of any planned bypass projects. She said there weren't any she'd heard of, and an effort to bypass North Branson would prove unpopular because it would kill off the business district.

"There's already too much movement away from downtown," she said. "Five years ago there was a group tried to get a bypass petition going, but it was beaten down by Mylon Taylor and Paul Sherman—he was the mayor then. No sir, anybody tries to bypass North Branson would catch it." I asked about So-Mo Holding, but she didn't know who owned the company.

Why would a group of North Branson's movers and shakers buy land between two highways when any bypass project would result in a lynching? And how could a policeman afford land around here? And a better question: Why was he allowed in on the mix? Was it a reward for his loyalty? Or something more? And who or what was the So-Mo Holding Company?

As Chick and I left the courthouse, we encountered Velonne Cavalerri, attorney-at-law, walking up the sidewalk, her high heels clicking in a brisk rhythm. I wished her good morning. She looked up at me, jaw set, and increased the length of her stride. She didn't stop to hug me or even speak. To describe her look as cool would be to call the North Pole chilly.

"She's crazy about you," said Chick.

"We're going to be married."

"Her ex-husband will be glad to hear that," Chick said. "She bled him like sticking an ice pick in his carotid in the divorce settlement. You gotta love lawyers, don't you? They'd hump a landfill if they thought there was a wallet in it. Cavalerri says his ex-wife, the lawyer, has been getting her oil changed regularly by Chief York. Started happening before they were divorced. He caught them at it in his own bed one afternoon. Said neither of them seemed the least concerned. York even asked how things were going for him. Mrs. Cavalerri told Mr. Cavalerri to shut the door until they were dressed."

I raised my eyebrows and looked at him.

Chick smiled. "That's what the man said. He also said York was welcome to her."

"There's a progressive attitude," I said, unlocking the Bronco.

"Just your regular Norman Rockwell kind of people. Makes you feel all gooey-warm inside, doesn't it?"

"Found out something else which was interesting while I was there," Chick said.

"Which is?"

"Mrs. Cavalerri defended Chastity on a couple of soliciting charges."

My hand was on the door handle when the police unit pulled up next to me. The driver's side door opened, and Officer Bredwell stepped out of the car.

"Just when you thought it was safe to go in the water again," Chick said.

"Chief York wants to see you," Bredwell said, without preamble, which seemed to be his normal operating procedure.

"I'm all booked up this afternoon. First, I have to go to the drugstore and buy some comic books, and then I'm going to watch *Oprah*. Today's topic is 'mouth-breathing bed wetters who become dysfunctional cops with bad manners.' "

"You can eighty-six the comedy routine, Storme. I'm not impressed."

"See," said Chick. "Told you you weren't funny."

"I try and I try."

The muscles around Bredwell's ears tensed. He said, "Chief York would appreciate it if you would come by his office. He wants to meet you. You don't have to come." His fingers squeezed and wrinkled his patent leather gun belt. "He wanted you to know it was up to you."

"See," Chick said. "Wasn't so hard, was it? We'll be glad to swing by and see the chief. Probably wants to pick our brains about police etiquette."

"Don't push your luck, asshole," said Bredwell, getting back into his car. He left, his tires squirching against the pavement.

"You tell him I was an asshole?" Chick said.

"Nope. Probably just brilliant detective work."

"It is hard to tell, isn't it?"

12

The North Branson municipal building was a neo–Frank Lloyd Wright construction of brick, glass, and steel trimmed with smooth mortar ribs built upon the base of a gently rising slope of grass; expertly landscaped and nonthreatening. We entered through glass doors and walked into the foyer. The receptionist directed us to the third floor. We rode a whisper-quiet elevator to the third floor. The elevator doors whooshed open, and Chick and I stepped into a huge open room that smelled of the dusky electric aroma of electronic machines and the burnt-brown odor of stale coffee. Phones jangled and computer keys clicked as we weaved our way through desks and chairs toward the back, where another receptionist told us we would find York's office.

There was no cigarette smoke curling up into thick clouds. No plainclothes detectives with loosened ties and rolled-up sleeves grilling suspects. It was more like the main floor of a corporation than a police squad room.

At the rear of the squad room we came to a glass-walled receptionist's office. The words ALEX YORK—CHIEF OF POLICE were stenciled in gold leaf on the glass. We walked through the door, and the secretary, who looked like actress Rachel Ward's sister, asked if she could help us.

"We're here to see Chief York. My name is Wyatt Storme."

She picked up the phone, pressed a button, and announced us. She hung up the phone and said, "Chief York said he'll be a few minutes. Would you care to have a seat?"

"No thank you," I said. "I'm not going to wait."

Her large dark eyes widened. "I don't understand."

"He asked to see us. I don't have the patience to play power games with him." I turned and started to leave.

"Wait. Please," she said. "Let me talk to him again."

I stopped and watched as she opened the walnut door marked ALEC YORK, CHIEF OF POLICE, PRIVATE. She entered the room, returned directly, and said, "Chief York will see you now."

"Another incredible example of your charm," Chick said.

"Tact and courtesy win the day every time," I said.

She ushered us into the maroon-carpeted office, closing the door behind us. Alec York, resplendent in a dark blue suit and rep tie, stood with his hands behind him and flashed his movie-star smile. He walked around his desk and extended his hand. "Alec York," he said.

I accepted his hand. The line of his suit was flawless, and the mahogany-tasseled Nunn-Bush shoes were uncreased. He looked like he'd just walked out of Bloomingdale's. "I know. It's on the door. It's everywhere. I'm Wyatt Storme. This is Chick Easton."

He shook Chick's hand, then offered us seats. We sat, and he walked around behind his desk and sat in the high-backed executive chair. On the wall behind him were plaques proclaiming him "Rotary Man of the Year—1995" and "Outstanding Law Enforcement Professional—1994," alongside pictures of himself with the governor, and with pro baseball and football players. On a cherry credenza to his left and behind him was a fishing trophy for winning the Law Enforcement Bass Tournament.

"Gentlemen," began York, leaning forward and folding his

hands in front of him, placing them on his desk. "I need your assistance. It seems we have a problem."

"I don't have a problem," I said. "Be glad to help you with yours, though."

He smiled and nodded his head. "You are correct. It is myself, and more specifically, my police department, that has the problem. A public relations problem."

"It's a little more than that."

He pursed his lips and nodded his head. "You may be right. Still, I'm hoping that we can resolve this uh . . . misunderstanding. It is Ms. Collingsworth I need assistance with. She seems to be under the impression there is a conspiracy of silence within this department. I assure you that this is not the case." He said it as if his assurances were sufficient and there could be no reason to doubt. Then he assumed a demeanor of resolution, his eyes looking straight at us, his shoulders squared. "Ms. Collingsworth, like most women, is excitable and prone to leap to conclusions."

"Some women, maybe," I said. "Not Sandy."

"Regardless, she is creating an unnecessary flap in the community, which threatens the morale of my officers and also the confidence of the citizenry, and I must take steps to deal with this false impression."

" 'Confidence of the citizenry'?" said Chick, looking at me and smiling.

Alec York sat back and eyed us. The look was flat and devoid of emotion. No one spoke for an extended interval. Most people are uncomfortable with long strings of silence. York, buttressed by his position and his confidence, knew this and had probably used the tactic before. First person to talk was the loser. For most of the last decade I had lived in the mountains of Colorado and the backwood timber of the Missouri Ozarks; long periods of solitude without hearing a human voice were nothing new. As for Chick, I had yet to see him ill at ease in any situation. The present one seemed to amuse him, as most things did.

I folded my arms across my chest, rested an ankle on top of my knee, and leaned back in my chair. York gave us a grave, practiced administrative look. Chick looked amused some more. The building hummed with a gray vibration like a huge sigh.

Finally, York gave up and asked, "What is it you do, Mr. Storme?"

I shrugged. "I'm retired."

"From what?"

"From answering questions about what I do."

He smiled at that. "Touché, Mr. Storme." He looked at Chick. "And you're a skip tracer, a modern-day bounty hunter. Is that correct?"

"Actually, I'm an armadillo rancher."

"Excuse me?"

"There's nothing like sitting on a horse at sunset, watching armadillos shimmering in the West Texas sun like a thousand Brillo pads," said Chick.

York put his hands together on the desk. "Very humorous."

"Glad you appreciated it," said Chick. "You care if I smoke?"

"I'd prefer you didn't."

"What I heard," Chick said, placing an unlit cigarette between his lips.

York leaned forward and placed his forearms on his desk. "Checking your backgrounds reveals some interesting, even astonishing, information."

"He's interesting, I'm astonishing," said Chick.

York ignored Chick. "Storme, you left pro football at the height of your career and disappeared from public life. When you have reappeared, it has been to irritate law enforcement officials and complicate their investigations. I hope that is not your intention here, because I guarantee it will not be tolerated. This is my town, Storme."

"Odd they named it North Branson, then," I said.

"It is not my intention to be unpleasant and confrontational. I am merely trying to be up front with you. As for you, Mr. Easton, checking with NCIC, I learn that your activities before 1975 are classified. Which indicates one of two possibilities—either you are in the witness protection program, or you worked for one of the federal intelligence agencies. I prefer the latter since a protected witness would not be rambling around the country picking up bail-jumpers. What do you think?"

"You got a match?" asked Chick.

"Why are you running a check on us?" I asked.

"According to Ms. Cavarelli, a local attorney, you made some rather ugly insinuations about our professional relationship."

"There you go," Chick said to me. "Making ugly insinuations again."

"Sometimes I can't stop myself," I said, looking at York. "I've met your wife. She was working out on some college girl. Seems she also labors under the false impression that you're spreading yourself around too much. Not to mention that one of your cops tries to take advantage of Francine Wilson after she makes allegations about Travis Conrad. Everybody has reason to wish her to go away and shut up, and then she conveniently turns up dead. What have you got, some kind of police outreach program to undersexed females?"

His face gathered itself like a fist. "I don't appreciate your irresponsible accusations. They serve no useful purpose."

"And I don't like being rousted every five minutes by your storm troopers."

"I'll admit that Officers Bredwell and Pethmore are a little over-enthusiastic, but they are good policemen. Highly decorated."

"And Sandy is a good reporter," I said. "She's honest and fair and persistent. If nothing is out of synch in your department, she'll shine you on. But if there is a bad actor in your department, she'll burn him. Right before your eyes. You can bet on it."

"Her information is wrong, and her suspicions are unfounded."

"Then why is Francine Wilson dead?"

"She may have committed suicide."

"Her roommate said it wasn't her style."

"That is almost a cliché in suicides. Close friends always assert that the suicide wasn't that type of person."

"She had her calendar planned for the next month. She was a very organized young person. Not the type to commit suicide as a spur-of-the-moment decision. She also had an appointment with Velonne Cavarelli. It would have been her second visit. I don't have any faith in coincidence, and there are too many of them here."

"We have not yet dismissed the possibility of homicide."

"How did she die?"

"We are not prepared to release that information. We are still investigating the rape charge, despite what you and your woman think."

"Her name is Sandy."

"Pardon me for offending your progressive sensibilities."

"No chance of that."

"Regardless, I did not invite you here to discuss the particulars of outstanding investigations, nor to engage in verbal volleyball. I merely wish for you to control Ms. Collingsworth while we complete our inquiries."

Chick laughed. It was a low staccato burst. "You want him to control Sandy?" Chick said. "Now, that's funny."

"Wrong choice of words," said York. "*Influence* might be a better term."

"I am Sandy's fiancé," I said. "Not her trainer. This is her ball game."

"Then I have wasted my time," said York. "Yours as well. Have a nice day." Then he dismissed us with as much regard as if we had suddenly evaporated.

13

⸺〰⸺

So, what next?" Chick asked as the waitress set an Amstel Light beer in front of him. It was four o'clock, and we were sitting in the motel lounge waiting for Fred Merrill to come by after work for a drink. The weather had turned muggy and unusually warm, and the air-conditioning was on, drifting through the muted lighting like the cold air that escapes when you open a refrigerator door.

"I don't know," I said. "We have a lot of disconnected information. The same people keep popping up, yet I don't know what any of this has to do with Francine Wilson's death. That, and I don't think York brought us to his office just to talk about Sandy."

"Sizing us up?"

"Yeah. But for what reason?"

"We're trampling the vines in his garden. You pissed off his girlfriend, the hot-blooded Mediterranean lawyer with the great legs, and around these parts, York is the bull stag and he doesn't like us scattering the herd. You're going to have to get a better handle on the way things work."

"Who hired the muscle?"

"That's a good question." He poured beer into a glass. "Seems heavy-handed for what we know. Then there's the fact that people are prone not to like you. You *are* kind of a scumbag when I think about it. Not surprising that people want to work out on you. I've got a theory about . . . well, look at this," he said, looking past my shoulder. I turned around in my seat and saw Mrs. Alec York walking our way. She wore a long-tailed blouse over dark slacks, with a gold belt that accented her thin waist and wonderful hips. Her eyes were set, as if concentrating to maintain a course through a maze.

She stopped at our table and looked at me with eyes that shimmered like the luster of windowpanes struck with a pale winter light.

"Are you going to offer me a seat?" she asked.

"I was under the impression you didn't like me."

She laughed. It was a harsh, braying laugh that erupted from her throat. Then, abruptly, her face turned serious. "Are you a gentleman, or not?" Her purse slipped down her shoulder, and she made no effort to adjust it.

"Won't you join us, Mrs. York?" I said, nodding at the chair. Chick rose from his seat and pulled the chair out for her. She sat down with a grace that belied her condition. A waitress bustled up.

"Will one of you gentlemen buy me a drink?"

"I'm not an enabler," I said.

"How fucking noble," she said. "Interesting that your gallantry does not preclude your insufferable smugness."

"I was first in my class in smugness. I also find your language inelegant." Finally got the chance to use the word.

Chick looked at me and shook his head slightly, then said, "I'm always willing to buy a drink for a lovely woman. What are you drinking?"

"Double Chivas with ice, please."

Chick nodded, and the waitress left.

"And who might you be?" she asked Chick.

"I might be Doc Holliday if I weren't Chick Easton."

The waitress returned with the Scotch. Mrs. York swallowed a quarter of it immediately before setting it on the table. The wetness of her drink glistened on her upper lip. She touched the back of a hand to her cheek.

"Heavy stuff for this early in the day," I said.

She cocked her head, put a hand to her throat, fluttered her long eyelashes, and said, "Your solicitude is so touching. It's comforting to be in the company of concerned gentlemen. I notice you're not drinking. Why is that?"

"I threw away my crutches years ago."

"And your etiquette with it, I'd say," she said, her eyes flaring up. "I understand you had a little tête-à-tête with my husband. Is that correct?"

"We had a conversation, but there were three of us there. One more than the requirement for a tête-à-tête."

"I don't need grammar lessons from bumpkins. I have an English degree from Wellesley. You do know about Wellesley, don't you?"

"Isn't that where they send rich girls to erase all trace of humanity before brainwashing them?"

"You are an asshole, aren't you?"

"Trying to hold up my end."

"What did my husband, the double bastard, talk to you about?"

"Not much. It was mutually frustrating."

"As most conversations with you probably are."

I shrugged. She took another knock of the Scotch. I said, "If you don't like your husband, why don't you leave him?"

She laughed the short braying laugh again. "Seems simple to you, doesn't it? Why doesn't the nasty Wellesley bitch just leave the manipulative, adulterous husband?"

"Sounds better every time I hear it."

"You have no understanding of power and position, do you Mr. Storme?"

"I have no respect for it," I said.

"How wonderful for you."

"You know about your husband's affairs then?"

"Yes, darling, I know all about them. I'm self-indulgent, not stupid." She spat the last word of the sentence at me.

"What do you get from your relationship with York?"

She drained her drink, then stared off into a distance beyond the walls of the lounge. Chick sipped his beer and studied her. "I'd like another, please," she said, holding up her glass. Chick nodded to the waitress, who brought another drink for Mrs. York and a beer for Chick.

"What we're wondering, Mrs. York," said Chick, "is why such a well-made, intelligent woman would continue in an unhappy relationship?"

She looked at Chick, smiled, then reached out and stroked the side of his face with the back of her hand. "You are a charming man," she said, cooing. "And such a bullshitter. Still, it's nice to hear. And you have an interesting face. The face of a complex man. There is a strength in it and a depth to your eyes that speaks of a man who seldom allows . . . oh, what are the words I'm looking for? . . . Yes, of course. A man whose eyes do not betray the passions within. What is it you have seen that you will not share, and why are you trying to look inside me where there is nothing but rage and self-loathing?"

It was as close as I'd seen Chick Easton come to being taken aback. Even half in the bag, Felicia York was a remarkable woman. Chick's eyes flickered once like static electricity before recovering. He said, "Mrs. York, there is some truly bad Karma in North Branson, and a girl has died. A girl who didn't deserve to."

"And," she said, gesturing with her hand, "you and the bumpkin are here to clean up the town like the Lone Ranger and Tonto?" She looked at me. "Is that correct?"

"Something like that."

She leaned back and said, "Well, I hope you don't end up dashed against the rocks." She swallowed Scotch. "Some of the best have. But I have been elusive, haven't I? You are wondering why I remain wedded to the billy-goat king?" She held up her empty glass. "This is my lover now. The ambrosia of the goddess of late afternoon ennui. Once, she was young and fair, bursting with the rapture of imagination's promise. And then . . ." Her eyes narrowed with the heaviness of whiskey and depression. "I am shackled to a man who brings me no happiness, and I am either too indolent or too codependent to free myself. I am the coauthor of his sickness and complicit in his dark schemes." Once again she stared off into a dimension only she could see.

"What dark schemes?" I asked.

"What?" she said, shaken from her reverie. "I need another Scotch. More nectar for the goddess." She stood up from her chair and waved her glass in the air, causing the ice cubes to fly through the air and rattle on an empty table nearby. She stumbled, and I rose from my chair and caught her around the waist. Her body sagged against me before she recovered enough to place her arms around my neck. Breathing the fumes of distilled malt into my face, she said, "Ah, Quixote, thou art the truest and brightest of knights."

At that moment Detective Fred Merrill entered the lounge, his bulky frame darkening the entrance. When she saw him a small cry escaped her lips, and she ran to the astonished Merrill, her arms out as if she were a drowning victim reaching for her rescuer.

She hugged herself to Merrill. Merrill, for his part, appeared confused and embarrassed, arms at his side—not knowing what to do with them or the lady. He glanced around the room, then, satisfied no one of consequence was watching, put a beefy arm around her, and walked her back to our table.

He helped her into her seat. "What's going on here?" he asked. I thought I detected a note of irritation in his voice.

"We've been pumping alcohol into the Duchess here, in hopes she will molest us," I said. He gave me a funny look. "What do you think, Fred? She came in like that; we didn't force it down her throat."

"You okay, Felix?" Fred asked her. Not Felicia, Felix. Like a pet name. Chick looked at me and raised his apostrophe eyebrow questioningly.

"Yes, Freddy. Felix the cat is wonderful. A wonderful cat." She held up her glass. "But Felix needs another saucer of cream." She placed her hand on his leg. "Please, Freddy, another."

Fred swallowed, enjoying her attention yet not wanting to show it. He ordered another drink for her and bourbon and water for himself.

"Not wise," I said.

"Butt out," Felicia, the wonderful cat, said.

"Glad to." I turned my attention to Merrill. "We've been visiting with Mrs. York's husband—"

"The double bastard," said Felicia, interrupting. Her eyes were drowsy, and her jaw was slack with the weight of alcohol.

"Anyway," I said, "he assures us our suspicions are unfounded and all is well in the magic kingdom."

"Where'd you run into him?"

"We were summoned to his office for an official audience."

"We may never wash again," said Chick.

"How do we get to talk Travis Conrad?" I asked Merrill.

"That might be tough. This town's pretty touchy about things like that."

"Is he in town?"

"Came in last night. Private jet. He and the Fire Creek Band will be playing the Hickory Wind this weekend. Starts tonight. You could go watch him."

"Where does he stay?"

"Usually rents out the Blue Bayou. The entire place. He and his entourage stay there. The Fire Creek Band, his roadies, and the technicians. And his bodyguards. They take over the whole thing. Throw parties for other celebrities. Sometimes he recruits local girls to come out and entertain."

"Like Francine Wilson?"

"And others like her."

"Sounds unwholesome," said Chick.

"We get complaints from time to time. Drug use, local girls who lose their dignity. That kind of thing."

"Then it's the job of the local police and power brokers to look the other way."

"Exactly."

"So Conrad might be at the Blue Bayou right now?"

Merrill gave me a tired look. "Dammit, Storme, don't get into shit I can't pull you out of," he said. "Guys like Travis Conrad have the key to the city. They're untouchable here. He can do whatever he wants. Including bouncing some nosy retired football player and his sidekick around the ballroom. You go out there and stir things and . . ." He hesitated, then said, "And you're not listening to me, are you?"

"You want to go out and visit an honest-to-God country star, Chick?" I said.

"Thought you'd never ask."

Felicia York, who'd been drinking quietly, slumped over on the table, passed out.

"Looks like you got your hands full, Detective."

Merrill shook his head. "Don't go out there, Storme."

I shrugged. "Thanks, but in the immortal words of the Four Tops, 'I can't help myself.' You take care of the Duchess, and we'll see you later. Ready, Chick?"

"Always," he said. "My Indian name is Ever Ready."

14

The Blue Bayou Resort was set on a hill looking down on the twin cities of Branson and North Branson. It really was blue, but there was no bayou. It was a New Orleans French–style building with iron gates and large rectangular windows on the main building. Brick commons in front. Vines growing off the wall. The marquee said, WELCOME TRAVIS CONRAD AND THE FIRE CREEK BAND.

"First-rate detective work," said Chick, looking at the marquee. "We're looking for the guy, and there's a sign three times the size of Rhode Island announcing where he's staying. I am mortified."

We went inside the main office. A man and his wife were at the desk arguing with the woman at the registration desk. The male tourist was mid-fifties and his neck was red, but the sun hadn't caused it. Their luggage was on the floor beside them, and he had both arms up on the desk.

"I don't care who he is," said the tourist. "I made reservations three months ago, and I want my room."

The manager, a tall woman in her early thirties, was not enjoying herself but did her best to deal with the problem handed down from the corporate office.

"I know it's an imposition, Mr. Morris," she said. "But Mr. Conrad's business manager said Mr. Conrad will comp you anyplace in town as well as give you tickets to his show."

"I don't even like his voice," said the man.

"Please, Sam," urged the man's wife, "let's just go somewhere else. We can stay anywhere we want, and it's free."

"I don't care. I work hard all year and don't like being pushed around by some guy who hasn't worked a day in his life." Mr. Morris didn't like Travis Conrad.

The argument went back and forth until the couple surrendered, but not before Morris had been offered free tickets to Glen Campbell's show as well as limousine service to tonight's performance. Mrs. Morris liked Glen Campbell. Before they left, Morris apologized to the manager and to Chick and myself for his outbursts.

After they had departed, the manager asked, "May I help you?"

"We'd like to make room reservations," I said.

"Forgive me," she said, "but for the rest of the week Travis Conrad has booked every room."

"Oh, that's okay," I said. "I'm bringing my wife down next summer and was in the area so I thought I'd drop by and make reservations now. It will be our tenth wedding anniversary, and I want it to be special. What's your best room?"

She smiled. Relieved. I smiled back. We were very happy. Another victim of the incomparable charm of America's sweetheart of the gridiron.

"We have several rooms that are very nice," she said. "We often have honeymooners come here."

"I want the biggest room in the place," I said. "Don't you have something special? Something like Travis Conrad would stay in. Big and roomy, you know. We'll need lots of room." I winked knowingly at her. I heard Chick chuckle softly.

"That would be the Evangeline Suite," she said.

"That sounds perfect. Where would that be located?"

She produced a diagram of the resort grounds, and with a felt-tipped pen she showed us how to get to the Evangeline Suite. I thanked her, and as we were leaving she said, "I hope you and your wife have a nice time when you come."

"Oh, she'll love this place."

We walked back outside into the warm Indian summer air. I said, "He'll be in the Evangeline Suite, or I'll admit Raymond Berry had better hands than me."

Chick lit a cigarette and said, "You do the corniest midwestern accent I've ever seen. How can you take advantage of that poor lady?"

"She didn't mind kicking the Morris couple out of the resort. Besides, I am from the Midwest."

"I already don't like Travis Conrad, and I haven't even met him."

"Well, we're about to."

We got into the Bronco as if to leave, but doubled back and drove to the rear of the resort lot, where we disembarked and made our way to the Evangeline Suite. It was situated in the inner court. It was of a similar motif as the rest of the motel, but larger and more elaborate. It was easy to see why Conrad had chosen it. I knocked on the door in a tentative manner. No answer. I knocked with more authority.

"Who is it?" said a gruff voice.

"Farley Tidwell. *Country Music* magazine," I said. "I'm here to interview Travis Conrad."

"An interview?" said the voice behind the door. Then there was the sound of muffled conversation. A voice, deeper inside the room, said something that sounded like "check it out."

The knob turned, and the door opened, revealing an accountant type in his late thirties—suit pants, tailored shirt with wide stripes, power tie, and suspenders. Receding hairline. Gold-rimmed glasses. He smelled of new money and the old South. "I'm Swope Archibald, Mr. Conrad's business manager." He barely touched the *r* when he pronounced his last name. "I usually coordinate these things. I don't remember talking to you."

"I'm sorry," I said, giving him my best humble yet persistent life insurance salesman manner. "But I set this up with Mr. Conrad personally. We were at a party in Nashville last summer, and he said to drop by when he was in Branson. So here I am. We're doing a series of interviews with the stars who have built this area into the new Nashville. We've talked with Roy Clark, Andy Williams, Bobby Vinton—"

"Godammit, Swope," said a familiar voice from inside the suite. "Don't keep him standing outside like a Baptist minister. Invite 'im in."

"Come in, gentlemen," said Swope. He opened the door to a large room furnished with pastel fabric couches and chairs and French-accent end tables. Monet prints. A wet bar against one wall. A wrought-iron stairway ascended to a landing with French doors leading to what appeared to be a sunroom. This room was built for parties and convention hospitality. Standing in the middle of the room, drink in hand, was Travis Conrad.

Conrad was dressed like a Marin County yuppie: Levi's, tennis shoes, collarless silk shirt, Armani jacket. But the curls framing the boyish face, the eyes that twinkled like the west Texas sky at night, and the trademark smile, which Rex Reed described as "the most famous good-old-boy smile this side of Burt Reynolds," gave him away as the man whose song "One Hell of a Woman and a Very Bad Man" was the Country Music Association record of the year in 1979.

"Come on in, boys," said Conrad, "and we'll have us a sitdown. Get these boys something to drink, Swope."

I thought I saw the business manager's jaw tighten at the mention of bartender duties, but he dutifully asked if we wanted anything. Chick said he'd drink whatever his host was having. We shook hands and sat. Chick introduced himself as my photographer. Archibald brought Chick a tall brown drink and sat. Travis Conrad sat in an overstuffed chair and crossed an ankle over a knee—relaxed, imperial. Country royalty.

"Well, son," he said, "what do those other old boys say about how they made this into the new Nashville?"

"Various things," I said. "Most agree it was phenomenal. Like spontaneous combustion is what Roy Clark said."

"Shit," said Travis. "Roy ain't been inside a recording studio except to fart in the last ten years."

"That's off the record, of course," said Swope Archibald, leaning forward.

"Of course," I said.

"Good to keep the farts off the record," said Chick.

"And them other guys you mentioned," said Travis, "bunch of losers who sing elevator music. I'd appreciate it you didn't lump me with them. They're all from yesterday. I'm as current as two hundred twenty volts. You ever seen Vinton's place? Looks like a Mexican whorehouse. A really nice Mexican whorehouse, though." He smiled, then said, "But you didn't come here to listen to this shit. Go ahead, let 'er rip."

He leaned back, and the flesh under his neck gathered like a sack of oatmeal. The crow's feet, the wrinkles at the mouth corners more visible in repose, and the unnatural darkness of the curly hair, colored to beat back the gray, combined to reveal a man fighting fifty. And losing. Gravity and time eventually claim us all. But he was current.

"How does the nightlife here compare to Nashville?" I asked. "I mean, is it as fast and loose as Nashville?"

"You mean women and drinking and staying up late?" He smiled as if we were sharing some inside secret.

"Yeah. Like how does a big star like yourself entertain himself in southwest Missouri? This is the Bible Belt. The Branson area is geared for family entertainment. You know. Silver Dollar City. The Shepherd of the Hills. How does a fast-lane guy like yourself, a guy who hangs around with movie stars, find a good time in North Branson?"

"Well, hell, son, you know how it is. Doesn't matter which pasture you turn the bull loose in if there are heifers available. Besides, you make your own . . ." He hesitated and looked at me with eyes the color of faded leather. "You know, you look more like a movie extra in a Clint Eastwood western than a magazine writer. How you gonna remember all this?" he asked. "I notice you don't have a recorder. Or a pencil, for that matter."

"Photographic memory," I said. "Like Dustin Hoffman in *Rain Man.*"

He nodded his head slowly, then looked at Chick. "You don't have no camera, either."

"Photographic eyes," said Chick. "Like Christopher Reeve in *Superman.* Or is it X-ray vision? Always get that confused."

"You-all wouldn't be running a shuck on old Trav now, wouldja?"

"Shucks no," said Chick.

"What Nashville party you and me meet at, anyway?"

"They run together in my head."

The faded saddle eyes considered me momentarily, as if recording my face, then he said, "You're not a reporter, are you? What is it you want?"

"Ask you some questions."

"Ain't got time for it. You better leave."

"I hear you like college girls," I said.

"Arch, call the boys up here."

Swope picked up the phone and punched in three digits, waited four seconds, then said, "This is Swope. T.C. says get up here right now. We have a little problem." Then he hung up the phone and looked at me. "They're on the way." He looked at us as if we were hanging meat. Chick chuckled.

"Anything else you boys like to know before you leave?" said Travis.

"Sure," I said. "Do you know Francine Wilson?"

"Who's that?"

"College girl you had sexual relations with a couple of weeks ago."

"I can't remember all the women who've jumped on ol' Maxie Python. I got more notches in my belt than John Wesley Hardin'."

"You'd remember this one. She didn't want to be a notch in your belt."

"Sometimes they say no, but they really mean come on," he said. He looked at Swope Archibald. "You gotta help them."

"In other words," I said, "if you want to buy a car from me, and I know you want to buy it but you don't want to pay my price, then you're saying it's okay for me to pin your arms and take the money."

"Now you're twisting things around," he said. "And that ain't exactly how it is."

"I think no always means no. Otherwise, you become just another bully. A sex mugger. Another thing, Trav, ol' buddy. I don't have any use for guys who think women are trophies. The whole bull-heifer thing? Offensive."

He laughed a throaty laugh and stood up. "Well, what do you know, Swope," he said, "we got us an honest-to-God prude on our hands." Swope looked down at his hands. "What's the matter, boy? Don't you like a taste of poon now and then? They like a taste of ol' Maxie Python, that's for sure."

Chick said, "I always heard guys who name their testicles do it so a total stranger won't be making all the important decisions."

Conrad laughed again. "That's pretty good. I like that one. You're all right. But I'm afraid I'm still gonna have to ask you to leave. Better do it before my boys get here and make you leave. They're real good at that."

"They'll have to be better than real good," Chick said, holding up his glass. "Because I'm not finished with my drink, and being anal retentive I'm all hung up on the completion thing. I try to fight it, but . . ." He smiled and shrugged his shoulders.

There was a knock on the door, and Swope walked over and opened it. Two men walked in, one of them a huge guy with long hair, gargantuan hands, and a face that widened at the jowls like a bullfrog. The other man was a six-footer with red beard and sleepy eyes. He watched everything with a disinterested expression and eyes the color of a lizard's tongue. He watched us by moving his eyes without moving his head. He looked familiar, but I couldn't place him.

The bigger guy said, "What do you need, T.C.?"

"Might be, Tad," said Conrad, nodding his head at us, "that these boys need some help leaving. I'll ask them. You boys got someplace to go?"

Before I could say anything, the big guy with the flaring jowls said, "Easton! You son of a bitch! Get up outta that chair so I can kick your ass." He was unhappy to see my friend.

Chick leaned back in his chair. Smiled and said, "Why Toad, how good to see you."

"It's Tad, you asshole."

"Like tadpole?"

"You know him?" asked Swope Archibald.

"Yeah, I know him," said Tad. The red-bearded guy crossed his arms and looked bored. "He trussed me up in Vegas and stripped . . ." He hesitated. "Doesn't matter. He's got one coming."

"Appears Tad don't like you much," said Conrad, smiling and swirling the contents of his glass.

Chick shrugged. "Almost a recommendation, isn't it?"

He looked at Chick as if seeing him for the first time. "Must be more to you than meets the eye. Both of you."

"Aw shucks," said Chick. "Twarn't nothin'. Like shooting toads with a BB gun."

"I was drunk, or you wouldn't have gotten away with it," Tad said. The outsized cheeks bellowed.

"Drunk or sober," Chick said, "same result."

"Let's step outside and settle this."

"Why that just suits me so much, Toady," Chick said. "You go on outside and wait, and I'll be around in a minute or so."

The corners of the red-bearded bodyguard's mouth raised an eighth of an inch in a bemused smile. "Come on, Tad," he said. "How many times I have to tell you? Be a pro. You're letting him yank your chain."

"This sonuvabitch's gonna pay."

"Grow up a little, man," said Sleepy Eyes without emotion or rancor.

"We don't need any fussing, anyway," said Conrad. "Do we, boys?"

"Not today," I said. "We'll talk again."

"Be looking forward to it," said Conrad, smiling.

Chick and I stood to leave, and Tad took a step in Chick's direction. Sleepy Eyes put a hand out to stop Tad. "T.C. said no problems, Tad."

"That's right, Tad," said Conrad. "You just go on back to your room and leave these boys alone." Tad glared at Chick some more until Conrad said, "Now, Tad."

Tad left the room, looking back at Chick as he went out the door.

"And now, boys," said Travis. "If you don't mind. I've got to get ready for tonight's performance. Come out and see it if you got time."

We walked to the door, and Sleepy Eyes opened it for us and followed us out.

Once outside on the veranda, our escort fanned his hands out on both sides of his face as if widening his jaws, and said, "Toad, huh?"

"Yeah," Chick said nodding.

Sleepy Eyes smiled broadly. In a soft voice, to himself, he said, "That's great."

15

We hadn't gathered much information, but I'm better face-to-face. I'd gotten a look at Travis Conrad and could infer a few things from the impressions I received.

Travis Conrad was used to doing pretty much as he pleased. He didn't feel the need to explain himself to us. There were no frantic denials of dalliances with college girls, the normal reaction. He considered us little more than an annoyance. In fact, he wasn't interested enough to ask our names, though he figured there was more to us than we were telling. He was smart. He sized us up quickly, cataloged us, then dismissed us.

"So where do you know Tad from?" I asked. We were heading back down the hill in the Bronco to North Branson proper. John Cougar Mellencamp was singing on the radio.

"There was a bodyguard competition in Vegas," Chick said. "You know, how far you can throw guys, real he-man stuff like that. I wasn't a contestant. I was working for Janet Sterling then. She likes to gamble but doesn't like to be crowded while she's doing it. Tad the Toad got drunk and started coming on to Janet, and I sort of nudged him away from her before a couple of guys from casino security escorted him outside. Anyway, when Janet left he was waiting outside her hotel. He got mouth problems, so I had to subdue him a little."

"He said you trussed him up and said something about being stripped."

"Yeah," said Chick, rubbing the side of his nose. "I hung him upside down off the high dive of the hotel swimming pool. But he wasn't naked. He still had on his underwear and shirt."

"How'd you get a guy that size up on the high dive, then hang him off the board?"

"Trade secret. I tell you how I did it, it'll lose some of the magic."

We stopped at a restaurant for supper, then killed some time in a bar Chick had seen earlier. At seven o'clock we returned to the Hickory Wind. I called Sandy and told her to meet us there. I sat at a table while Chick once again positioned himself where he could best view the room while keeping an eye on the rear exit.

Sandy arrived fifteen minutes after the call and sat down with me. There were a Dr Pepper on ice and a glass of chablis on the table between us. We were waiting, hoping actually, that Chastity would return tonight and tell me who the policeman was that had propositioned and perhaps killed Francine Wilson. While she was at it, maybe she would also tell us what was going through Jack Ruby's head in '63.

A live band was playing, and the room pulsed and throbbed with music and bodies. I told Sandy that if Robby Blue showed up, it might not make for a pleasant evening. She made the point, well taken, that whereas Chastity had refused to talk to me, she had been less reticent with Sandy.

"This wine tastes like paint thinner," Sandy said.

"Should have ordered the Dr Pepper," I said. "It has a fruity bouquet with a nice array of flavor notes on the palate and a wonderful aural nose."

"Do you think she's coming?"

"She doesn't, we've got a problem running this thing down. The other trails are blocked and will require work to open up."

"How does he do that?" Sandy asked, looking across the room

at Chick. "I've never seen anyone drink so much and still function. Can't you get him to quit?"

"Short of sewing his lips shut, I don't know what to do."

She sipped her wine, made a tight-lipped face, then said, "I've known Chick for two years now but still don't know much about his background."

"He doesn't talk about it much."

"Neither of you talk about it much."

"Not much to say."

"What kind of work did he do in Vietnam?"

I wiped sweat from the icy glass, pushing it down along the side of the glass with my thumb. It formed a tiny wave, leaving a narrow band of clear glass behind it. "He was some kind of government hit man. Went behind enemy lines. There were seven like him. Three made it back. He doesn't like to talk about it."

"And neither do you."

I nodded.

She changed the subject. "So, you met Travis Conrad."

"Yeah, but he wouldn't give his autograph so we left in a huff." I told her how it went. "You get the sense, talking to Conrad, that he considers himself untouchable."

"Celebrities get that way."

"Are you that way? I need to know so I can plan the rest of the evening."

"No," she said. "I'm very accessible, in fact. Who'd you have in mind?"

"America's all-time greatest wide receiver."

"Jerry Rice?"

"Okay, that does it. I'm going to start returning Diane Sawyer's phone calls."

"Actually," she said, "Travis Conrad *is* close to being untouchable in this town. He and Alec York are drinking buddies. York likes hanging around with the country stars, and they like the protection he affords. I've been inquiring around and discovered that wild things occur when the celebrities are in town. There have been several Francine Wilsons, and they have been deflowered by various celebrities, some of whom are considered "family" entertainers. The parties and the orgies get out of hand, the police are called, the girls are hustled out, maybe a couple of roadies or band members take a trip to the police station. Sometimes the celebrity apologizes, but he is never accused, arrested, or implicated."

"Bad publicity for the tourist trade."

"Exactly."

"Jerry Rice, huh?"

"Diane Sawyer?"

"Connie Chung got fired so I crossed her off the list. Take away Rice's speed, intelligence, and hands, and what have you got?"

"A handsome man with a great body."

"Diane Sawyer, on the other hand . . ." I looked up and saw Chastity walk into the lounge. I leaned forward, and Sandy placed a hand on my arm and said, "Don't scare her off." I caught Chick's eye and nodded in Chastity's direction. As she walked by him Chick spoke, and she smiled and stood next to him brushing his shoulder with hers. He ordered her a drink. When he paid, he made sure she saw the contents of his wallet. Chick was carrying four hundred dollars—fifties and twenties, salted with a few tens and some fives. She probably wasn't above rolling a guy for that amount, particularly if she had police protection.

Chick threaded through the writhing press of dancing bodies, carrying both drinks without touching anyone or spilling a drop, as if he were walking through an empty auditorium. They sat. She placed a hand on his leg and whispered something in his ear. As she did, Chick looked at us and gave us a wide-eyed, open-mouthed look as if shocked.

"What a ham," Sandy said.

The band finished, and a crew came on stage, rearranging the setup. Chick ordered Chastity another drink, then scanned the room, his eyes settling on Sandy and me as if seeing us for the first time. He stood and waved, then taking Chastity by the hand, led her to our table.

"Wyatt Storme," he said, as if he hadn't seen me in years, "how are you doing? And Sandra. Lovely as ever. I want you to meet a friend of mine. This is Charity."

"It's Chastity."

"I was hoping for Charity," Chick said. "Either way it's deceptive labeling. I may call the Better Business Bureau."

"Screw this," she said. She started to leave, but Chick pulled her back and into a chair. He did so without struggle or strain. Her eyes registered surprise, and she sat. With her free hand she took a swipe at Chick, but he calmly caught her wrist and kissed the back of her hand.

"Come on," he said. "Be nice." He placed her hand on the table, patted it, and released her. "Give it a chance, huh?"

The surprise in her face was replaced by an uncharacteristic softness. In her world—a world of rough passions and ugly appetites—there was little legitimate tenderness. She left her hand on the table.

"I can't tell you nothing," she said, looking into Sandy's face with pleading eyes.

"Anything," Chick said.

"What?"

"Can't tell you anything. Watch the double negatives."

"We understand that you are frightened," said Sandy. "But we can't allow this man to continue to abuse and intimidate women."

"What's the cop's name you had the encounter with?" I asked.

Chastity put a cigarette in her mouth. She lit it, took a short draw, blew out the smoke, looked around the room with the quick eyes of a cornered animal, and clicked her fingernails. She looked at me, then closed her eyes and sighed. "I can't tell you."

"We need to know," I said.

"You want too much."

"Chastity," said Sandy, "we don't want any harm to come to you, but at the same time, we want to make sure this doesn't happen to someone else."

"Even if I tell you," she said, then gave a harsh snort, "what makes you think it won't happen again? These guys make the rules around here. You don't live here. You'll be going back to Rodeo Drive in Beverly Hills." She pronounced *Rodeo* with a long *e*. "And I'll still be here renting it out and dodging these guys."

"I don't live in Beverly Hills," said Sandy.

"Wherever."

"Who are 'these guys' you are referring to?" Sandy asked. "Are you talking about Travis Conrad and Alec York?"

"Uh-uh. You've been real nice to me, but I've got nothing else to say on it." She took a big swallow of her drink. The long ash on her untoked cigarette fell off on the table. "Anyway, it's not that big a deal. Sometimes you get roughed up, sometimes you pay a cop off with it. 'Hazards of the business,' Robby says." She looked at Sandy. "You don't know what it's like. You're beautiful and refined and got nice clothes and you talk good, but you don't know what it's like. I'm just a dumb little girl with a good body. Nothing else."

"I don't agree," Sandy said. "Give yourself a little credit. There are many opportunities women can pursue."

Chastity laughed derisively. "That feminist shit? We're all sisters, right? Vote for the right people, and everything will get all better, that it?" She made a dismissive gesture with a hand, took a drag on her cigarette, and stubbed it out in an ashtray.

Sandy remained composed. She didn't look sympathetically at the hooker. She didn't patronize her, and she didn't speak as if she had a higher, more noble perspective. She spoke direct and straight. Sandy was not possessed of the do-gooder mentality that many of her colleagues affected and had been inflicting upon the less fortunate for three decades.

"You're right, I don't understand your situation and can't speak for you, and I won't be here to help you the rest of your life." Her blue eyes were bright and keen. "What you do from this point is up to you. I realize you can only give us the information we need at personal risk, and it will require courage to do that. It's your decision. But if you do decide to help us, these men will do everything possible to protect you."

"And there is nobody better at it," said Chick. "Nobody."

She looked at me, and I nodded my head at her. She chewed her lower lip with tiny teeth and considered the proposition. Fired up another cigarette. She swirled her drink with a swizzle stick.

"I . . . I just don't know. I'd like to . . ." She stopped in mid-sentence, mouth open, as she looked across the room.

Robby Blue was making his way across the crowded dance floor. There were two guys following him.

"Oh, boy," Chick said.

"Oh, shit," said Chastity.

16

Robby Blue was accompanied by the two men who had bounced me around the parking lot of the motel. I felt anger roll like lava inside my head, but in its wake was a residue of anxiety. They had beaten me. Easily. Hard to forget.

They stopped at our table, and Robby Blue said, "Let's go, Chastity."

Chastity started to rise, but Chick put a hand on her arm and she hesitated. Robby Blue didn't like that. "Get your ass up, and let's go," he said.

"I don't think it's nice," Chick said. "You talking that way. It's rude. You think it's rude, Wyatt?"

"Yeah," I said, watching the blond man's single wet-concrete-colored eye. The shifting artificial light painted hollow shadows on the hard bones in his impassive face. "I do."

"Me too," Chick said. "I thought it was rude, too."

"Who're you?"

"I'm the Big Bopper," said Chick. "You've already met my friend, the Duke of Earl. And who are these two grad students?"

"Employees," Robby Blue said. "Cecil here used to work for Wayne Newton as a bodyguard."

"You wouldn't think that many people would want Wayne's body," said Chick, looking at Cecil. "Cecil, huh?"

Robby Blue ignored Chick's question. "Come on, Chastity, get your ass up."

"He absolutely has no idea how to act, does he?" Chick said.

"No upbringing," I said, looking at Cecil.

Chastity's eyes were nervous. Chick left a hand on her arm. With his other hand he reached out and raised the shot glass to his lips, and smiling, he drank, his eyes on the men, the music thumping heavily in the smoke-filled air.

Chastity looked at Chick and said, "I've got to go with him. Please." The leg-breakers shifted a half step.

"You got a hearing problem, cowboy?" said Cecil. "Thought you were supposed to be moving on? You need some help?"

I smiled at him. "You're not as effective facing me. Just a pair of errand boys being ordered around by a low-rent pimp. All you'll ever be."

"Don't make us ask again."

"Don't come around anymore," I said, the anger now stronger than the anxiety.

"What's that mean?"

We were attracting attention from nearby tables. Also from the bouncers. Two beefy young men in burgundy-colored sweaters with the Hickory Wind logo on the chest pushed their way through the crowd in our direction. As they reached our table, Chick released his grip on Chastity, patted her hand, and smiled up at Robby Blue.

"Everything all right here, gentlemen?" asked one of the bouncers, a dark-haired man with football player's pectorals swelling his sweater. There was no way for him to know that he and his partner—whose experience was manhandling tourists and frat brothers drunk on Corona beer—would be insufficient for this situation were it to escalate. Cecil and Eye Patch were carrying. There was too much collateral danger for bystanders, especially for Sandy, to push the issue. Chick and I knew that. Robby Blue knew it and was prepared to use it to his advantage.

"Everything's okay," I said. "A misunderstanding."

He pulled Chastity to her feet by her arm as if she were a wayward child. She offered no resistance. Robby Blue looked at us, grinned smugly, and said, "See you around, chumps."

"Hey, Blue Boy," said Chick. "You take care of her. Anything happens that shouldn't, you understand that Underdog and Fido won't be enough to prevent you becoming unrecognizable to your next of kin." Then he smiled. "Always good to meet interesting people, though."

Robby Blue started to say something, thought better of it, turned on his heel, and pulling Chastity along behind him, pushed through the crowd, Eye Patch following them. Cecil stayed behind, briefly, to glare at us with washed-out eyes. Chick looked at him and said, "So, now your name is Cecil?"

Cecil said, "What's that to you?"

"Beats Dog-ass, I guess."

The dark-haired thug bared capped teeth and said, "We'll see you around." He turned and left us.

Chick smiled to himself, then lifted his glass to the departing man and said, "Semper paratus, semper fidelis."

I looked at Sandy and shrugged, then I asked Chick, "What was that thing before the marine motto?"

"Ever ready," said Chick, before tossing down the remains of the shot glass. "Ever faithful."

"You know him from somewhere, don't you?" Sandy said.

"Yeah," Chick said, dragging on a cigarette. "As a matter of fact I do. He was with Tad the Toad that night in Vegas."

17

I leaned forward in my chair and said, "You're saying the night you hung Tad from the diving board Cecil was with him?"

"Who is Tad?" asked Sandy. "And you did *what* with him?"

"Long story," I said. "If Cecil knows Tad, there may be a connection between Travis Conrad and Robby Blue."

"Probably," Chick said. "Cecil would be high-speed for a guy like Robby Blue. I doubt Robby Blue knew how to get hold of 'Rude Dog' Chaney."

"That's his real name?"

"Might be," Chick said. "The agency used him once. They had him pop a Mexican drug dealer that had burned an agent. Chaney knew the Mexican, and the company paid him five grand to do the dealer."

"The CIA had a thug kill a drug dealer in a foreign country?"

"You can't have some upstart foreign drug dealer popping a state-of-the-art Langley operative," said Chick. "You let those third worlders get away with that, why next thing you know they'll want their own country and hold elections."

"Those were the two guys in the parking lot," I said.

"Figured that," said Chick. "Anyway, Rude Dog is go-fast and high-dollar. Too chic for a punk like Robby Blue."

"But not for Travis Conrad."

"Something blows foul in the Hickory Wind."

I turned the details over in my mind. We had connections between Travis Conrad and Alec York. And now we had connections between Robby Blue and Travis Conrad through their bodyguards. Cecil could have been provided by Tad the Toad. But why? Travis Conrad didn't appear to know who Francine Wilson was. Or maybe he didn't care. He at least didn't appear to care enough to kill her. He was also an actor who had been in three movies, but I got the feeling he wasn't lying. Another thing was that if Cecil and Eye Patch were provided to prevent Chastity from talking to us, what did Chastity know that could harm them? What did Francine Wilson take to the grave with her?

A crew was setting up for Travis Conrad's performance. Conrad's Hickory Wind was different from other live-performance nightspots in the area in that it was set up like an old western saloon in ambience, though the furniture and trappings were modern. The rest of the live-performance nightspots were theater-style. Conrad must've liked the feel of playing like a bar band.

The Fire Creek Band came onstage and began warming up. Then, with a room-vibrating flourish, they sailed into "Ghost Riders in the Sky." Halfway through it Travis Conrad, suspended by cables, descended from the ceiling to the stage. Landing, Conrad raised his arms to thundering applause as two stagehands ran out and removed the cables from the country star. A leggy woman in a bikini, boots, and a cowboy hat came out and handed Conrad his guitar. Conrad took the guitar, and he and his band smoothly segued into their trademark song, "Smokey Bars and Hot Guitars," without missing a beat. It was visually stunning and professional.

Standing at either side of the stage, like bookends, were Tad the

Toad and his partner, Sleepy Eyes. They were a study in contrast. Tad wore a tight-fitting T-shirt and stood with his arms crossed so everyone could get a look at his biceps. Intermittently, he would steal a look at them himself. Tad paced and watched the room as if a sniper were waiting in the shadows. His partner, on the other hand, wore a sports jacket and looked like a man waiting for a bus. I couldn't shake the feeling I had seen him somewhere before.

My impressions of Travis Conrad weren't good, but you had to give the guy his due. He was good at this. He could play lead guitar while singing lead vocal, which put him on a shortlist of musicians with Eric Clapton and Waylon Jennings.

During a pause between songs Conrad launched into a monologue laced with jokes, and teased with the audience. A pair of hecklers in the front row—who looked like hard-core Hank Williams, Jr., fans—began shouting vulgarities at Conrad. Conrad bobbed and weaved rhetorically, a veteran at such things, until he angered them with a comment about "being born at the shallow end of the gene pool." One of them stood and pointed his finger at Conrad, then took a step toward the stage. By the time he had stood up, Sleepy Eyes had quietly worked his way close to the man.

Sleepy Eyes said something to the man, trying to get him to settle down. The man, a big guy with shoulders like used tires and a beer gut, tried to push the bodyguard away, but Sleepy Eyes slapped the man's hands away. The bodyguard still did not seem upset, but his knees were bent and his hands were above his waist and relaxed. The heckler recovered and took a swing at the bodyguard. A mistake. The red-bearded bodyguard stepped inside the arc of the blow and hit the man three times—two shots to the body and one to the neck—then danced away. The big man staggered and fell over his chair. The other heckler jumped out of his chair, and the bodyguard pointed at him and told him to sit down. The man looked at his buddy, nodded, and sat.

By this time, Tad and a couple of the bouncers had the fallen heckler in hand and were hustling him out. Sleepy Eyes backed away, straightened his jacket, and resumed waiting for the concert to end.

"Sorry about that, folks," said Travis Conrad from the stage. "The only other thing I got to say is this:"

> *In my time I've seen lots of things*
> *Dusty rodeos and busted dreams,*
> *But I ain't seen nothing*
> *quite as fine*
> *as visions colored*
> *by country wine.*

The band picked up the cue, and they followed "Country Wine" with "One Hell of a Woman and a Very Bad Man."

The crowd and the moment belonged to him.

And now I remembered where I'd seen Sleepy Eyes.

"You notice anything about Tad's buddy?" I asked Chick after Sandy had excused herself to make a trip to the ladies' room.

Chick nodded. "Yeah, he's good. Looks like he boxed some."

"More than some," I said. "That's 'Sleepy' Joe Shaunessy. He was a middleweight in the seventies. Lasted five rounds with Marvin Hagler before Hagler TKO'd him. Shaunessy cuts easy. But he held his own until then."

"Good we don't piss him off, then," Chick said.

"That's my plan."

"Or we could pop him if it came to that."

I shook my head. "No."

"Easier to cap him than dance with him."

"I'll think of something."

"Hope you think of it before he takes a swing at you. You're a big, tough guy, old buddy, but boxers are a different breed. No offense."

"That's what I keep you around for."

"I am somewhat amazing," said Chick. "Of that there is no doubt."

The phone, programmed by the front desk to ring at 6:00 A.M., awakened me. I stirred, lifted the phone, and dropped it back on its cradle since there would be no human voice on the other end—technology had made our lives easier, not necessarily better. I extricated myself from the tangled cocoon of sheets and blankets, and padded to the bathroom to wash the lingering, stale aroma of the Hickory Wind from hair and body. The hot water cascaded relief on a body nicked, bruised, battered, and abused by AstroTurf, linebackers, and an unpopular war.

I turned off the water, stepped out of the shower, and toweled off. I looked into the mirror and flexed my biceps like Arnold Schwarzenegger. Maybe not exactly like Arnold Schwarzenegger. There was a knock at the door and a male voice saying, "Room service." I wrapped a towel around my waist and answered the door. A short man with a barber-shop-quartet mustache brought in a pot of coffee and a newspaper. I tipped him, and he thanked me, then said, "Excuse me, sir, but I recognize you. You're Wyatt Storme. I'm a big Cowboy fan. And . . . I know it's a little irregular, but would you mind giving me your autograph."

I nodded, and he handed me the room-service ticket and a piece of paper, both of which I signed. That done, I retrieved my wallet, removed a twenty-dollar bill, folded it, ran my thumb and forefinger along the fold to sharpen the crease, then carefully ripped the bill into two pieces, handing him one half and keeping the other.

"You get the other half when I leave," I said. "All you have to do is keep anyone else from dropping by for my autograph. You handle that?"

"I'll do my best, sir."

"That's all anybody can do, partner. Thanks for the coffee."

After the waiter left, I poured coffee and thought about our dilemma. Chick was right. A cheapjack pimp like Robby Blue couldn't have ordered up muscle like Cecil and Eye Patch. There was a circle of corruption in North Branson that enveloped its white-columned, red-bricked, vanilla center and stank like the rotted carcass of a road-killed coyote.

There is a point in these things where you have run your traps, found nothing, and the only option left is to repeat the process or wait. Waiting has its reward if the quarry is nervous or greedy. If waiting doesn't work, then you've got to poke a stick in their burrow. In the present situation we seemed to be stirring them up merely by being here. There was a payoff in all of this. Somewhere. For someone. And as it neared realization, they might become anxious and greedy. The trick was to figure out what the payoff was and then position yourself close to the trail. But what was the payoff?

My bet was that it all had something to do with a parcel of land running between two highways and a bypass nobody wanted. I opened the nightstand drawer, and inside, next to a Gideon Bible, was a Branson area phone book. I pulled it out and thumbed through the business white pages looking for a number for the So-Mo Holding Company. There was no listing. I looked under "Southern Missouri" and "Southwest Missouri." Still no listing. I wasn't surprised. I accessed an outside line and dialed the information operator and asked for a number for either the So-Mo or the Southwest Missouri Holding Company. After a wait the operator informed me that the So-Mo Holding Company's number had been unlisted at the customer's request.

"Unusual that a business would have an unlisted number, don't you think?" I asked her.

"There are a few," she said. "Depends on what kind of business they are conducting. For some, anonymity is an advantage."

I'd certainly agree with that, I thought. There was certainly no law against it. I hung up and went out to the Bronco, got a Missouri road map and a Branson area tourist map I'd picked up at a restaurant, and walked back to the motel. Back in my room I spread the maps on the bed and poured more coffee. The strip of land owned by So-Mo and the leading citizenry of North Branson ran between the two highways with one narrow tip touching the banks of Lake Taneycomo and a small tributary forming a triangle. I folded the map. A bypass connecting two highways and access to a docking point on the lake. What did it mean? Having land that could be turned into a bypass I could understand. That was a license to print money. You sell a narrow strip to the state, which puts in a highway, then you sell off the highway frontage at a high price. That was one way to make a killing. Gambling was another way. Riverboat gambling was only allowed on the river in Kansas City and St. Louis, not on the lakes, and not in southwest Missouri. It made no sense. Maybe it was just part of the deal and had no significance, yet the strip of real estate reached for the lake like a reptile's hungry tongue.

I opened the paper and searched the headlines. There was a high court appointee in the D.C. district being contested by the opposition party, another uprising in an obscure province in the former Soviet Union. I checked the local-interest section, and there was an article about preserving a Civil War battle site, one on the struggle between Kansas City and Branson over a proposed Walt Disney theme park, and one dealing with a federal grant for an enterprise zone in downtown Springfield. Nothing of any real interest.

I punched numbers into the phone and waited for the information operator to answer, then asked for information for Paradise, Missouri.

"May I help you?" asked the operator. I asked for the number for the Paradise County *Herald-Examiner*.

She gave me a recorded voice, which informed me that the number requested could be automatically dialed by pressing "one." I chose the path less traveled and dialed it myself for I was bound by my rebellion against this frantic, fast-track world of bells and whistles and information highways. A male voice answered on the second ring, and I asked for Jill Maxwell. He transferred the call, and I heard a voice which I knew to be attached to nice legs, chestnut hair, and a high-speed brain.

"This is Maxwell," she said.

"So who cares?" I said. "This is your favorite ex–football player."

"Storme. What a nice surprise. Who're you and your cute little buddy ticking off this time?"

"Just about everybody."

"Where are you?"

I told her, then asked what she knew about North Branson or the So-Mo Holding Company.

"Fastest-growing area in the Midwest," she said. "I'm not familiar with So-Mo Holding, though. But I'll see what I can find out. Where are you calling from?"

I told her. She said, "Is my little sweetheart around?"

"Yeah. He's here."

"I know. He called yesterday."

"So why'd you ask?"

"Checking to see if you'd cover for him. You still dating the fluff?"

"If you mean am I still in love with Sandy, the answer is yes."

"What are you guys into down there?"

I gave her a brief history of our life in North Branson.

"Hmm," she murmured into the line. "Interesting. A country music legend, possible police corruption and murder in mom-and-pop entertainment land. That may actually amount to a headline with a little work. I think you've got something."

"What?"

"I'll let you know after I've researched it a little."

I gave her my number and hung up and punched in room number 120.

Chick answered and said, "Not now, Sandy, I think Wyatt's onto us."

"The boyfriend's always the last to know."

"That you, Wyatt?"

"For humor to be effective it must at least be plausible. Besides, she's in Springfield, remember."

"That's what she tells you."

"You bring your sailor suit with you?" I asked.

"Never go anywhere without it."

"Good. Because I want to go out to the lake. Maybe we can build a raft and do the Tom Sawyer thing."

"Can I smoke a corncob pipe and drink from a jug of McCormick's whiskey?"

"Whatever," I said. "Just get dressed and meet me in the parking lot."

"Sure. Just as soon as I throw Collingsworth out. 'Take me.' 'Take me.' It's all she ever says."

I hung up on him.

18

Chick and I drove out to Lake Taneycomo and parked the Bronco at a roadside observation park named after Missouri and America's famous World War I general, John J. Pershing.

World War II was prosecuted by another Midwesterner, a Kansan named Eisenhower, and presided over by Harry Truman from Independence. Abraham Lincoln was from Illinois. My Uncle Fred often remarked that when the country got into trouble, it took people from the Midwest to straighten it out. I went to Vietnam but was unable to resolve anything. So much for my uncle's theories.

We got out of the Bronco and were greeted by conflicting sensations—the soothing sound of water lapping at the shore and the sounds of construction: whirring power saws, thumping jackhammers, and the trip-crack sound of hammering.

"Looks like they're renovating that dock," I said, pointing to where the sounds of construction were coming.

"That close to the point you told me about?" Chick asked.

"Close."

"Not much here."

I looked up the shore to the construction site. "Makes you won-der why they're working on the dock."

"Well. No use waiting. Might as well go over there and ask around."

"Might make them mad."

"Yeah," Chick said, smiling. "I can't wait."

We walked down to the construction site, where we were met by a wide-faced man in Carhart coveralls and a yellow hard hat; a cheap, fat cigar stuck in the corner of his mouth. He had the straight-ahead eyes and bulldog stance of a man used to telling people what to do and them doing it.

"I help you guys?" he asked as we invaded the work site.

"What are you guys building here?" I asked, giving my words the right flavor of open-faced Midwest vacuity.

"Who're you guys?" the foreman asked.

"We're just passing through and saw you guys working here, and we were having a discussion about your project. I said I think you're building an observation deck, and my buddy here says, no, they're building a fishing dock. So this goes on awhile, and I thought, what the heck, let's just go on over and ask. So here we are."

The foreman's eyes shifted from me to Chick, then back. "It's a dock," he said, as if this was the end of the discussion.

"For fishing?"

"What?" he said, irritated.

"Is it for public use?" I asked, continuing the curious tourist act, as if his answer would give me something to talk about at the next Lions Club meeting back in Terre Haute.

However, he wasn't buying it.

"Who the hell're you guys, anyway?" he said. "You got nothing better to do?"

I widened my eyes in feigned shock. "I'm sorry. I didn't mean to make you mad. Like I said before, me'n Joe Bob were just passing through on our way to Silver Dollar City, and we just stopped for—"

"You're way off the path for Silver Dollar City," said the foreman. "So why don't you just put your country butts back in the car and get the hell out of here." He said the last sentence as if spitting something unpleasant out of his mouth. "I got work to do." He started to walk away.

"No need to be unfriendly, fatso," Chick said. "We don't like unfriendly."

The man whirled around as if Chick had spit on the back of his neck. "You talkin' to me?"

"No," Chick said, "I'm talking to the twenty other rude fat people around here."

The heavyset man's eyes narrowed, and his head nodded slowly. "You want some shit? That it?"

"You notice how his little piggy eyes kind of sparkle when he's upset?" Chick said to me.

"He's probably overworked," I said. "What with concealing this secret project and all."

"He'd better keep it a secret," Chick said. "That's the way we want it."

"You guys here from Conrad?" he asked, recognition dawning on his face. "Shit, I don't know why they keep sending you guys out here to check on us."

"We're thorough," Chick said. "You understand *thorough*?"

"We got it covered," said the foreman. "Look, we'll be done on time like we promised. So relax and take the day off, huh?"

"Mr. Conrad don't like it when we take the day off," I said, allowing the impression to persist. I took a chance. "York, either. They just want to make sure everything comes off like it's supposed to. You follow?"

The man reached up and rubbed the side of his face. He was changed now. Somehow he'd become our friend. "You guys know how it works," he said. "We'll take care of our end. York makes sure the state guys get the thing extended out here, and we'll get this done in plenty of time. Okay? Look fellas, I'm on the clock here and gotta get things done. Next time you come by, forget the Joe Bob routine, huh?"

"Sure," Chick said. "My partner watches too many movies. Y'know? Thinks he's Harrison Ford or something. We'll tell them everything's cool here. Okay?"

The foreman smiled. Glad to help. "Sure. But you guys better get out of here. State guys been dropping by like they're smellin' something. Nosin' around. Hey, next time you guys come by, bring a case of Budweiser or something. Guy gets thirsty out here, ya know?"

We bid our new friend adieu and drove back to town.

"See, I was right," Chick said. "They're up to something."

"But what? It's got something to do with the string of land. Has to. Something's coming in we don't know about and maybe nobody knows about except York and Conrad. But what is it, and how soon is it going to happen?"

"Somebody has a lot at risk here. I'm talking the kind of money where they remove obstructions."

"Interesting, isn't it?"

The weather had warmed into the kind of false spring Missouri sometimes offers before winter elbows its way in—hard, flat, and cold. We ate lunch at a little Mexican place run by second-generation Mexican Americans who knew how to clear your sinuses and warm your belly. I ordered fajitas, and Chick had chimichangas, gleefully washing them down with Tecate beer and Dos Reales tequila.

"Now, that was truly the Mexican cuisine experience," Chick said, back in the Bronco. "Any restaurant with the good sense to stock Dos Reales tequila gets my business every time. In fact, I must now begin a quest to seek out and purchase a fifth of Dos Reales and will not rest until I find some."

"Well, you can begin your quest after we drive out to the college. I want to talk to Francine Wilson's roommate again."

Sharon Keltner met us in the lobby. She ushered us into a study room where we could talk in private. After we were seated in the spare furnishings, I asked if she knew how her roommate had died.

"No," she said. "I was doing fieldwork at the high school the day she . . . the day it happened. They won't tell me how it happened."

"I know this is hard for you, but she was electrocuted. She was found in the bathtub of the Red Cedar Motel, an electric blow-dryer in the tub with her."

She looked perplexed, as if something was out of place.

"You okay?" I asked.

She nodded. "I'm okay. But they found her in the bathtub like she was taking a bath?"

"Way I understand it."

She shook her head slowly. "There's something wrong."

"Like what?"

"For one thing, Francine never took baths. 'Sitting in your own dirt,' she called it. She was funny about hygiene. Ultrafastidious. She would never take a bath, only showers."

"But if you were going to take your own life, that might not matter."

She shook her head again. This time more forcefully. "No. That's not all. She was scared to death of being electrocuted. She used to get on me for blow-drying my hair over the sink with the water running. When she was little, she had a Saint Bernard that was struck by lightning. She said she could still remember the smell of burnt fur and that the dog's tongue was burnt black. She said it was a horrible way for the poor dog to die. I did a research paper on suicide once, and suicides never kill themselves in ways that frighten them."

"In other words," I said, "you're afraid of high places, you don't jump off a building?"

"Because you're afraid of the fall. Right."

"Doesn't the fact she was found in the Red Cedar Motel surprise you?" I asked.

"Not really. Sometimes she would check in there to cram for tests or to do research papers. The dorm's kind of noisy some-times, and"—she paused, her face coloring—"she liked the adventure of being in a motel. You know? Francine was kind of a romantic."

"She ever meet anyone there. Boys?"

She thought about her answer as if deciding something. "Somebody. She had somebody she met there."

"She tell you who?"

"No. It was like a secret."

"Could he have been married?"

She nodded her head. "She never said, but that's kind of what I thought. She'd get calls and would talk low so I couldn't hear."

The door to the study room opened, and a tall, thick-bodied young man with brown hair and a green-and-white letter jacket stepped in and pointed a finger at me. He appeared out of breath and agitated. "What are you doing here?"

"We know each other?" I asked.

"You're the guy came to town asking about Francine, and now she's dead." He took a step toward me, and I could see it wasn't so he could shake my hand. "You sonuvabitch. I'll knock your head off."

He took a big roundhouse swing, which would have done just that if I hadn't leaned away from it. It wooshed by my face, causing him to lose his balance, which I helped along by slapping the back of his elbow as his arm went by. He stumbled and landed with the upper part of his body over the table, but he wasn't done.

"Kenneth!" said Sharon. "Stop it. Right now."

While he recovered from his awkward position, I took the opportunity to move away and push a chair between us. I didn't want to hurt him, but more than that I didn't want him to hurt me. As he started toward me again, Sharon stepped in front of him and hit him in the chest with the palms of her hands, which was like trying to stop a Mack truck by throwing a beer can at it. As yet, Chick hadn't moved.

"Out of the way, Sharon," said Kenneth.

"No," she said. "You shut up and stop it. Mr. Storme is here to help us. He didn't even know Francine. He was trying to find out what happened to her. And whether someone raped her."

His face and shoulders visibly sagged at the last statement. "Somebody raped her?" He sat down like a sack of cement and looked at his big hands. Tears formed in his eyes. "Who?"

"We're not sure at this point," I said. If I gave him too much information he might complicate things by going after Travis Conrad. Stability didn't seem to be his long suit.

"I'm sorry," he said. "Nobody told me."

"It's okay," I said.

"It's bad enough finding out she was dead. And now this. I . . . can't take this shit."

"Had you recently had sexual relations with her?" I asked.

"What?" Kenneth said.

"Mr. Sensitivity," said Chick, as much to himself as anything.

"Sorry," I said, "but I don't have much time. I need to know when was the last time you had sex with her."

"She was a virgin." I saw Chick's eyes widen.

"Are you sure?" Chick asked.

"What do you mean 'am I sure'?" he said, his eyes hot as he looked at Chick.

"Nothing. Nothing," Chick said, putting up his hands. "It's just . . . ah . . . unusual in a college student."

"What he means is that she was seeing other guys," I said.

"That's a bunch of crap! Francine would never do—"

Sharon touched his arm and said, "She was, Kenneth. She didn't want you to know, but she occasionally went out when you were on a road trip." He pursed his lips, and his throat broke out in blotches of color. His fists clenched and trembled. "She wanted to tell you, but she was afraid to."

"Afraid of what?" he bellowed.

"Your temper. You seem to lose your temper quite a bit anymore."

"That's 'cause I've got a lot of pressure on me. With the team and all. Who was it?"

"Are you taking steroids, Kenneth?" I asked.

"What? No," he said, but his eyes were elusive. "Maybe a little, you know. Before a big game. You know how it is. I want to play in the pros, and Coach says I got a chance but I've got to be bigger. Stronger."

I looked at him. Saw the round moonlike face and swollen neck. Thought about the temper tantrums. I made a mental note to have Merrill check the semen found in Francine for steroids. I didn't know if it would show up, and I knew Kenneth was supposed to be in Cape Girardeau at the time of her death, but I asked anyway.

"Were you with the team the entire time you were in Cape Girardeau?"

"What kind of question is that?" Kenneth said. "Everybody knows I was."

"It's the kind of question the police are going to get around to asking when they admit it wasn't an accident."

He looked away from me and said, "I was with the team the whole time."

"They'll ask your coaches and teammates, too."

His head jerked around quickly. "Won't make any difference." He tried to look at me defiantly. "Why don't you guys get outta here. You're not helping nothing."

Hard to disagree with that.

Add one more person to the list of people who might have killed Francine Wilson.

19

Some bodyguard you turn out to be," I said. "That kid wanted to rip my lungs out. What were you waiting for?"

"What a baby," Chick said, smiling. "You were okay. My spider sense hadn't even started to tingle yet."

We were back at the motel. Sandy hadn't returned from Springfield. Before talking to Sharon Keltner and the boyfriend, I'd been convinced whoever killed Francine Wilson did so to protect something or somebody. Adding the boyfriend to the mix was messing that theory up. I called Merrill.

"You'd better check on Francine Wilson's boyfriend, Kenneth," I said after getting Detective Merrill on the line. "He's a football player. I don't know his last name."

"Kenneth Mantle?" said Merrill. "Big kid? About your height? Two-sixty-five? Brown hair?"

"That's him."

"He was in Cape Girardeau at the time of her death."

I told him about the steroids and the jealousy and the hunch I had that he was holding something back.

130 W. L. Ripley

"Pretty thin," said Merrill.

"Maybe. I don't think the kid did it, but if you can confirm he was with the team the whole time, then you can cross him off the list. Check his thighs for needle tracks. Then check the lab report on the semen found in the girl for steroids. He insists she was a virgin, but the roommate says otherwise."

"Why would he hurt her if he loved her?"

"He came at me like he wanted to kill me, and I don't even know him. Using steroids is like abdicating responsibility for being a rational human being. At Dallas I watched a guy destroy a bank of lockers because he missed a tackle in practice." In fact, I watched from a safe distance armed with a pair of dumbbell bars. You soon learned not to take chances with a hopped-up lineman. "You've got to see this kid and dry up his connection before he starts growing horns.

"Also, you might want to look into the So-Mo Holding Company. It's connected with York and Conrad." I explained about the string of land purchases and our visit to the lake construction site. I told him what Sharon Keltner had said. "I agree with her. No way Francine dies that way. Not even by accident. Somebody with a badge is covering up, which means the police know, or at least suspect, who did it."

"Messing with York and Conrad in this town's like pissing on a spark plug. You're not making my job any easier."

"You got anything to share?"

"Not much," he said. "But I'll tell you this much. The Wilson girl's best friend back in her hometown had a car wreck two days ago. Bad one. She didn't make it. How you like that for a coincidence?"

"I don't. Had they visited each other recently?"

"No. But phone records show six phone calls between the time you say she was raped by Travis Conrad and her death and only two calls in the month previous. See if you can guess where the friend was heading when the accident occurred?"

"To the college to visit Francine."

"You got it. Keep that under your hat because I'm flying solo on this. Accidental death is what we're giving the media, but unofficially we're considering Francine Wilson as a possible homicide. I was you, I'd get my girlfriend out of town. This thing is hot, and everybody near it is getting burned."

"You're not going to like the next question," I said.

"Then don't ask it."

"Got no choice. You and Felicia York got something going?"

"You're right," he said. "I don't like the question."

I decided not to push it. I hung up and looked at Chick. Gave him the other end of the conversation with Merrill. He listened without interruption.

When I finished he said, "I'm like you. I don't like coincidences, and there are too many. I also agree with Merrill. Get Sandy out of town. She's running through the cemetery kicking over tombstones, and the vampires are waking up."

"Getting her to leave may be the difficult thing."

An hour later Sandy hadn't returned, and I called the Springfield TV station. The manager told me Sandy had left instructions to leave her line open until after 7:00. I said I'd call back after 7:00 and hung up.

No sooner had I placed the phone back on the cradle than it began ringing. I picked it up and put it to my ear.

"This is Storme," I said.

"This is . . . Chastity." Her voice sounded weak and strained.

"You all right?"

"He . . . beat the shit out of me."

"Who did?"

"Can't tell you over the phone. Can you meet me someplace? I'm . . . scared."

"Okay," I said. "Tell me where."

"Not here. You know where Park's Marina is?"

"I can find it."

She said, "I'll be across the water from the marina. At the picnic area."

"I'll be there," I said. It was 6:45 by my watch.

"Please hurry," she said. "And come alone."

20

~~~

Probably a setup," Chick said.

I nodded and loaded the Browning Hi-Power. I shoved it into the clip-on holster and slipped it inside the back of my jeans. "That's why you're going with me."

"Sorry, there's a *MacGyver* rerun on cable. True-to-life tales of espionage and intrigue. Tonight he makes a communications satellite out of Tinkertoys and an old eight-track player. It's a can't miss. Thought I'd pick up some tips."

"Come on," I said. I pulled on a black sweatshirt and a black baseball cap. "I'll buy you an ice cream cone."

"Two scoops? Cherry cheesecake in a waffle cone?"

"Shut up and get your stuff."

"Sure get short-tempered whenever you think somebody's trying to kill you. That's a character flaw."

It was 7:30 P.M. when we exited the highway and hit Lake Road 37. It was turning dark, and the sky was bearded with a inky bank of clouds in the northeast. Before we left I had disconnected the fuse to the Bronco's interior lights. Chick was lying on the floor in the back when I opened the door and stepped out, tugging on a pair of black driving gloves. The evening air felt cool and thick with moisture as I walked across the park grounds.

The place Chastity selected was dark and remote. There was a pole light nearby, but the light was out. Or had been put out. I closed my eyes and placed a hand over them to help me adjust to the darkness. Opening them, I made a quick reconnaissance assessment of the area.

I had experience. Who said you didn't learn anything in the military? Join the army, learn a skill. My skill was getting close to the enemy without him knowing I was there. Then calling back coordinates for screaming metal birds to drop loads on their prey. I was good at it. I could field-strip an M-16, reassemble it, and be spraying metal jackets in seconds. I knew how to avoid the bouncing Bettys, the Claymores, dig a foxhole, fill sandbags, lob grenades, lead a patrol, and stay awake for hours on watch. I could also block wide bodies, remember a galaxy of numbers and check-offs, run grass drills, and catch a football in a crowd of blood-lusting track stars built like Arnold Schwarzenegger.

What I couldn't do would fill a résumé. I'm not gregarious. I fidget when I wear a tie. I'm not a mixer, and I have the phone etiquette of a Visigoth. I despise rhetoric and climate-controlled buildings. I don't remember names and cut people off who take the scenic route when they're talking.

But I can get close when I want to.

There was a huge, spreading oak tree thirty yards from the place I was to meet Chastity. I slipped under its darkness and waited. I didn't see Chastity or anyone else. I waited some more.

Chick was right. It smelled like a setup. "Come alone" was the tip-off. I waited for forty minutes and was on the move to a different spot when the whitetail buck burst from cover seventy-five yards away and bounded through the sparse trees of the campground, its white flag flying.

I hit the ground just as I heard a sizzling sound followed by the rolling crack of a rifle. It originated from the spot where the buck had burst from the tree line. I rolled on the hard ground, jumped up, and sprinted for the shelter. En route, I heard the crack of the weapon, again, followed by two staccato pops from a different source. Reaching the shelterhouse, I crouched behind a large brick barbecue, pushing myself against the rough brick. My lungs were pumping like pistons, and my forearms shivered as I struggled to beat back the adrenaline rush of fear. I'd been shot at before. Daily in Vietnam. Not something you adjust to.

The deer had saved me. No reason for him to be running through the exposed picnic area at night unless he had been spooked.

But it wasn't over yet. I heard the double staccato report of a handgun, followed by the roar of a shotgun, then silence. I didn't know how many were out there. The shelter was open and exposed to a field of fire if I tried to leave it. The Browning was no match for a concealed rifleman.

I waited, gun in hand, eyes and ears straining to detect movement. After two minutes passed, I heard the sound of a boat engine followed by two more pistol shots. I moved out of the shelter and started for the trees, running low and fast.

I was near the tree line when I heard Chick's voice.

"Wyatt," he said, "it's clear."

I relaxed.

"What happened?" I asked.

"There were two of them," he said. "I got a couple shots before the guy with the shotgun opened up on me. They had a boat stashed."

"Could you tell who it was?"

"No. Don't think she's gonna show, do you?"

"No."

"We better get out of here. Wouldn't be a good idea to be here when the cops show. I got a bad feeling about this."

So did I.

21

Somebody wanted you dead or at least out of town," said Chick. "And me with you, which is what I get for hanging around with you. Telling you to come alone is a nice touch if they figure that would pull me along, too."

I stopped at a convenience store pay phone. Called the TV station. The woman that answered said Sandy had left an hour ago. About the time we were en route to the marina.

I pulled the Bronco into the motel lot.

"Maybe somebody found out and kept her from coming." Thinking that made me worry about Sandy and the same thing happening to her. When I saw her rental car wasn't in the motel lot, I pulled back out into the traffic. It was 8:45. She should have returned by now.

Sandy was the type of person who lived by her planner. The type of person who thought she was on time only if she was early. My disdain for the tyranny of time and appointments often annoyed her, proving that opposites attract. She was the punctuality princess in an industry that depended on it.

And she wasn't on time.

I drove to the police station and didn't find her rental. Drove out to the college campus. Same result. I sailed the Ford past the Hickory Wind. No luck. It was now 9:57. I drove back to the motel, my left leg tense, the foot pushing against the floorboards. I felt like I often did in such situations. Impotent. And with impotence came frustration. As a closet control freak, I was uncomfortable when I was unable to govern things around me. One of the attractions of being a wide receiver was that on each play I was out there—separate from the rest of the team and in control of my actions—whether that meant running my route or blocking down on a linebacker. And after each assignment we would line up and do it again.

All of which had something to do with living back in the woods of Missouri and on the mountains of Colorado. Only God and nature had any say in those places; the rest was up to me. I could never live as Sandy lived—sent from place to place, subject to the whims of the corporate mentality.

Despite my independence I wanted to be near Sandy, and the conflict between autonomy and interdependence was a high-wire act. I couldn't live in her world yet could not conceive of a world without her.

Which results in the anxiety I was feeling. Anxiety I seldom felt. It was coming in waves now, overpowering and consuming.

"Where is she?" I said as we pulled into the motel lot. Once again, her parking slot was empty. I slammed on the brakes and shut down the truck.

"I don't know, Wyatt," Chick said. "I wish I did, but I don't. She's all right."

"I shouldn't have listened to her. I should've gone ahead and had you tail her. I should trust my instincts."

"If you could control her, she wouldn't be who she is and wouldn't mean what she means to you. Man, you can't have it every way. You're stuck with it, buddy. She is high risk, high speed, and high maintenance. No changing it."

I returned to the motel to check for a message from her while

Chick took the Bronco to look. When she returned, I wanted to be there.

There were no messages.

Chick called from a pay phone at 10:45. He had nothing to report. I hung up and tried to watch television, but the actor's lines washed over me like a fan pushing hot air: it didn't help, and it left no residue.

At 11:05 the phone rang. A voice I didn't recognize said, "You were warned, asshole, and you don't listen so good. Everything from now on is your fault." Then the person hung up. I called the front desk and asked the clerk if she knew who called my room. She didn't.

"Did the caller ask for me by name?" I said.

"He asked for your room number. Is something wrong, sir?"

I hung up and called the police station and asked for Detective Merrill. He wasn't in. I tried his house. No answer. I got up and paced. That didn't help either. Panic gripped my heart with nailed talons and began squeezing. Tighter.

Only liars and sociopaths claim they are never afraid. In my life I had been afraid often and for long periods. I was afraid now. Afraid for Sandy. Afraid of the possibilities.

Afraid of being alone.

The last fear, though patently selfish, was real, and I was not proud of myself for it. However, experience had taught me that fear was an opponent to be subdued if not defeated. Fear sapped your strength, your will. But properly channeled fear could be utilized. If you could suppress and focus your fear, it could work to your favor, adding strength to purpose. So even as the red demon squeezed, experience was devising ways to redirect it.

It provided no relief, only resolve.

And the night passed like a long train.

22

~~~

Chick rustled me awake at 6:00 A.M. My eyes felt raw and dry and swollen. Sandy had not returned. Chick ordered a pot of coffee and some pastry. I tossed back the coffee, burning my tongue. Refused the pastry.

"Didn't have any luck, partner," Chick said. "Tried. Sorry. I saw Merrill, so he's looking for her, too."

"I'm going to look some more," I said. "You go ahead and stay. You were up all night."

"I'm going," he said. "I don't, you'll just get into trouble, and then you'll call and wake me."

We walked out to the parking lot. The first pinkish light of dawn appeared on the horizon, and it turned the asphalt purple-black. There at the rear of the lot sat a maroon Cadillac Seville. One I'd seen before. I walked back into the motel, down the hall to a place on the wall where a red fire extinguisher sat enclosed behind a glass door. A crimson cloud was swirling and fomenting in the front of my brain. No turning back. No prisoners. I shattered the glass with the metal rod and jerked the canister from the wall and walked back outside. Chick was silent as he followed me.

Outside, Chick circled to the rear of the lot while I walked to the Caddy, careful to keep cars between me and its occupants. I crouched low to the ground and approached the Cadillac. Nearing the car, I saw the blond hair and eye patch of the driver.

I stood, lifted the red cylinder, and drove the base of it through the driver's side window. Glass exploded, and I felt a satisfying surge of electricity up my forearms as the canister thudded off the thug's head.

Chick materialized on the passenger's side with his gun drawn as I jerked the door open and pulled the driver out by his collar. The blond man tumbled out of the car and onto the black asphalt like a broken rag doll, the side of his head bloody. When he hit the ground, I kicked him in the ribs.

"Just relax, asshole," I heard Chick say to the other thug. "Move once, never move again. Your call."

"Where is she?" I said, pointing the nozzle of the fire extinguisher at the blond hood.

"Where's . . . who?" said the blond man. The impact had knocked the eye patch askew, and I could see the mangled scar tissue of his ruined eye.

"Not good enough," I said. I shot carbon dioxide foam onto his torso. He sputtered and tried to turn away, but I stepped on his forearm.

"One more chance, then I make you completely fireproof. The lady with us last night. Where is she?"

"I . . . dunno . . . what you're talking about."

I put the muzzle of the canister against his lips. "I've heard this stuff is poisonous, but I'm skeptical. Either I find out where she is, or you're drinking this."

"I . . . I don't . . . know. Truth."

"Why are you here? Why are you working for Robby Blue?"

"A favor."

"Favor? For who?"

"Can't say."

"Here it comes." I put my thumb on the extinguisher's trigger.

"No! All right. It's not worth this. Damn. You split my fucking skull, you sonuvabitch." He put a hand to his head.

"Who?"

"Somebody in Jeff City."

"Who in Jefferson City?"

"You're a bright guy; you figure it out."

"The lieutenant governor?"

"No, the fucking water department. Hell, I don't know. We were told to scare you off. That's all. It's a job."

"Scare us?" Chick said with mock incredulity. "We fear nothing. Except . . . you know, maybe spiders."

"You guys soldiers?" I asked.

"You mean like Mafia?" he said, a sneer on his lips. "That's some imagination you got."

"I've got no time for your mouth," I said. "Answer straight, or you're going to look like Frosty the Snow-thug, inside and out. Got it?"

He nodded his head, then rubbed it. He pulled his hand from his head and looked at it stained with blood. He looked up at me as if I'd just stepped on a freshly mopped floor. "I'm bleeding all over the place."

"This family business?" I said.

"We're out on loan. Boss says get the hooker away from the reporter. Scare the cowboy off. Says it's a down payment. That's all we know. They tell us to go, we go."

I looked at Chick over the top of the car. He shrugged, then said, "Probably true." He looked down, said, "Excuse me a moment, Wyatt." He looked into the car and spoke to the other hood. "Hey, Cecil, you wanna hand me the pistol you've been trying to get from under the seat for the past couple minutes? Butt first. That's the boy." He took something from the thug and put it in his coat pocket. "Thanks for your contribution, sir."

"Get him out of the car and bring him here, Chick," I said, remembering the cheap shots and the beating I'd received.

Chick opened the door and pulled Cecil along by the collar. He stopped him in front of me.

The dark-haired hood sneered at me and said, "The fuck you want, country—"

I dropped the fire extinguisher on his foot, interrupting him. He yelped in pain, and I brought an elbow up alongside his jaw. He stumbled against a car, and I ripped a left into his kidneys. He slid down the car to the pavement.

"You feel better?" said Chick.

"Yeah," I said, chest heaving. I pulled the Browning out and dug it under Cecil's chin, pushing his head back. "Now, Cecil, tell me again how you want me to leave town. Were you out at the marina last night?"

"The . . . fuck you talking about?"

"Somebody tried to shoot me. With you talking so tough all the time, figured it might be you."

"We weren't at no marina."

I jabbed with the gun, and he grunted in pain. "Don't lie to me, Cecil. If I don't find her I don't care what else happens, so don't harbor any fantasies about me being afraid to bust a cap."

"It's the truth. Me 'n' Jerry followed you back to the motel last night, then we went to get something to eat, and we get back here and your truck's gone. Picked you up later, followed your buddy around town when he took the truck. Followed him back here. Been sitting out here most of the night."

I looked at Chick. "What do you think?"

"Could be. They could've followed us out to the marina, but I can't see them getting into position in the dark. They're city boys. Wouldn't be how they set it up. They'd do it up close and make sure. Don't think they'd sit out here overnight if they'd just shot at us. Too sloppy."

"We wouldn't miss either," said Eye Patch.

"This doesn't get us any closer to finding Sandy," I said. "Where's Robby Blue, Cecil?"

He had his hand on his jaw where I'd hit him. "Never met him before yesterday. Guy's a genuine case of diarrhea. Got a hard-on for you so he can't be all bad. Wanted us to wait on you and pop you. I told him he wasn't in the fucking Wild West; these things gotta be handled right."

"Where you guys work out of?" asked Chick.

"Saint Louis."

"When you going back?"

"Soon as you assholes cut us loose."

"Good," I said.

"You don't, Cecil," said Chick, "you know I'll take you out."

"Yeah?" said Cecil. "Maybe not as easy as you think."

"Cecil, Cecil, Cecil," said Chick, shaking his head. "You never learn. Do what you think best, then." He looked at Cecil and smiled. "Either way, sure will miss you."

23

~~~~~

At 9:30 A.M. Detective Merrill found Sandy.

He had put a call out with a description of her rental and the tags. Something Chick and I couldn't do. For all the criticism they receive, the police remain the undisputed champions at finding automobiles and running down information.

After finding her, Merrill dispatched a unit to locate me, which the young cop did, telling us Sandy was at the emergency room.

When we arrived, Merrill was waiting for us.

"She's okay, Storme," he said. "Found her wandering around in a daze in the high school football stadium. She doesn't know why or how she got there. I talked with her for a while, but she's still a little fuzzy. Last thing she remembers was waiting in her car to meet a hooker named Chastity—"

"Wait a minute," I said. "She was meeting Chastity? Where?"

"In the parking lot of the stadium."

"And that's the last she remembers?"

"Yeah. No bumps, no bruises on her. But her hair and clothes were a mess. Grass stains on her clothes, like she'd been rolling around on the field. And, a . . . one more thing." His eyes dropped away from mine. "You're not going to like this. When they found her, she wasn't wearing hose, though she was wearing a skirt."

Realization flooded my neck, causing an electric tension to pulse along my spine. "Are they . . . checking her for it?"

He pursed his lips, his jowls slack in the heavy face. "Already did." His eyes dropped to the floor. "Sorry, Wyatt."

I closed my eyes and felt a sickening weariness settle into my joints. I placed a hand to my forehead and massaged my temples. He, whoever he was, had taken her. Robbed her of that which could not be returned. A faceless tormentor. I felt the hopelessness of impotence and the wispy-cold breath of anxiety. There was also a sense of something lost. Something that could never be regained.

And I stood there on the cold linoleum floor in the bloodless hospital corridor, my heart screaming into the darkness forming in my head.

"I'll do everything I can to find the guy," Merrill said.

I opened my eyes and looked into the heavy face and Saint Bernard eyes of the small-town cop. "I appreciate it," I said. "Does she know?"

"Not yet. Wanted to talk to you first. You want one of us to tell her?"

I thought about it. Struggled with it. I never lied to Sandy but sometimes held back—kept her from knowing about the danger I sometimes faced, even courted. It angered her when she would find out about things after the fact.

But this was different. This was a black monster of a revelation. Horrible in its complexities and possibilities. Sandy was strong. But she remembered nothing about the rape. Why jolt her with it? But what if at some future date she remembered? Was it better to tell her now and deal with it, or hope she never did? And if she never remembered, would she be better off? What about pregnancy? Venereal disease?

As if reading my mind, Merrill said, "She's been tested for AIDS and any . . . uh, social diseases. We'll have the results by the end of the day."

"Pregnancy?"

"No way to tell this early."

"And the HIV could show up months from now."

"Yeah."

"How could she not know she was raped?" I asked. "That doesn't seem possible."

"I know," said Merrill. "Believe it or not, I worked a case three years ago. Same thing. Woman had been raped and said she didn't remember it. She even passed a polygraph. She was too drunk to remember but we had an eyewitness."

"Let me think about it."

"Think about what?" he asked.

"Whether to tell her or not."

"Shit, Storme, you can't . . ." He stopped and looked at me. "All right. Up to you. It's a load, though."

"Thanks."

He nodded. "I'll be back later to talk with her some more, see if I can find out anything else. You better get some rest, man." He shook Chick's hand, turned, and lumbered down the corridor, leaving us.

Chick looked off down the hall. His voice sounded detached. "Whatever you decide, man," he said. "Okay with me."

The hospital personnel wouldn't let me see her. She was groggy, and the doctor wanted her to sleep. The doctor tried to get me to rest. He appealed to Chick to reason with me, but Chick said nothing.

I sat in the waiting room. Stared at the floor. Chick leaned against the wall, one leg crossed in front of the other, and looked out the glass door, an unlit Camel cigarette dangling from his lips. As unmoving as a palace guard.

The light from the waiting-room television flickered on the scarred tile floor.

At 11:00 Chick uncrossed his legs and pushed away from the

wall. Something outside had his attention. "Well, look at this," he said.

"What is it?" I asked, rubbing grainy eyes with my hands.

"Cops are here."

"Probably Merrill. He said he was coming back to talk to Sandy."

"It ain't Merrill."

"Who then?"

"Take a look. They're coming through the doors right now."

24

I walked into the emergency room corridor in time to see Police Chief Alec York burst through the double glass doors, the bottom flaps of his London Fog raincoat trailing him. Two uniforms were with him. Spotting me, he strode purposefully in my direction, hand extended.

"Sorry about this, Storme," he said, favoring me with a brief look of compassion. Then, my hand gripped in his, he turned to the receptionist, identified himself, and asked where Ms. Collingsworth was located.

"Follow the yellow arrow," she said. "Second door on the right."

He turned his attention back to me, then said, "Right after we ask her a few questions, I'll try to see that you have some time alone with her."

"I'd like to go in with you."

"Sorry," he said, lips pursed. "Can't do that. Afterward perhaps." He released my hand and walked briskly down the hall and disappeared into the room, second door on the right. The two policemen went in with him. Moments later the badges were back in the hall, escorting the doctor. The doctor appeared flustered, but the police ushered him away from the room and positioned themselves on either side of the door. The doctor disappeared down the long corridor.

I looked at Chick, and he tilted his head to one side and gave me an ironic grin. I walked down the hall in the direction of the two cops. When I got to the door, each took a step toward the other, blocking my entrance to the room.

"Help you, sir?" said one.

"My fiancée is in there. I want to see her."

"Sorry. Nobody goes in. Chief's orders."

I nodded and walked back down the hall.

"Can't go in, huh?" said Chick.

"Chief's orders," I said.

Chick nodded. "Chief's a busy man."

"Lucky he had time to come down and take a personal interest."

"Yeah. Lucky."

I looked down the hall in the direction of the two policemen. Thought about it some. Why was he here? I wanted to know what he was asking her.

"Forget about it," Chick said.

"Forget what?" I said, startled by the intrusion on my thoughts.

"You're not getting in there until they let you in. Have a little patience, huh?"

I crossed my arms and leaned against the wall. Waited.

Ten minutes passed before the door opened and one of the posted cops leaned into the room, nodded, then motioned to me with a hand in a "come here" gesture. I unfolded myself from my spot on the wall and walked down the hall, Chick following. When I got to the door, the cop who motioned to me said, "Chief said you can go on in now."

Wordlessly, I entered the room. I wasn't going to thank them for deigning to allow me to see the woman who completed me.

Her face was bloodless under the fading ski tan. Half-moon

shadows underlined the intelligent blue eyes. The expressive mouth was slack and down-turned, another half-moon shadow formed in the aperture between her parted lips.

"She is very listless," said York as I made my way to the side of the bed.

"Sandy," I said. "It's Wyatt."

Her eyelashes fluttered spasmodically at the sound of my voice. Haltingly, she lifted a hand, and I grasped it between mine like a precious stone. It was cold and smooth. Dry. As if something was wicking the life from within.

"She remembers nothing," said York. "Which doesn't help us any, but may be the best thing for her."

I leaned down and kissed her forehead. "Wyatt," she said hoarsely, as if from the back of a dusty cave. She smiled wanly.

"Yeah, I'm here, sweetheart. Going to stay right here, too."

"I'll leave you two alone," said York. "If you need anything, please call me. I promise you we will find the person who did this."

I swallowed the words forming in my gut. I didn't look up as he left.

"Sandy," I said. "Can you talk?"

"Yes," she croaked.

"What did York want?"

"Asked what happened."

"Did you meet Chastity last night?"

"Can't remember . . . no. Don't think so."

"When did she contact you?"

"Early evening the first time. Weird. Said she . . ." Sandy paused, as if winded, before continuing. "Said she would call back later. That she had important information. Told me to keep my line open and not call anyone until she called back."

"When did she call back?"

She closed her eyes and wet her lips with her tongue. I watched as she struggled with her memory. "Six thirty, no, before seven. Said to meet her at the football field."

"And to come alone?"

"Yes."

"You should have called me."

"Tried. No answer."

They set it up neat. No way for me to call Sandy, who was keeping her line open for a call from Chastity. Then they called me and got me out of town and out of my room so they could lure Sandy to the football stadium. She couldn't call me because I had left by the time Sandy's line was free.

"Do you remember anything after arriving at the football stadium?"

She closed her eyes again and thought. "I remember pulling into the parking lot."

"Anyone else around?"

"No. So I . . ." Her brow pursed. "Wait. I remember my door opening . . . then . . . nothing. Can't remember anything after that."

"Your door opened? Did you open it?"

"I don't think so."

"So it's possible someone opened it. Is that what you're telling me?"

She nodded. I told her about Chastity calling me and my trip to the marina. Left out the part about being shot at for now.

"So what did they gain?" She was becoming more lucid now.

"I don't know," I said. I didn't tell her what Merrill had told me. Couldn't tell her. Couldn't even think it.

"I'm thirsty."

There was a glass of water on a portable stand with a plastic pitcher next to it. I picked up the glass of water and handed it to her. She sat up, removed the hinged straw, and drank deeply from the glass. "Oh, my head. Drank too fast. I'm getting an ice cream rush." She smiled at me. It was good to see. "Thing is, I don't see—"

She stopped in midsentence, and her back arched as if stabbed with a metal rod.

"You okay, Sandy?" I said as apprehension snaked up my spinal cord.

The glass slipped from her hand and broke on the floor. Then her eyes rolled back in her head, her body shivered violently, and she lay back against the pillow, unmoving.

After checking her pulse and breathing, I rang the nurse's buzzer.

And I prayed.

25

The doctor and two nurses hustled me out of the room and at-
tended to Sandy. They rushed her to a different part of the hospital. I followed them but was rebuffed at the door. I didn't fight it.
Chick had followed me, but I didn't know it until I felt his hands
on the backs of my shoulders.

"Come on, man," he said. "They know what they're doing."

I nodded and walked down the hall with him. Once again, we
sat and waited. It was a different waiting area. This waiting room
had a floor-to-ceiling window with a view of the city below. I
stared out the glass, seeing nothing. I hadn't cried since Vietnam.
Not because I didn't want to sometimes, and not because I
thought it unmanly. My tears had dried up inside me, years ago,
drawn away like a sponge by the misery of war and death and loss.
And loneliness. Loneliness like a hammer chipping away at what
had been me.

Then I'd met Sandra Collingsworth. And her bubbling-brook
laugh and summer-blue eyes had thawed and warmed me and
brought me back. God, who watches over the soldier facedown in

the rice paddies and forgives the selfish football player's transgressions, sent her to me—an undeserved gift and evidence of his patience. And as I prayed He would spare her, I knew I was also asking Him to spare me her loss.

Then, realization. The water!

I jumped up from my seat and hurried down the hall toward the emergency wing.

"Hey," Chick said. "Where're you going?"

I didn't answer. My only thought was to get back to the room Sandy had been in when the paramedics first brought her in. She drank the water just before she was overcome by the attack. As I turned the corner to the corridor leading to the ER, I saw an elderly janitor, thin and wiry, coming out of the room where Sandy had been. He was pushing a yellow mop bucket. His eyes grew as I ran up to him.

"You already clean that room?" I said.

"Yes sir," he said, swallowing. Unsure what I wanted. "I did."

I closed my eyes and rolled back my head in frustration and disappointment. Then I slapped my hands together. "Dammit!"

The old janitor was confused. "I couldn't leave that glass on the floor. That nurse, she wanted it cleaned up right away. Did I do something wrong?" There was an edge of anxiety in his voice.

"No. It's okay," I said. "I'm sorry. I didn't mean to snap at you." I looked into the bucket. Looked into the dirty water. Chick had arrived by this time. Then I had another thought. "Anyone remove the water pitcher in there?"

He knit his eyebrows, trying to fathom my reasoning. "Far as I know nobody's touched it."

"Thanks." I went into the room and recovered the pitcher. It was half full. Good. Maybe I had something. Maybe nothing. Maybe her attack was brought on by something else. A delayed reaction of some sort. I wished I had gotten there before he mopped up the water and the broken glass. I handed the pitcher to Chick and said, "Get this to Merrill and see if he can get it analyzed."

Chick nodded. Without another word, he left.

I waited out the afternoon, alternately pacing and dozing. As I dozed I dreamed I was back in the jungle, humping through the elephant grass, an M-16 slung across my back. Oddly, I was wearing my football uniform, urethane mouth protector clinched between my teeth. Somehow I had become separated from my squad, and the faster I walked the thicker the jungle became. The foliage began to twist and grab, wrapping itself around me with damp green tendrils. I tried to scream, but the mouthpiece muffled it. I heard someone yell "incoming" and tried to free myself from the vegetation as my ears filled with the banshee shriek of artillery fire.

But there was no explosion.

Something thudded off my football helmet, and I lifted my head to see a football in the wet tangle. I reached to pick it up, but it rolled away from me.

Then Chick's voice said, "C'mon, we gotta get out of this place." He pulled me out of the twisted vines, and we were on solid ground, hiking along a village that transformed itself into the rolling Missouri countryside. A familiar house appeared on a slight rise. I was home! Thank God, home. I looked up and saw Heather hanging clothes on a line. She waved to me, her long auburn hair fluttering in the breeze like a flag. As I raised an arm to wave back, I saw my daughter, Aubrey, toddling my way with the stilted new-colt gait two-year-olds have. I dropped my gun and opened my arms to hold her. So good to see her. Glorious.

"You too late, Daddy," Aubrey said. "It already happened without you."

I started running toward her.

Then, just as I was just about to pick up Aubrey, I heard the harsh bray of a diesel horn followed by the sharp hiss of air brakes. The house and Aubrey and Heather disappeared, and I was jerked awake.

My breathing was quick and syncopated. I felt my pulse in my ears. Panic shipped into my nervous system. Electric. I fought to breathe slow and deep, to control the wild stampede of fear rushing down the slope of my medulla to my spine. My teeth ground together with the ferocity of an epileptic fit, yet this was no epileptic attack. From deep inside my soul came a wave of anguish I'd suppressed for so long, and it broke and slammed against the rocks violently.

I leaned forward and placed hands on my knees as my chest heaved. Finally, the panic subsided, and my breathing returned to normal with only an intermittent catch. Aubrey. Heather.

Sandy.

Why? The question screamed in my mind and echoed in my soul. Why? I'd asked it a thousand times. Clamoured for an answer. There was none. I felt a bursting, like lesions tearing in my heart.

I rubbed my face with my hands.

And felt the dampness of my tears. Two decades' worth.

26

I washed my face in the waiting-room bathroom. Looked into the cadaverous eyes in the mirror. Saw the brown-and-gold whiskers on my face. It was 4:00 P.M. I asked the desk nurse—a different one than before—if there'd been any change in Sandy's condition.

"No," she said, appearing oddly uncomfortable. "I'm sorry."

"Something wrong?"

"No," she said, shaking her head quickly. "We'll let you know as soon as there is any change."

I ordered coffee in the hospital coffee shop. When the black liquid reached my stomach, I became conscious of the emptiness inside. I ordered a sandwich and nibbled at it. It tasted soggy and flat but made the coffee more palatable. I finished the sandwich, got another cup of coffee, and returned to the waiting room. Sat and looked out the window. During the afternoon the sky had darkened and thunder now rattled the glass, echoing and rolling away to recede into the distance.

I was overwhelmingly tired, the kind of trudging fatigue I used to feel in Vietnam—a soul-numbing limb heaviness that was physical and spiritual in nature.

A bolt of lightning rent the autumn horizon. As it reached for the earth, it broke into forked tentacles of furious cobalt electricity. Blue cracks in the dark, mattered heavens. Blue chained lightning shimmering briefly in the sky, lighting the universe, leaving only the rumble of its passing.

Chick walked into the waiting room five minutes after I returned. His eyes looked like mine, yet there seemed to be no attendant weariness in his mannerisms.

"Any word?" he asked.

I shook my head. "No. Same."

"I found Merrill and gave him the water. He said he'd get it to the lab and give the technicians some kind of story about where it came from. Said he'd know something tomorrow, but he thought you . . . we were clutching at straws." He paused, then said, "You okay, man?"

I looked at him absently. "Yeah." Rubbed my face. "Yeah, I'm okay."

"You look fabulous."

"Shouldn't have let York in there alone," I said.

"How could you have stopped it? He's the main cop, and this is his turf. Besides, he may not have done a thing. Other than the fact we don't particularly like him and vice versa, we don't have much reason not to think he's squared away."

"I told Sandy not to go anywhere without telling me."

"Seems we've had this conversation."

"It doesn't make—" I stopped in midsentence when I spotted my old buddy Officer Bredwell and another uniformed cop walking in our direction. The second cop was a larger man, a weight-room type, with unusually long arms, a neck like a redwood stump, and a head shaped like a cinder block. His shirt buttons were pulled tight across the chest, and his biceps swelled the sleeves like twin pythons trying to digest something thick and heavy. He looked like Li'l Abner, only dumber. His name tag said HERRMAN.

"I need you to come with me, Storme," said Bredwell, who had yet to learn anything about protocol. "You too, Easton. We want to talk to both of you downtown."

I shook my head. "No."

"Where's your buddy, Officer Peckerwood?" asked Chick. He moved closer to the slab of beef in the cop's uniform. He was smiling up at the big cop. "You're a big one, aren't you?"

The cop named Herrman said, "What're you? Some kinda fag or something?" Sounded like Li'l Abner, too.

Chick chuckled. Smiled. "I turn that way, the suicide hot line'll jam up with calls from distraught females. Can't have that. But I would like to point out that it is rude, not to mention stupid, to address others in such a manner."

The big man's eyes narrowed. "You saying I'm stupid?"

"No," said Chick, smiling. "That would be superfluous."

Herrman looked confused. He leaned forward and looked down at Chick. "I'll bite off your head and spit down your neck, city boy."

"Make him stop," Chick said. "He's frightening me."

Herrman started to say something else, but Bredwell cut him off. "That's not what we're here for." He turned to face me. "We're authorized to place you under arrest if you refuse to accompany us."

"What charge?"

"Murder," said Bredwell.

"Who are we supposed to have killed?" I said.

"Chastity Yablonski."

27

I sat in a windowless room and stared at the walls. There were four of them. Off-white. The police had separated Chick and me after our arrival at the station, left me in the twelve-by-eighteen room to ponder my situation. Though I hadn't been officially charged, I learned Chastity had been found murdered on the picnic grounds at the state park.

Found in the park. Strangled to death with her own nylon hose.

Someone or several someones had gone to a lot of trouble to cover the rape and subsequent demise of Francine Wilson. Francine dead, Chastity strangled, Sandy comatose.

And the longer I thought, the more I wanted whoever had touched Sandy. Ached to get at him. I had to wait. I had to focus. My hands felt along the tabletop; its wood veneer was scarred by blackened cigarette burns and gouged with graffiti. The lone sign in the room said NO SMOKING!

I reached into my shirt pocket and pulled out the stubby Chateau Fuente, removed its cedar sleeve, clipped one end and lit the other, drew on it, then released a cloud of blue gray to swirl and drift into broken lines of dissipated heat in the enclosed room. Rebellion lay in his way, and he found it. William Shakespeare said that, and he was right again. I was halfway through the robusto when the door opened.

"You'll see what I mean when—" said Bredwell as he entered the room. "What the hell is going on? You can't smoke in here, Storme. Put that out."

Following him into the room was a younger cop-looking guy— an African American wearing a tweed sport coat, a white shirt, and a striped tie loosened at the collar. Officer Pethmore was with them this time.

I took another pull on the cigar. I couldn't tell which was more satisfying—the taste of Dominican tobacco or the look on Bredwell's face.

"You smartass," said Bredwell. "Put that out before I make you eat it."

I was getting tired of Officer Bredwell's belligerence. I released a stream of smoke in his direction, then, looking into his eyes, I stubbed out the cigar on the pockmarked table. I reached into my jacket and pulled out another cigar. "I'd rather eat a fresh one," I said, unwrapping the new one. Bredwell's eyes blazed up, and the veins in his temple turned red.

"Please, Mr. Storme," said the plainclothes cop. "Don't do that. We don't want any trouble. We realize you've had a bad day. I'm Detective Snipes." He stretched out a hand. I stopped unwrapping the new cigar and accepted his hand. Bredwell and Pethmore remained ready in case I made a break for the door or tried to light another cigar. Snipes pulled out a chair and sat down. "I understand you used to play pro football."

I looked at him. "Just get to it," I said, without venom.

Snipes's eyes looked to Bredwell, then back to me.

"Okay," Snipes said, "a working girl named Charlotte Yablonski, also known as Chastity—"

"No wonder she changed it," I said, interrupting him.

"Huh?" he said, momentarily losing his train of thought. Then he smiled and nodded. "Yeah. Hard to get picked up in a noisy bar with a name like that. Anyway, you knew her, correct?"

"Yeah."

"How did you know her?"

"She had information Sandy Collingsworth needed."

"Miss Collingsworth is your reporter friend?"

"Yeah."

"What was that information?"

"Ask her."

He sat back and chewed the corner of his lip. "You know we can't do that."

I nodded. "Yeah," I said, looking at Bredwell and Pethmore, then back to Snipes. "I'm aware of that."

"You and Miss Collingsworth, as I understand it, are close?"

Pethmore said, "They're shacked up together at the Holiday Inn."

I rolled my head in his direction. Looked at the smirk on his pinched face. "You know," I said, "you say anything else even remotely derogatory about her, I'm going to accelerate your toilet training." Pethmore's freckled face flushed pink.

"Are you threatening an officer?" he asked.

"Just want to make sure you know where the lines are."

"That's enough!" said Snipes. "Pethmore, you keep your head closed."

"You can't talk to me like that," said Pethmore. "I ain't takin' no shit off a—" He hesitated.

"Go ahead, Pethmore," said Snipes. "Say it. You aren't going to take no shit off a nigger. That it? Just—"

Snipes was interrupted by the door swinging open and banging against the doorstop. "What the hell's going on here?" said Detective Fred Merrill. His bulk filled the doorway, and his bushy eyebrows hung like awnings over the fierce brown eyes. "And what are these two doing here?" he asked, meaning Bredwell and Pethmore.

"We're here to assist Snipes," said Bredwell.

"Well, you're relieved."

"But we were told—" started Pethmore.

"You got something in your ears, or are you just stupid? I said get out of here. And I mean right now."

Bredwell started to protest, but Merrill cut him off. "Was there something I said you didn't understand, Bredwell?"

Bredwell pursed his lips. He shook his head and said, "We'll see what the chief has to say about this."

Merrill stepped in the uniformed cop's path and looked down on him. "Let's get this said, Bredwell. One of these days you're not going to have York to cover your butt, and when that happens you're going to be working night security in condom factories for minimum wage. If there's anything else I can do for you, just let me know." He jabbed a finger at Pethmore. "And that goes for your redneck buddy, too."

The two men glared at each other, briefly, before Bredwell left, Pethmore following him. Then Merrill turned to Snipes and said, "Dammit, Dave, why'd you let those assholes in here?"

"They said York told them to. Sorry, Fred."

"Is Storme charged with anything?"

"Not yet."

"Then we'd better hurry before they get to York." Merrill put a size thirteen up on a chair and said, "Okay, Storme. Did the hooker call you last night?"

"Told me to meet her in the park."

"The state park?"

"Yeah. She also called Sandy and told her to meet her at the high school football stadium. Told us both to come alone. To different places. At the same time. Sandy did. I didn't."

"Sounds like somebody's trying to set you up. Anybody confirm your story?"

"Chick was with me. The desk clerk will be able to confirm the time of the phone call."

"What did you want from the hooker?"

"The name of the officer she traded out for sex to get him to drop a soliciting charge."

"Any idea who it might be?"

"Not really," I said. "But Pethmore and Bredwell come to mind. They always seem to be around."

Merrill thought about it for a minute, then said to Snipes, "Take a walk, Dave."

"You sure?"

"Yeah. They're trying to milk this investigation for publicity reasons. I just want to find out who did it. You stay any longer, it's just going to get you into shit with the boss."

"I don't care, Fred. You know I'll stand with you."

Merrill smiled. "I know. But something happens to me, I need you to be free and clear to conduct the investigation or to keep me updated. Whatever's needed. So get going."

Snipes left the room.

"That's a good man," said Merrill.

I nodded.

"He'll stay hitched. He's the smartest cop on the force and my best friend."

"And he doesn't like Pethmore."

"Another plus," said Merrill. "I think they're going to try to hook you up to this killing somehow. I don't think it's going to fit, though. Whoever did it was probably hoping to draw your lady friend off so she wouldn't go with you and hoped you wouldn't take Easton. Where is he, anyway?"

"I don't know. They separated us when we got here."

"Will they be able to trip him up?"

"No. In fact, the cop interviewing him is probably going crazy about now."

"We gotta get on this fast, before the trail gets cold. The longer you wait on these things, the tougher they get. The forensic guys're already on the scene. I've taken a look at the body. They never look quite real, you know? Never get used to that. How did she sound on the phone?"

"Scared. Nervous."

"How did she know where you were?"

"I gave her my number in case she decided to give us some information we wanted."

He thought about it for a moment, then said, "What do you know that I don't, Storme?"

"Maybe nothing. But York and the Gestapo have been in a full-court press since Sandy arrived."

"Sorry about your lady friend. You weren't involved with the prostitute, were you?"

I looked at him.

"Sorry," Merrill said. "Gotta ask it. Were you?"

"No."

"Easton?"

"No."

"Why was she seen in Easton's company along with you and your lady friend at the Hickory Wind?"

"How do you know about that?"

"My job to know," he said, pulling a pack of cigarettes from his jacket pocket. "If you keep answering questions by asking questions, you're going to slow this up. What were you doing with Chastity at the Hickory Wind?"

"What I told you before. We needed information she had about a cop." I told him the whole story while he lit his cigarette. When I finished, he said, "So you have been in contact with her on more than one occasion. Did you touch anything at the park?"

"Nothing they can take prints off."

He thought for a moment, then said, "They'll also be looking for fluid samples, strands of hair, that kind of thing. You're okay there?"

"We got out of the truck while we were waiting. They may find Chick's cigarette butt. Other than that, nothing."

"This is a damn mess. The kind of mess that occurs when nonprofessionals stick their noses in things."

"Especially when the cops are doing such a crackerjack job."

His chin raised a half inch. "Give me a break, huh."

"Two local women and a national media person have been sexually assaulted, maybe by cops. The locals get killed. This stimulates the police to increase traffic surveillance and harassment of a reporter who is presently incommunicado. Then they drag in two guys who need Chastity alive instead of bringing in a pimp named Robby Blue. When it comes to making a mess, no one can touch the North Branson police force."

"I'm doing the best I can."

"I know," I said. "But there is too much peripheral damage."

"Such as?"

"Are you sleeping with Felicia York?"

He glared at me.

"Can't help it," I said. "You got something going with her, or not?"

"What's that got to do with you?"

"If you keep answering questions by asking questions, this will take forever."

"You're kind of a wiseass, you know?"

"I've heard that. Are you sleeping with Mrs. York?"

He chewed his lower lip. "Yeah."

"Well, that's certainly bright of you."

"I'm not proud of it."

"Then why do it?"

"I don't know. Well . . . that's not true. There's the obvious reasons, of course. Then there are other motivations."

"Like you can get back at her husband, right?"

He took in a big breath. "I oughta kick your ass," he said, but without conviction.

"Well, you can't do it, so don't dwell on it," I said, smiling when I said it. "Besides, I'm not trying to put you on the spot; I just want to know how things stand. I'm not going to get into it with the one guy I trust in this place."

"You can trust Snipes. If it comes to that."

"I appreciate you finding Sandy. And do what you want, but it would be better if you stayed away from Mrs. York. Preferably forever, but at least until this is over. She's reckless and dangerous."

"You're right."

The door swung open again, and Alec York entered the room. Right on cue.

28

Alec York didn't look particularly angry or upset when he entered the room, but the animosity in the air was like a ball of barbed wire; some of it due to circumstances, some due to personality clashes. It had the residual flavor of class struggle and life choices: the nattily dressed and aristocratic administrator versus the rumpled, straightforward local-guy police detective who only knew how to run in a straight line. I was merely a distraction; a pawn in their long-running duel. As was Felicia York.

"What are you doing, Detective Merrill?" said York.

"My job," Merrill said. "I'm interviewing Storme about his possible complicity in the death of Chastity Yablonski."

"Why did you dismiss Officers Bredwell and Pethmore?"

"Because they're a pair of mouth-breathing morons. Not to mention the fact they think the Ku Klux Klan is a viable political organization."

"Do you think that's a proper way to describe your colleagues?"

"My colleagues were prejudicing this investigation and alienating Mr. Storme, who has been cooperative. I'm not familiar with the procedure for badgering witnesses. Is this something new I missed? I understand Storme hasn't been formally charged."

"We were prepared to do so, if necessary, to ensure his cooperation." He addressed me. "We wish for you to cooperate freely, without coercion, if possible. Regarding poisoning the air, who has been smoking in here?"

I raised my hand. "I did. Please forgive me. I'm not up on interrogation protocol. But I promise to do better."

He looked at the table and saw both the stubbed-out cigar and Merrill's cigarette butt. I'm sure he picked up on the nuance of the situation. He said, "Bredwell tells me you did so willfully, ostensibly to annoy him."

"An added bonus."

"Someone strangled Chastity Yablosnski. Did you know her?"

"Yeah."

"What was your relationship?"

"I was her pimp."

His eyes narrowed an eighth of an inch. "A more substantive answer, please."

"Maybe I need a lawyer," I said.

"That is your prerogative."

"I could get Cavalerri. Would that be an advantage? Or a disadvantage?"

"You seem determined to provoke me with Ms. Cavalerri."

"Mrs. Cavalerri," I said, correcting him.

"There seems to be no pleasing you."

"You could try singing to me."

"Do you wish representation or not?" he said in clipped tones.

"Won't need it if you're not charging me with anything. Are you?"

"No."

"Okay, ask me what you want."

"Your relationship with Chastity Yablonski?"

"No relationship. Sandy was interviewing her."

"Meaning Ms. Collingsworth?"

"You know who she is."

"Did Chastity Yablonski contact you last night?"

"Yes."

"Why?"

"I don't know. Someone killed her before she could tell me what she wanted." I watched his eyes closely to see if they would reveal anything. He was ice. I didn't tell him she was possibly going to reveal her killer's identity. "She wanted me to meet her."

"Where?"

"You know the answer to that, too. I've already told Merrill and Snipes."

"Tell me so I'll feel involved."

"The picnic grounds at the state park."

"Her body was found in the state park," he said.

"Should I confess now, or allow you to pick me apart using your clever interrogation tactics?"

He ignored that. "Did you go to the park?"

I nodded.

"Did you go alone?"

"No. Chick was with me."

"Were you and Easton together the whole time?"

"No."

"Did you kill her?"

"No."

"What about Easton?"

"No."

"How do you know?"

"He had no reason."

"His past is rather shadowy. How do you explain that?"

I shrugged.

"Be less evasive, Mr. Storme. Your position is precarious. By your own admission, you were at the scene of the murder and were the last person to speak to her. Also, I have information that says someone of your description busted the window out of a 1996 Cadillac Seville with a fire extinguisher. Why would you do that?"

"Interior of the car was on fire. I'm a junior fire chief."

"You assaulted the driver."

"Did he file charges?"

York pushed back the tail of his coat and placed a hand on his hip. "No. He didn't."

"There's a surprise," I said. "A pair of leg-breakers who didn't file charges. Probably wouldn't look good on their résumés they get slapped around by their victim. Interesting you knew about it, though."

"I know everything that goes on in my town."

"Except which policeman was hitting on prostitutes and perhaps killed Francine Wilson."

He slammed a fist down on the table. The gesture was theatrical, and I was unimpressed. "I am growing tired of your insinuations."

"I'm not insinuating, I'm declaring. Where were Officers Bredwell and Pethmore last night? For that matter, where were you?"

"I'm asking the questions."

"And doing a bang-up job."

"Tell me why I'm not having you arrested at this moment, Storme?"

"Because you don't have jack. I didn't do it, and you know it. Chick didn't either. There's no law against being at the state park, nor is there any law against being at the scene of a murder you didn't witness. You've been intent on tagging me since we've been here, and there is no legitimate reason for it. You police your territory like a feudal lord and are worked up because I'm not paying tribute."

"What were you doing down at City Hall Records?"

Time to run a counterplay.

"I'm thinking about investing in a string of land outside of town," I said. "I'm hoping they'll put in a new bypass."

Like a good defensive end, York should've stayed home, but no matter how good they are, the temptation to pursue the flow catches the best of them.

"There is no bypass being planned."

"And you'd know, wouldn't you? Being the lieutenant governor's little brother."

"That kind of information would be unethical as well as a violation of public trust."

I scratched my jaw. The folksy touch. "Well. That kind of throws me. I guess for the life of me I can't figure why you and your father-in-law, your lawyer friend, and your other flunkies have bought up all that land. And who is the So-Mo Holding Company?"

He tried to recover, but I was already through the hole and into the secondary.

"I fail to see," he said, "how that bears upon the discussion at hand."

"Why did you buy that land, York?" I said, pressing.

"How would you like to be charged with murder?" He was getting angry. Good. A crack in the cool facade was to my advantage.

"How would you like to be sued for false arrest?" I answered, smiling at him. I wondered if I should light a cigar, à la Red Auerbach. Probably a trifle smug at this point. Had to avoid over-confidence. "I am a genuine American folk legend, engaged to America's sweetheart, as a matter of fact. Probably wouldn't look good in the morning papers, not to mention what Sandy's network would do with it. Your problem, as I see it, is that if I killed Chastity, not to mention why, then who lured Sandy to the football stadium? These two incidents occurred several miles apart at approximately the same time. There are other inconsistencies. I haven't been Mirandized, nor do I have an attorney present. This is sloppy work for a slick political operator like you. If you weren't so lathered up to jack me around, you'd see that, too."

York placed balled-up fists on the tabletop and leaned toward me. These movements looked practiced. "Don't you mess with me, Storme." he said. "Others have tried it."

"Seen it before," I said. "Lloyd Nolan does it better."

"I don't appreciate your flippant manner."

"Flippant? Where'd you learn to talk? You been reading *Wuther-*

ing Heights? You came in here with this tired George Sanders, smooth-bully act, and it isn't working. Charge me or cut me loose. I think *Seinfeld* is about to come on."

York's lips pursed into a thin line. I'd hit him in a soft spot with the land deal. He hadn't expected it straight at him. Then I'd pimped him in his own place, which was pushing it a little. That beats what I wanted to do, which was punch him in the mouth. It was at least more subtle.

York pushed himself away from the table and said, "I'm not prepared to charge you at this moment, Storme. However, do not assume that we won't come back to you. Detective Merrill, get Storme and his associate out of my sight."

Merrill, for his part, had been enjoying the whole scenario. A wry smile played on his lips as he escorted me from the room.

Once out of earshot of Chief York, Merrill said, "He wanted to hang that on you, bad. You'd better not even spit on the sidewalk in this town. He didn't like that one bit."

"I didn't see you coming to his defense."

"Yeah," said Merrill. " 'You could try singing to me'? I thought I was going to bust a gut. You're nuts."

I shrugged demurely.

29

I collected Chick, and we returned to the hospital. En route, we exchanged notes.

"Pretty standard stuff," Chick said. "They asked cop questions, I gave them my comedy routine. They frowned, and I smiled. Then they threatened me with jail and roommates who would Roto-Rooter my waste-removal system. A terrifying experience. Mostly, I think they were pumping me to find out what I knew about things besides Chastity."

"You didn't smoke, did you?" I asked.

"That would be rude. I would never hinder a police investigation."

We arrived to good news at the hospital. Sandy had come out of her coma, but I couldn't see her yet because the doctor wanted her to rest.

"I think the worst is over," said the doctor. "She is in excellent physical shape. I'm not sure what caused her to become comatose. The lethargy and dilated eyes suggest drugs. I see no evidence of trauma on the CAT scan. Fortunately, her condition was temporary. The memory loss is inexplicable. Sometimes, shock causes it. The system protects itself from the memory of a traumatic experience."

"What about the . . . a . . . ?" I rubbed my forehead. Was having trouble saying it.

"The assault?" He said, helping me. "Doesn't seem to be any long-term physical damage. Some contusions on the biceps and shoulders where she was restrained by her attacker. The vaginal lips were irritated, which is consistent with rape. The police want semen samples. It is my understanding you do not wish us to tell her of the sexual assault."

"I'd appreciate it if you didn't."

"I don't know what to advise on that," he said. "It is a complicated matter, and my expertise is the human body, not the mind." He leaned closer to me. "I would advise you to get some rest. Your eyes are bloodshot, and you look as if you're on your last legs."

I thanked him, and he said I would be able to see her tomorrow and that she might be released then.

As Chick and I left the hospital, I said, "You know who everybody, including the police, has forgotten, don't you?"

"Sure," said Chick. "Our buddy Robby B., the friendly neighborhood pimp."

"That's right."

"So how do we find him?"

I thought about it. There was one string we could pull.

"I think you deserve a beer for all your trouble," I said. "I'll even buy."

"Well," Chick said, "whenever you offer to buy, it usually means one of two things. One, you want a favor. Two, hell *has* frozen over. But this time I'll buy a vowel and select door number three and guess we're going to talk to the bartender at the Hickory Wind."

I smiled. "And they call you a burnout."

"Hah!" he said. "Chick Easton, master of the mixed metaphor and king of the cosmic cowboys, cares little for what they say."

It was early evening when we entered the bar of Travis Conrad's Hickory Wind. It was that hammock of time between crowds. The late afternoon office types were finishing up before heading home for dinner and sitcoms, while the tourists were starting to filter in for dinner and the show. Bob the bartender and a couple of his colleagues were wiping glasses and placing them on towels under the bar, getting ready for the evening crowd. We slid onto barstools in front of him. Quickly, he placed two napkins with Budweiser logos in front of us. Trying to keep the customer satisfied.

"What'll you have, guys?" he said.

"I'll have a beer," said Chick. "Too late in the day for any serious drinking. Hate a late start."

"What about you?" Bob asked me.

I held up a twenty-dollar bill. "Information," I said.

He concentrated on the glass he was wiping down. "Fresh out. Can I get you something to drink?"

"How do I get hold of Robby Blue? Other than waiting for him to walk in."

He shrugged. "I don't know anybody with that name." He flipped a glass mug up, filled it from the tapper, then placed it in front of Chick and said, "Two dollars, please."

Chick patted his pockets. "Whoops. Looks like I forgot my wallet. Can you get this, Wyatt?"

"Be glad to," I said, looking at Bob. "But all I have is this twenty. And I want my money's worth."

Bob eyed the twenty. "I'd like to help you guys, but I can't. Beer's on me." He started to turn away.

"Whoa! Slow down, hoss," said Chick. "We ain't asking for your firstborn. We just want to visit with our favorite businessman, Robby Blue."

"What makes you think I know how to get hold of him?"

"Because he couldn't operate so freely here unless you allowed it," I said.

He wiped his hands on a bar towel. "He just comes in here, that's all. It's a bar, not a church."

"You heard what happened to Chastity?"

He nodded. "Yeah. A dead whore. So what?"

"Your disrespectful tone is beginning to disturb me," I said.

Bob's mouth worked as if his lips were dry. Unusual for one who worked around liquids. "Look, I don't want no trouble."

"Where's Blue?" I said.

"He's a wicked bastard," Bob said. "He won't like it if I say anything."

"And we won't like it if you don't," said Chick. "Seems you need to deal with the more immediate problem."

"Not here," he said.

"Right here," I said. "Right now. I'm tired of everybody putting me off to a later date, then disappearing."

"I need to make one call," he said.

"To who?"

"Guy I know. He'll know how Robby operates and from where."

"Chick goes with you and listens in."

Bob looked at Chick. Chick smiled broadly. I would have smiled, too, but didn't want to overwhelm the guy. Bob gave in and motioned for Chick to follow him. They disappeared into the rear of the establishment.

I swiveled around on the bar seat as three smartly dressed females entered the bar. Their jewelry sparkled whitely, and they reeked of Chanel No. 5. I recognized one of them. Velonne Cavalerri. The late Francine Wilson's attorney and Chief York's steady punch. I was developing a crummy attitude about their relationship.

She looked at me. I smiled and nodded my head. Her one-hundred-dollar-an-hour smile disappeared. Hmm. Was I losing my charm? I smiled at the tallest of the trio, a blonde. She smiled in return. Still had it.

They sat at a table, and a waitress hustled over to take their orders. These were women in ascendancy. Perched on the lower edge of middle age, at the peak of their powers; delicate in their grace, terrible when moved to displeasure.

It is my theory, formed by experience, that in any power structure, women often hold the key to the storehouse.

I slid off my barstool and sauntered over to the table where the trio of women were sitting. I can saunter with the best. Accompanying Mrs. Cavalerri was a petite brunette and the taller woman who had smiled at me. As I approached the table, Cavalerri's marvelous cheekbones tensed and the corners of her mouth formed little commas, and I felt the heat of her midnight-black eyes. Fortunately, I had recently powered up with Wheaties and took it head-on. I was, however, impressed by the force of her presence and was beginning to see what Alec York saw in her beyond the obvious. Adultery was not my cup of tea, but York deserved high marks for degree of difficulty.

The petite brunette leaned back in her chair to look up at me, and her sidelong glance at Cavalerri told me she would look to the attorney for guidance in this situation. As for the tall blonde, her head was cocked to one side, and she traced a lock of hair from her face. So I addressed her when I asked if I could join them.

The blonde, smiling, looked at Cavalerri, then back at me, and said, "Of course you can. My name is Christine." She extended a hand, which I accepted. She kept my hand in hers as I sat.

Christine introduced the petite brunette as Joyce, "and this is Velonne."

"I've already met Mr. Storme," said Cavalerri, still glaring.

"Storme," said Christine. "Wyatt Storme? The football player?"

"Long time ago."

"My brother had a poster of you in his room when he was in high school. You were his favorite player. He would just *die* if he knew I talked to you." She looked at Cavalerri and said, "Wouldn't he just die, Velonne?" I felt the competitive tension between the two women.

"Yes, Christine. When you consider his propensity for hero worship, he would most certainly die."

Christine gave me a conspiratorial wink, which Cavalerri couldn't see, then said, "You certainly don't seem very friendly toward Mr. Storme. Why is that?" She was enjoying herself. I liked Christine.

"Mr. Storme is an abrasive gossip," said Cavalerri.

"As opposed to a lubricated one," I said.

"Ooh," said Christine. Moving her chair closer to the table and to me, she patted my hand. "What kind of gossip do you have, Wyatt?"

"It would be indelicate to mention it in front of Mrs. Cavalerri," I said.

"That's usually the best kind," said Christine.

"Don't wet yourself darling," said Cavalerri. "He has a network bimbo for a girlfriend."

"Is that true, Wyatt?" asked Christine, slightly pouty, but in a humorous manner. She was having fun caricaturing a gossipy female.

"Which thing? That I have a girlfriend? Or that she is a network bimbo?"

"Do you have a girlfriend?"

"Yes." I looked at Cavalerri. "But I understand it's considered stylish in these parts to have several."

Christine, picking up on the unstated meaning, said, "I think he has your number, Velonne. Is there anything you wish to share with the group?"

Cavalerri gave Christine a patronizing smile. "Mr. Storme is a boorish clod with an overactive imagination."

"It's because my hormones haven't balanced out yet," I said. "Mrs. Cavalerri probably was unaware that another woman was murdered and that my friend, the network bimbo, has been assaulted and hospitalized."

Christine was taken aback by this. She was amused by the community intrigues and by vexing Velonne Cavalerri, but this was more than she'd bargained for.

"No," said Cavalerri. "I hadn't. Anyone I know?"

"Another former client of yours. A hooker named Chastity. Seems nearly lethal to contract your services, doesn't it?"

"I don't find you, or your conversation, very pleasant," said Cavalerri.

"That's funny, I was known as the best conversationalist in the county when I was younger."

"Well, both you and your conversation are getting old."

"Sure are touchy. I thought lawyers were inured to the unpleasantries of confrontational discourse."

"What is it you hope to accomplish by baiting me?"

"Why did Chastity come to you for representation?"

"I can't remember every client I've ever engaged."

"How many of your clients are prostitutes?"

"I don't think this is the appropriate time or place to discuss such matters."

"Thought you might like to know," I said. I stood. "Nice to meet you ladies." I walked back to the bar, dropping the saunter. Chick had returned. Bob looked as wrung out as a bar towel.

"Do any good?" I asked.

"Believe I did," said Chick. "You feel up to a little ride?"

"Always," I said.

30

Robby Blue operated out of a restaurant lounge called the Bistro. When we entered the place, Robby was seated at a back booth talking on a cellular phone. He was alone. The receptionist asked how many were in our party.

I said, "We're supposed to meet someone. There he is. Thanks anyway."

We walked to where Robby Blue was talking animatedly on the portable phone. There was a bottle of wine in a bucket on the table in front of him along with a pack of cigarettes and a chrome Zippo lighter. He was wearing a lime-green shirt underneath a not-of-this-world lapel-less jade jacket. Hanging from the collar of the shirt was a bolo tie with a yin/yang symbol for a slide. Alligator shoes. When he saw us approach, he swiveled the mouthpiece down and his shoulders sagged.

"I'll call you back," he said. He shut off the phone and laid it on the table. "The fuck do you guys want?"

"And you said he wouldn't be glad to see us," said Chick, pulling a chair over and sitting in it, reversed, the back of the chair facing the booth table. I slid onto the seat opposite Robby Blue. Chick reached out and picked up the cellular phone. Robby Blue tried to grab it first, but Chick snatched it up before the pimp could stop him.

"Now, I just want to look at it," said Chick, holding it away from him. "Don't be selfish."

"You guys better leave," he said.

"You forgot 'or else,' " I said.

"What?"

"The bad guy always says, 'You better leave or else.' "

"You're a smart guy, aren't you? You could end up dead being smart."

"I'm about to die from fright just talking to a genuine tough guy like you. That how Chastity died?"

"I don't know anything about it," he said, but his eyes were evasive.

"Who was the cop that's been trading out sex for favors?" I said.

"Ask her." He threw up both hands in mock surprise. "I forgot, she ain't saying much anymore, is she?"

"Your grief is touching. Did you have her call me and Sandy before you killed her?"

"I got nothing to say to you. Fuck off."

Chick was holding up the cellular phone. "Boy, these things sure are fancy. All kinds of little features on it. Mute button, call waiting, why I'll bet it's even got a redial on it. Well, look at that, wouldja? There *is* a redial button." He pushed a button on the phone and put it to his ear. "Wonder who we just got through talking to?"

Robby Blue's eyes were intent on the phone in Chick's hand. He leaned toward Chick as if to grab the phone, but Chick put a hand up as if refusing a cup of coffee.

"Toad!" Chick said, with genuine glee, into the mouthpiece. "Good to talk to you, buddy. That's right, this is the son of a bitch. How good of you to remember. We're sitting here talking to a friend of yours. Robby Blue . . . aw, come on, Toad. You know him. Six-one, crummy manners, dirty mouth, *Star Trek* ward-robe." Robby Blue was beginning to look ill. "Tsk, tsk, Toady. That any way to talk? You should hear some of the things Robby says when you're not around. Very loose-lipped." Chick winked at Robby. "Guess who I ran into the other day? Rude Dog Chaney. So good to see him. He's going by the name Cecil, as in Cecil the Seasick Leg-breaker. Robby said he appreciates you setting him up with a go-getter like Chaney. Well, gotta run, Toad. Places to go, people to hang upside down . . . no, thanks for the offer, but I only do that with females." Chick held the phone away from his ear and gave a mock shudder.

"Such rudeness," said Chick. "Boy, Robby, he seems ex-tremely pissed off. Maybe I shouldn't have mentioned you were talking to us."

"You stupid shit," said Robby, but the steam had gone out of his epithets. "You're going to get me killed."

"That'd be too bad. Shame to lose an inspired concept dresser like you."

"What do you guys want?"

"Who killed Chastity?" I asked.

"Not me."

"She said somebody beat her up. You do it?"

"I don't have to talk to you guys."

"Sure you do. If not now, then later in a quiet place with no one to interrupt. If that doesn't work, we can always let Toad know that you spilled about the project Travis Conrad and Alec York are working on."

Robby looked as if he'd just been told he was HIV positive. "I don't know anything about that."

"But we do," I said. "And when they ask how we know, we'll be sure to give you all the credit. You ready, Chick?"

"Wait a fucking minute," said Robby. He looked around the room. "Give me a break, huh?"

"Like the break Chastity got?"

He put both hands to his chest. "You think I did that? Uh-uh. I loved the bitch like a sister."

"I'm constantly impressed by your colorful language," I said. "Somebody did something . . ." The words stuck in my throat. "Something that someone is going to pay for in large coin. What do you know about the harassment of Sandy Collingworth or the murder of Francine Wilson?"

"I didn't do it."

"Who put Chastity up to calling Sandy and me?"

"Not me."

"Stop that."

"What?"

"Quit telling me who didn't do it. I want to know who did. Who would beat her up besides you?"

"I don't know, but it wasn't—" He stopped himself before he said it again. He reached for the cigarettes and shook one loose from the pack and put it in his mouth. Lighted it, his cheeks hollowing as he inhaled. Put his hand to his head.

"Soon," I said. "You have to tell us soon, or we're going to take you out of this place and you *will* talk to me."

The cigarette must have embolded him, because he said, "You guys aren't scaring nobody."

"That right?" said Chick, impassively.

"Yeah, mother—" Before he could finish Chick chopped him across the throat with the side of his hand. Robby choked and struggled for air, the smoke from his cigarette wavering like a swimming snake. He coughed and rasped for air. A waitress walking by asked if he was choking on something.

"No," said Chick. "He's all right. Just tried to swallow more than he can handle."

Satisfied, the waitress went about her business. When she left, Chick said, "You ready to act nice?"

Robby raised a hand like a traffic cop and put his other hand to his chest and nodded. He took a swallow from his wineglass. We waited while he regained control.

Robby nodded.

"You ever procure for Travis Conrad?" I asked.

"Procure?"

"I forgot. That's a two-syllable word. You ever get girls for Conrad?"

"Not for him. For his road guys and some of his friends. We got an arrangement. T.C. don't have no trouble getting laid."

"What about Alec York?"

"The chief?" He took a drag at his cigarette. "I got nothing to say about him. No way. He's fucking Dracula, man."

"This isn't working for me, Robby. You need to give me more."

"Like what?"

"Who made Chastity call?"

"Don't . . ."—he coughed hoarsely—"don't know."

"That's it," I said. "Let's take Robby for a ride."

"Wait," said Robby. "All right. I'm not sure who did. I didn't beat her up, though. I have, but not this time." He looked around the room quickly, as if invisible beings were watching him. He lowered his head and voice, and said, "How about the name of the cop's been boffing her?"

"Who?"

"Pethmore."

I looked at Chick.

"Did he have her call Sandy and me?"

"Figure it out, man," he said. "Cops got their own action going. I ain't no shooter, man. Only thing it's got to do with Robby Blue is I stay out of their way."

"You better be right," said Chick.

"Tell you something else, man," said Robby. "Pethmore? The dude likes it rough."

"You got any other clients like it like that? Rough?"

"Yeah. College kid named Mantle. Football player."

31

~~~

I went looking for Officer Pethmore but couldn't find him. Frustrating. I didn't believe everything Robby said—he was under duress and a liar by choice—but at least it was a direction. A flesh-and-bone lead. Four hours passed before emotion and lack of sleep combined to slow me to the point where even anger couldn't keep me going. I would find him. Soon enough.

"Better you don't see him tonight, anyway," said Chick. "You're all in, and you shouldn't front a cop in his own territory."

"Just want to talk to him," I said.

"Uh-huh."

Before lying down to catch some sleep, I called Merrill and told him what I had found out about Pethmore.

"Pethmore, huh?" said Merrill. "I'd love to cool him out."

I also told him about Mantle.

"Yeah, that's a shame," he said. "Unfortunately, I got something to go with that. Found out the night the team was in Cape Girardeau that Mantle was in the wind. Nobody saw him until the next morning. One of the players said Mantle popped a couple of amps and played the game. Coach didn't know about it because the other kids covered for him."

"Could he have made it here and back by morning?"

"Yeah." There was sadness in his voice. "I think we're probably going to arrest him tomorrow. York wants it. He doesn't like loose ends. Too bad. Mantle's a nice kid." A nice kid that used drugs and slept with prostitutes, I thought. I am still amazed the way society gives athletes a pass for their behavior. It was the same for me, I guess. Athletes are treated like spoiled children and then the public wonders why. If O. J. Simpson had been treated like a thug the first time he beat up his wife, instead of a football/media hero, maybe Nicole Simpson would still be alive.

Maybe not, too.

"Where's Mantle getting the dope?" I asked.

"Don't know yet. There's a couple local dealers I may check. Robby Blue's also known to distribute, but his clientele is a little more upscale than college kids."

"So you think Mantle did it?"

"I think he's going to take the fall."

"Not what I asked."

"We don't have anything else."

I hung up the phone and noticed the message light flashing. I called the desk. The message was from the room-service waiter. The desk manager put me in touch with the autograph hound with the handlebar mustache. He told me two guys had been asking what room I was in, ostensibly to get my autograph. One of them was a big guy with a large jaw. Tad the Toad?

"Come by sometime," I said, "and pick up the other half of the twenty. You earned it." I hung up and jiggled the room keys— mine and Sandy's. I grabbed the Browning and went next door to her room. No use taking chances. I opened her door, removed my shoes, and lay down on the bed fully clothed, the nine on the bed beside me. I didn't turn down the covers.

I slept for nine hours.

I awoke to the smell of coffee. Chick was sitting in a chair in the room watching television. "Did you know you snore like a bull elk?" he said.

"How'd you get in?" I asked, squinting through grainy eyes. I rubbed my face. "You got a key?"

"I don' need no stinking key," said Chick in a overdone bandito accent. "Coffee?" He poured some from a black plastic coffee carafe. Steam rose and released its aroma, and Chick handed the cup to me.

"How long have you been here?"

"Most of the night. Got a present for you. Put your shoes on, wash the sleep out of your face, and follow me."

I did so, and Chick opened the suite door between Sandy's room and mine. In my room, gagged with a tie and handcuffed to the bed frame, was Officer Pethmore. He was wearing civilian clothing—black jeans and sweater—and his legs were bound at the ankles with duct tape.

"How?" I asked.

"Called your room. There was no answer, so I picked the lock and let myself in. You weren't home, by the way. Checked Sandy's room and saw you asleep, so I thought I'd cover you. Figured you'd made enough people mad by now. Anyway, I wait, and Dick Tracy here picks the lock and is creeping your room when I jump out of the darkness and subdue his ass. Who knows what evil lurks in the hearts of men? I ask myself."

"Cut him loose," I said. "I want to talk to him."

Chick gave me a funny look. I said, "It's okay. Just want to talk to him."

"You can talk to him without me untying him," Chick said. He loosened the tie gag. I recognized the tie.

"That's my best tie. Why don't you use your own ties?"

"All of mine clash with his sweater."

"You guys caught big trouble here," said Pethmore after Chick removed the gag. His face was blotchy with pink shadows under the pale freckles. "Kidnapping a police officer is a felony."

Chick and I looked at each other.

"You have to admire a guy who breaks into your room and starts quoting law to you," I said.

"He could plead insanity," Chick said. "The minute he opens his mouth in court, they're going to suspect there's something wrong with him."

"Get these cuffs off of me, right fucking now."

"No," Chick said. "You'll just start acting silly and talking tough again. Besides, I let you go, and Storme'll start working out on you. I'd enjoy seeing it, but it'll get him into trouble. He goes inside, who'll I hang out with?"

"What are you doing in my room?" I asked Pethmore.

"Looking for evidence."

"And you were so excited about doing police work that didn't involve stopping cars with expired plates that you plumb forgot to bring a search warrant. That it?"

"Pethmore is an enterprising cop," Chick said. "He didn't need any of our nasty old evidence." He reached into Pethmore's jacket pocket and pulled out a pair of lace panties. "He brought his own. These yours, Pethmore? I'll bet they belong to Chastity."

"What are you doing with them?" I asked.

He glared at me.

"We know you were doing the ultimate naughty with her," said Chick. "Did you kill her?"

"I don't have to answer to you."

"Boy," said Chick, making a face. "He's tough to crack. I give up. Hate to be a cop in prison, though." He made a little circle with his thumb and forefinger. "This is your asshole before you go to prison." Then he held his hands about ten inches apart. "This is your asshole after one month in prison. Any questions?"

"I didn't kill her."

"Who did, then?" I asked.

"Thought you did."

"What would be my motivation?"

"Maybe that pimp killed her. Robby Blue."

"Maybe," I said. "He's the one told me you had a thing going with her. Said you were on his payroll."

"He's fulla shit."

"I can see the headlines now," said Chick. "DIRTY COP MURDERS HOOKER. You'll be a celebrity. Maybe after you get out of prison they can pump you full of Geritol and roll you onto the *Geraldo* show. That is, if Geraldo's still alive."

"I didn't kill her."

"So what are you doing with her underwear?"

"Stole it out of the evidence room."

"You're lying," I said. "You couldn't explain how it got from the police station to my room. Try again."

"She gave them to me."

"Ooh," said Chick. "You wear them, or just chew on them while you watch the news?"

"How many times were you and Chastity together?" I asked.

"None of your business."

"You killed Francine Wilson, didn't you?"

"You're crazy. I didn't kill nobody."

"Why try to frame me, then?"

He looked at the floor. Then up at me. "I thought you did it."

"Doesn't answer the question. Why the frame? I did it, then eventually some evidence will turn up. And if I did it, why haven't I tried to get out of town?"

"I got nothing to say to you."

I picked up the phone. "Fine with me. Say it to the police, then."

He shrugged. "Big deal. I'll tell them you grabbed me on the street and drug me back here. Who you think they'll believe?"

"I'll make sure Merrill is the cop who looks into it. Or maybe Snipes. Poetic if an African-American cop sends your cracker butt to Jeff City. Then we'll call the highway patrol and the media. Your buddy York is a politician. He's already had enough bad publicity. How quick you think he'll throw you to them? As for the highway patrol, they'll make sure he doesn't load the dice. York's got much more motivation to keep the state patrol off his back than to cut you loose."

"We'll see."

"Guess we will," I said. I called Merrill, and he said he'd be right out. I hung up the phone.

"Okay, Pethmore," I said. "The cops are on the way. Were you the other guy with Tad the Toad, asking what room I was in?"

"I don't know what you're talking about."

I reached down and lifted him by his hair. His face contorted into a mask of pain and anger. "I've had about enough of your petulant behavior. You're going to talk to me. Who attacked Sandy Collingsworth?"

He shook his head. I jerked him up by his hair and slapped him across the face.

"Again," I said. "What do you know about Sandy Collingsworth?"

He glared at me.

"No good," I said. I shook him by the hair. The dragons were loose in my soul, their leathery wings flapping. A red firestorm formed behind my eyes and clouded my thoughts. I saw Sandy comatose in a hospital bed. Thought of the violation perpetrated against her.

"Lighten up, Wyatt," said Chick, grabbing my arm. "This isn't going to work."

"We'll kill you," said Pethmore.

"Yeah?" I said. "Who's we? You and Tad? York? Bredwell? Who else?"

"It's all I got to say."

"There aren't enough of you," I said, "to get it done. Not after what you did to Sandy."

He looked up at me. His face had changed. He looked like a little boy accused of cheating on a test he'd flunked. "I didn't do that," he said.

"You'd better pray you didn't," I said.

Merrill showed up fifteen minutes later. Dave Snipes was with him. Snipes cuffed Pethmore. A state trooper showed, and Merrill thanked him for answering the call and told him there were sensitive circumstances involved, and that Merrill would keep him posted. The trooper nodded and left.

"They nabbed me on the street, Fred," said Pethmore as Snipes escorted him to the door. "Then they drug me back here."

"Why would they do that, Pethmore?" asked Merrill.

"Frame me for the whore's murder."

"Why you? Why not the pimp? We know about your little freebies with the hooker, Pethmore. Get him outta here, Dave."

"York ain't gonna like this, Merrill," said Pethmore as Snipes hustled him out of the room.

"I'll keep it in mind," Merrill said.

"All right, guys," he said. "True-confession time. What's Pethmore doing creeping your room? What have you assholes stirred up?"

I told him about our visit with Robby Blue. "Robby got nervous when Chick talked to Tad. Somehow, Pethmore must've gotten word about us talking to Robby. Makes you wonder if Tad told him, doesn't it? Pethmore and Tad are asking around about what room I'm staying in. Then Pethmore breaks in to plant evidence."

Merrill looked at Chick. "Where's Pethmore's piece?" Chick reached inside his jacket and handed Merrill a .357 Colt.

"Must've forgot," said Chick.

"Uh-huh," grunted Merrill. He looked at Chick some more. "How come you're so good at this?"

Chick shrugged. "Natural talent?"

"Anything on Chastity?" I asked.

"Not much. Either she didn't know it was coming, or it was someone she trusted. Maybe someone like Pethmore. Strangled. There was no sign of struggle."

"Seems to be the trademark of all of them."

"What do you mean?"

"No struggle from the coed, Francine Wilson. Even though she hated baths. No struggle from Chastity. No struggle from Sandy."

Merrill lighted a cigarette and offered one to Chick, who accepted. "Listen, Storme, I've been holding something back from you. They found traces of scopolomine in your lady's blood sample."

"What's that mean?"

"It's a drug. Grown in Colombia. It causes people to hallucinate, become disoriented, go into convulsions—"

"Memory loss?" I asked.

He nodded. "It can even induce a coma."

"York," I said.

"Don't jump to conclusions. We've busted three dealers in the last six months. All of them had some of the stuff."

"How is it administered?"

"In food. In gum."

"In a drink?" I asked.

"Yeah," he said. "You can even blow it in somebody's face. Believe it or not, it's used to treat Parkinson's disease."

The phone rang. We looked at it. I picked it up.

"This is Storme."

"Good morning, you gorgeous hunk of beef. This is Jill Maxwell. Got the info you wanted."

"Great. Give it to me."

"What do I get in return?"

"I promise not to strangle you next time I see you. Come on, Jill, there's a lot going on." I updated her.

When I finished, she said, "Sounds like you've been busy. Anyway, here's the poop. So-Mo Holding Company is owned by some interesting people."

"Like who?"

"Like Travis Conrad, the country-western star. A country-western star who is presently strapped for cash due to back taxes and some bad markers in Vegas. Like a high-ranking state official whose name I'll give you only if you promise I get an exclusive on this."

"Like a lieutenant governor with the same last name as the local police chief."

There was a pause at the other end. Then she said, "That's very good. It's hard to surprise me, but sometimes you take my breath away. If you know that, then you might know that they have some silent partners who play rough and also what they're involved in down in Missouri's neon country."

"A highway bypass," I said.

"A bypass? You do need me, don't you, you big dummy. These people think bigger than that. Much bigger."

"So what is it?"

"This is delicious," she said, teasing. "I know something you don't know. Something big. Really big. Want a clue?"

"Come on, Jill."

"You going to play, or not?"

"All right." I pursed my lips. "Give me the clue."

"Okay, here it is. Well, Wyatt Storme, now that you've won the Super Bowl, what are you going to do next?"

I let it sink in. "You're kidding."

"That's right," she said.

They were going for the brass ring.

Disney World.

32

The doctor released Sandy from the hospital later that morning, and I bought her lunch at the Boating House, a North Branson restaurant dominated by a glass wall that afforded diners a wonderful view of the Ozark resort area. She ate sparingly and smiled when I tried too hard to entertain her. We walked the Branson strip as I'd had enough of North Branson, and I bought her an ice cream cone which she didn't finish, but her eyes smiled when she tasted it. Come back to me, Cinderella Sunshine.

We went down to the lake and caught a ride on an excursion boat. The Indian summer breeze was warm, blowing her spun-honey-colored hair about her face, and the seagulls were white as snow as they rolled and pinwheeled against the azure Missouri sky. The color had returned to her face, and her eyes had regained their sapphire luster. Even the smell of diesel fuel from the boat's motors could not dim the moment as I looked at her. Against the backdrop of autumn, she was a golden leaf.

But the knowledge of her being raped hung over my mind like a circling raven. I hadn't told her yet. Didn't want to tell her. The thoughts turned over in my head. Was ignorance bliss, or was knowledge power? There was no solace to be found in trite clichés but rather a point in my thought processes where the thinking was no longer thinking but a type of smooth-grained torture, churning like a riverboat wheel, leaving nothing in its wake but the anguish of thought.

Sandy still tired easily, so I took her back to her room to rest. Merrill posted a man at the motel to keep an eye on things and specifically to protect Sandy. At 4:30 Merrill came by and offered to buy Chick and myself a drink. We accompanied him in his department unit, a Ford Taurus.

"I've got one errand to run before we get there," he said as we were getting into the Ford. "If it's okay with you gentlemen."

I sat in the front seat with the window rolled down as Chick, in the backseat, and Merrill were smoking cigarettes.

"We charged Pethmore with B and E," said Merrill en route. "That should buy some time to try to hang the murder bite on him for the hooker. You shoulda seen his face when we processed him through." He smiled hugely, then lifted his chin as if savoring something delicious. "It was great. Bredwell looked like somebody stuck an electric cord up his ass and threw the switch, pacing around trying to find out what was going down. 'This isn't right, Merrill,' he kept saying. 'It's those two out-of-town fucks we should have in the lockup.' " He swiveled his head and smiled at me. "Meaning you. I don't think he likes you guys very much."

"All our efforts, wasted," said Chick.

"I wanted to be the guy who told York, but I couldn't find him anywhere. He was incommunicado. But he still comes out smelling like a rose. Got the Mantle kid locked up for the Wilson girl and now Pethmore for the hooker. Makes him look like he is not afraid of sacred cows."

I said, "You hear anything about the Disney Company wanting to open a new theme park here?"

"Rumor's been around for years. There are people that would bulldoze the family cemetery to get Disney World in here. Word is

Kansas City and Saint Louis would like to have it, too, but K.C.'s already got Worlds of Fun and Saint Louis has Six Flags."

"What are the chances of it happening? Is there enough juice around here to pull off something like that off?"

The North Branson traffic slowed to its late afternoon crawl. "You know, when I was a kid there wasn't that much here. We've always had the fishermen and some tourism, but nothing like now. It's hard to imagine how much money has poured in here in the last ten years. We're in some kind of race with Branson. Celebrities and high rollers have bought up a lot of land on spec. Yeah, I think there are some people who could pull it off."

Merrill jammed on the brakes to avoid hitting a car that abruptly stopped ahead of us. "Fucking tourists. They ought to put us on bicycles," he said. "There's almost no way for us to respond quickly in emergency situations. I was a crook, I'd rob a bank and run away on foot. They'd never catch me."

"What if I told you that Mylon Taylor, Alec York, Velonne Cavalerri, your mayor, and even Bredwell along with a holding company owned by the lieutenant governor and Travis Conrad have their names on some prime real estate stretching from the highway to Lake Taneycomo?" I said. "Would that group be capable of making a big score?"

He thought about it. "Old man Taylor has a nose for land speculation. But he's honest, regardless of what you may think of his daughter. They need his money, but he plays it straight. Conrad wouldn't have any trouble either, but the rest of those, I don't see it. Especially Bredwell. There are some places around here where an acre of land's worth more than he makes in a year."

"Think you could find out who the previous owners of the land were if I show you on the map?"

"Probably," he said. "What've you got in mind?"

"Run a check on the previous owners. See if they were arrested, then the charges dropped."

"Extortion?"

"A possibility."

Chick said, "You might want to see if they're still living. Life's getting pretty cheap in North Branson. Lots of accidents. And if they are, if they're still living around here. We can find out how much they got for it."

"I'll get Dave on it, first thing tomorrow," said Merrill. He turned off the main drag onto a street that dropped off like the edge of a table. We followed the winding street down the hill and turned off again and pulled into the parking lot of an abandoned bar whose name, the Bull Ship Lounge, could still be seen on the dilapidated marquee. Directly east of the Bull Ship was an old bait shop, also abandoned. Grass grew up through the cracked asphalt, and there were cans and empty quart beer bottles strewn about. "Gotta meet somebody. Back in a minute."

The Taurus rocked on its chassis as he lifted himself out of the car and walked across the lot.

"Who would he be meeting here?" I asked.

"Probably a snitch," said Chick.

"Must be really shy."

"What I thought, too. Why not just call Fred on the phone?"

Merrill was halfway across the lot when he was jerked back as if pulled to the pavement by an invisible wire. He hadn't hit the ground before the rolling crack of rifle echoed across the lot. Then there was a smacking sound like a rock striking concrete, and the windshield of the Taurus exploded into a spiderweb of shattered glass. Chick and I bailed out of the passenger's side and put the car between us and the building where the shots were coming from. Two more shots rang out. One slapped the pavement by Merrill, and the other slammed into the Taurus.

"I got the shooter, you get Merrill," said Chick, who was up and running at a forty-five-degree angle to the building, gun drawn. Peering over the edge of the car, I saw Merrill lying on the asphalt. Twenty yards of open space between me and the wounded cop. Too much killing field between us. I jumped back into the Taurus, stomped the gas pedal, and drove to a point where it would shield Merrill from the shooter.

I leaned out of the car and checked him. There was a blackened area on his right side and a dark stain on the side of this neck, but he was still breathing. "Don't die on me, Fred," I said.

"I'm not dead yet . . . you unemployed has-been," said Merrill. His eyes squeezed together, and he sucked in a short breath. "Take more than one shot to . . . take out the king of Taney County. Besides, I'm wearing a vest."

I reached inside the car and pulled the microphone out. "How do I get hold of the dispatcher?" I asked. "We need an ambulance for you."

"Screw that," he said. "I can take care of that. Get that SOB who shot me." I handed him the microphone. "There's a shotgun in the trunk."

I released the catch for the trunk and, staying low, waddled humped-back to the trunk and took the short pistol-grip Remington twelve-gauge shotgun out. Back behind the car, gun in hand, I checked the action. Loaded.

"Double-aught buck," said Merrill. "You got five shots."

Merrill was calling in as I zigzagged across the parking lot, heading for the bait shop. No shots greeted me. I heard the sound of someone running behind the Bull Ship. I picked up the pace and ran at an angle I hoped would intercept the fleeing shooter, holding the Remington in front of me.

Reaching the corner of the ancient bait shop, I saw a flash of blue, then heard the slapping of brush. I looked down the slope, and thirty yards ahead was a man with a rifle running through the tangle of second-growth brush and weeds. It's times like these when you never know what to say. I placed the front bead of the shotgun on his legs and shouted, "Hold it!"

Robby Blue turned at the sound of my voice and raised the AR-15 rifle and rattled off a shot, which hit the bait shop fifteen feet away from me. I squeezed the trigger, and the Remington bellowed and bucked. The shot pattern caught Robby Blue full in the chest, and he was swept from his feet as if struck by a train. I shuffled another shell into the chamber and kept the gun trained on Robby's prone form as I stepped from the corner of the bait shop.

I had taken only three steps when a voice off to my right said, "Good-bye, asshole." I dropped to the ground and rolled, trying to bring the shotgun up to a shooting position. I heard two quick pops and looked up to see Tad the Toad as two crimson flowers erupted on his neck. He slumped to his knees. He sat briefly, his eyes staring in disbelief, as his life leaked out of his neck, before he crumpled over into the weeds behind the Bull Ship Lounge.

Chick Easton stepped out from behind the building, the Walther still pointing at the dead man. "You talk too much, Tad," he said. "Shoot, then talk." He looked at me. "What are you doing, layin' around? Every time I need you, you're rolling around on the ground. That Robby Blue down there?"

"Yeah."

"You okay?"

"Sure." I got to my feet. "You piddled around any longer, I wouldn't have been. What were you doing?"

"I needed a cigarette. Fred okay?"

"Think so."

"I was trying to get close enough to take one of them alive," said Chick. "But I didn't know you were going into a killing frenzy."

"Tried to take Robby Blue alive, but he wouldn't have it. Wasn't expecting two of them."

"I don't think they were either."

I heard a siren in the distance.

Detective Dave Snipes and Officers Bredwell and Herrman were the first on the scene. The blood on the side of Merrill's neck was from the errant shot that had struck the pavement. Chips of pavement had cut his neck. Bredwell tried to make a grandstand play by placing Chick and me under arrest, but Merrill interceded.

"You never disappoint me, Bredwell," said Merrill as the attendants strapped him onto the stretcher. "Whether you like it or not, Storme and Easton were assisting me. Dave, you're in charge. Either of these dipshits makes an administrative decision without written permission from Jack Webb, shoot him."

"Glad to," Snipes said, smiling.

The attendants loaded Merrill into the ambulance and left.

"Guess he spanked you guys," Chick said to Bredwell.

Snipes took our statements and released us. As we were leaving, Bredwell said, "This isn't over."

"But," said Chick, "the seconds are ticking off the clock, sweetheart."

33

It was a setup." Chick said as Snipes drove us back to the motel. Merrill's car had been taken to the station to match the bullets from Robby Blue's rifle. "Whoever tipped Robby and Tad knew the name of Merrill's snitch. Who knew it?"

"Only cops would know that," said Snipes.

"Cops like Bredwell and York." I said.

"Never prove that. Not in this town."

Snipes dropped us off at the motel and we checked on Sandy. She was sleeping, and the cop Merrill had stationed there was still on the job. "Quiet here," he said.

Chick and I left the motel to get something to eat. I drove through the thick, sluggish North Branson traffic. The neon reflections washed across the hood of the Bronco and flickered through the cab.

"Who gains from killing Merrill?" Chick asked.

"Can't figure it," I said. The traffic came to a standstill. "Thought once they locked down on Pethmore and the Mantle kid, it was over for them. I've been thinking the murders were to cover up the land deal. The Disney people wouldn't have anything to do with a scandal. But somebody wanted Fred Merrill and maybe even Robby Blue dead."

"Better if they do each other, isn't it?"

I nodded. "What are we missing here?"

"Beats hell out of me. Why do people kill each other? In war it's to gain ground, to further policy, to protect your country. In the private sector, people kill to gain power, to get money, for revenge . . . what else?"

The traffic edged forward haltingly. "There's a land deal cooking," I said. "Anything that casts a shadow on it could kill it, and millions of dollars are lost. So why risk it?" It was spinning furiously in my head. A dozen little gears spinning, none meshing with the others.

"Let's look at it from a sexual angle," I said. "We assume Pethmore raped Francine Wilson, but we don't know he did it. Then there's Travis Conrad and Francine. But Conrad isn't worried about his night with her, yet he is neck-deep in the land deal and one of his apes is connected to Robby Blue. Francine is engaged to the football player who doesn't know she has another boyfriend. Maybe a married boyfriend.

"She is discreet, though. And not the type to engage in an affair without there being some emotion attached to it. Then we have Alec York." The traffic slowed again, and I rested my foot lightly on the brake pedal. "He's involved with Velonne Cavalerri and is known to chase other women. Many other women."

"Yeah," said Chick. "How does he do that when a blue-chip guy like me has to beg to hold their hands?"

"Francine Wilson goes to see Cavalerri, and she is killed. Likewise, Chastity had used Cavalerri, earlier, and the same thing happens."

"Which means Cavalerri may know something she isn't telling."

"Or she revealed something she didn't know was important to someone else."

The traffic was moving briskly now, like an ice floe broken loose from the polar cap.

"Either way, there is a connection we've missed. And what does Felicia York know?"

"Everything seems to revolve around Alec York and his women," said Chick.

I turned off the main road and took a side street. "I wonder. Was York intimate with Francine Wilson?"

"Holy shit, Batman," said Chick. "I think you may be onto something."

"But how to run it down? Francine is dead, and York isn't going to tell us."

"We could try the roommate again."

"And we could try Cavalerri and Mrs. York, too."

"Nothing to be lost by it."

"We haven't tried Mylon Taylor," I said.

"Sounds good to me," said Chick. "Fortunately, being a top-notch bounty hound, I happen to know where he lives. But before we do that, pull into the nearest liquor store. I need to renew my quest for Dos Reales tequila."

"I thought you were hungry."

"First things first," he said.

Twenty minutes later, with Chick sipping the neck of a tequila bottle, we pulled off the main highway and onto a long paved lane nestled into one of the myriad valleys formed by the Ozark Mountains surrounding the Branson/Table Rock lake resort area. Mylon Taylor's home—estate would be a better term—was situated on twenty acres of manicured Kentucky bluegrass and second-generation oak and walnut trees. He met us in a high-ceilinged, leather-and-oak-furnitured study, volumes of classic literature and professional books on high shelves, where his maid had seated us to wait for the great man.

More impressive than the house was Mylon Taylor's hospitality. He could have easily turned us away.

"Mr. Taylor never turns anyone away," said the maid, a sturdy woman in her sixties with laugh lines at her eyes and mouth. "It's his way. Would you men care for refreshments while you wait?" We declined.

Chick looked around the room after she left. "This ain't much," he said. "Why, it isn't much bigger than a basketball court."

Mylon Taylor entered the room and shook our hands. He was wearing a loose-fitting white guayaberas shirt, the kind cigar plantation owners wear, outside a pair of khaki slacks, and Topsiders. He had snow-white hair, and though he was in his late sixties, he was tall and handsome and walked with the smoothness of a much younger man.

"Welcome to my home." He shook our hands and sat. "What is it you gentlemen wish to see me about?" he said. No messing around.

"Thank you," I said. I gave a brief history of our stay in North Branson, including Sandy's assault. Then I said, "You're trying to court the Disney people to buy some land you own. That right?"

He put his hands behind his back. "Why would that be any of your business?"

"Fred Merrill says you're a straight shooter. He doesn't think you'd be involved in anything illegal or underhanded."

"I know Fred," said Taylor. "But I don't know you. And I don't know what you're talking about."

"People are dying because of a strip of land you own in conjunction with your son-in-law and a group that calls itself So-Mo. So-Mo is owned by Travis Conrad and Justin York and maybe some nasty guys with a history of getting their way. Also, someone is building a dock on Lake Taneycomo." I made a guess. "A dock for riverboat gambling?"

"I'm aware that So-Mo is owned by Conrad and York. I loaned money to Alec for the venture. I have nothing to do with the dock personally, nor will I have anything to do with the gambling industry. The people Alec has hired to build the dock, I think, are connected to some unsavory characters, and I have people check-ing on them."

"A riverboat gambling venture will require legislation, of course."

He fixed eyes the color of folding money on me, and said, "Any state that props itself up on gambling money is a state that is selling its soul. I told Alec that and also that it was a questionable enterprise as speculating on political decisions often are."

"So why lend him the money?"

He sat down and put his hands together. "Felicia talked me into it. I've never liked Alec much, but since my wife and son died, Felicia's all I have so I am careful not to criticize Alec in her presence. She is a much better person than she shows. I will al-ways believe that. Alec has become quite powerful. He's power drunk, in fact. He runs the local women and treats Felicia badly, which is one of the reasons she drinks too much. Started when her mother died. They were very close. When Felicia was a little girl, I was too busy making money to pay attention to her." He shook his head. "It was wrong of me, and now I don't know how to be a father except to indulge her."

"It's not too late," I said.

He blinked his eyes. "What do you mean?"

"Not too late to be her father. She's highly intelligent, and there is a substance to her that I didn't immediately appreciate," I said. "Explain it to her." Talking to Mylon made me identify with his sense of opportunity lost. Once, Felicia had been his little girl, the apple of his eye. He was a good man. One of the real tragedies of the American dream is that we are so busy buying into the dream that we don't see the reality of family and love and living life. Or, as in my case, too young-headed when we get our chance. The tragedy is that we think it is too late even while the promise re-mains. For some, the chance will never come around again, a consequence of human mortality.

"Don't miss a chance to enjoy her," I said. "At least she is still around. I lost my daughter." The words were in my mouth and out before I thought about them. "She was two years old," I said. The weight of the pain broke loose like a rock slide in my mind and slid down the mountain, gaining momentum. "Aubrey and my wife were killed . . ." I hesitated. "They were killed when a truck driver, who'd been pushing it too hard and too long, came off a ramp and hit them."

Chick was looking at me. There was surprise in his usually impassive face. "I married Heather before my second tour of Vietnam. Aubrey was born while I was overseas. I came back a year later and was recruited to play football at Missouri University. There was a lot of travel involved, and I was gone frequently." I sucked in a breath. I was lost in a maelstrom of despair and repressed memories, memories I had kept inside like a jagged scar on my soul. There were several there to keep it company. It was merely the one that hurt the most. The one I had kept hidden the most. Only Sandy knew of it. I had no idea what made me share it at this point. Maybe I felt some sort of compassion for a father's loss, a father's pain.

"We were flying back from USC when it happened. Heather and Aubrey were coming to pick me up at the airport to celebrate Aubrey's birthday. I had a present for her. A present that was never unwrapped." I looked Mylon Taylor straight in the eye. "I left MU the next spring and transferred to Colorado State. I ran away from the pain. I didn't want anything to remind me of it. I was young and just back from Vietnam, and I was tired of hurting. There's nothing I can do about it now. Except endure it. And it's not any fun living with it. Aubrey's not going to grow up, and I wasn't there for her. I can't change that. But you can change what is happening between you and Felicia. You can still be there for her."

I felt emotion well up inside me, choking off further discussion. I nodded my head at him, lips pressed together. I wanted him to know the ball was in his court.

Mylon Taylor rubbed his hands on his pants and looked down at the parquet floor. His head began to nod, as if agreeing with some thought inside his head. "Yes," he said. "Yes. I've been making excuses. I've lost my wife and son. No reason I should lose my daughter, also." He looked at me. "Is there?"

I shook my head. "None," I said.

He nodded at me. A nod of affirmation. He said, "I appreciate you coming here and . . . sharing something so painful with me. I wish I could give you something that would help you. But I know little except that I bought that land on spec years ago. And I would like to sell it to the Disney people. Other than that, I can't help you. But if you need anything—money, introductions to people in the community who might help you—I'll be more than happy to assist you. I've endured my son-in-law and his escapades long enough. I'm a foolish old man who thought he could pretend everything is all right."

"It isn't foolishness," I said. "Everything isn't all right for most of us."

We stood and shook hands. For a moment he looked as if he were going to embrace me, but propriety got the best of him and the moment passed.

"It's okay, Mr. Taylor," I said. "I understand."

He nodded again, and we left.

I would never see Mylon Taylor again, but I would never be the same for meeting him.

Maybe it meant something. And maybe not.

34

⁓⁓⁓

A cold rain was falling when Sandy and I arrived at the Boating House restaurant the next morning. The glass wall was darkened like cheap sunglasses, and a smoky mist hovered over the tree-covered hills.

We ordered coffee and waited. Hoped our guests would arrive. I had dispatched Chick to talk with Francine Wilson's roommate, Sharon Keltner, while Dave Snipes had driven up to the Blue Bayou to interview Travis Conrad regarding the late Tad Bodrine, also known as Tad the Toad.

Sandy had rebounded quickly. The wan look had vanished, replaced by the quiet confidence I associated with her. I brought her up to snuff on what had been happening, once again leaving out the violation perpetrated against her. I told her what I had in mind, and she agreed to help.

I had called Felicia York and asked her to meet Sandy and me at 10:00 A.M. When I called, her husband, the public servant, was already at work. Her speech had been thick with sleep and hangover, and I was worried whether she would show, but she mentioned that her father had talked with her. "Father has good instincts about people," she said. "He was merely unlucky with his family."

I didn't comment.

Cavalerri was a little tougher, according to Sandy. Her lawyer instincts made her wary of an invitation from a media person. Finally, Sandy won her over. Sandy didn't tell her Mrs. York would be there. She didn't tell her I would be there, either. Sandy told her she would meet her at 9:45. I wanted her there ahead of Felicia York because I figured she would walk out if she saw her lover's wife sitting with us.

We drank coffee and got ready for our guests. A pair of older ladies, fully equipped with blue hair and lilac perfume, bustled over to our table, giggling like schoolgirls, and asked for Sandy's autograph. Neither asked for mine. How soon they forget.

"Your public," I said as they left. "They pant for you."

"What are you going to do when our guests arrive?" Sandy asked.

"I don't know," I said. "I want to get them together and see what happens."

"There's a great plan."

"Any suggestions?"

She sipped her coffee, holding the cup delicately between both hands. "I think it would be to our advantage to avoid a hair-pulling."

"Agreed."

She sat her cup down and tapped a manicured finger against her lips. "Well," she said, "they're both powerful figures in this community. As such, they will try to maintain their images. But, regardless of what the sisterhood may wish broadcast, they're women sharing one man. They won't like this. And it could prove dangerous for that man."

"Sweet is revenge—especially to women."

She gave me a hard look.

"I didn't say it; Byron did."

"And you relish every word."

"You'll not trap me with your subtle journalistic wiles."

"Anyway," she said, repositioning herself in her chair, "this is a prickly situation and will require you to control your predilection for fireworks."

"I love it when you talk dirty."

"I'm telling you that you will need to shut up for a change."

"Will I be allowed an occasional smile of appreciation as you weave your magic?"

She smiled and shook her head. It was good to see her smile. "Just don't instigate anything. From what you tell me of these two women, the situation will be touchy enough. What we must do is convince them that we"—she gave me an appraising look—"at least I, sympathize with their situation and emotions." She gave me the hard look again. "Are you sure you should be here when we get this pair together? It could get nasty, and neither of them has any particular fondness for you."

"I can't understand it either. Maybe they're lesbians and are overwhelmed by the tangency of my aura of maleness."

She reached out and patted my hand. "Relax, Wyatt. It's not quite as overwhelming as you might think."

"That's because I turn it down a couple of notches when I'm around you."

"Thank you so much."

"The least I could do."

Velonne Cavalerri, attorney-at-law, arrived at 9:55, fashionably late, which was all right since I figured Felicia York would likewise be late owing to her dependency on alcohol.

Cavalerri approached the table with the wariness of an ocelot. She wore a long, scalloped V-neck sweater in a leopard print over a dark skirt, all of which was set off nicely by almond-shaped ebony eyes, olive skin, and the lean, hungry look of the huntress. Her effect was palpable. I harbored sexist thoughts. She stood at our table. Looked at me. I smiled. Her lips narrowed in a thin line. Oh well. Everybody can't love me.

"I didn't realize he would be here."

"Like waking up Christmas morning, isn't it?" I said.

Sandy gave me another hard look, then she said, "I apologize for not telling you. However, he is my fiancé and is given to pouting if I don't take him everywhere."

I tried giving her a hard look, but it bounced off her. Maybe I needed to practice it a little. The well-appointed barrister sat and ordered coffee.

"What is it you wish to discuss?" asked Cavalerri. She addressed Sandy, acting as if I didn't exist. Maybe if I burped or started humming Nilsson's "You're Breaking My Heart" on my pocket comb.

"There has been a tragedy. Several, in fact," said Sandy. "You know about Fred Merrill?" The lawyer nodded. "Wyatt has been attacked by thugs. I was lured to a place where I was rendered unconscious." I felt an icy breeze whistle past my heart. "Is this normal for North Branson?"

"Of course not. But I fail to see what this has to do with me."

"Perhaps nothing. But somebody is going to great lengths for some unknown motivation. Whether it is for money, or power, or vengeance, or jealousy, we don't know. I was hoping you might have some information. Information that you might not be aware is pertinent."

It was then that Felicia York walked into the restaurant, surprising me by arriving at straight-up 10:00. She was resplendent in a cobalt-blue pantsuit, her hair pinned away from the delicate neck. Her turquoise eyes flared up, momentarily, at the sight of Velonne Cavalerri, then she smiled a venomous smile.

Cavalerri was not as amused by the appearance of her rival. However, she remained composed. As cool as a Mediterranean breeze.

I introduced Sandy and pulled a chair out for Mrs. York. The waitress came by, and Mrs. York ordered a glass of wine. Then I sat and waited for the fireworks to begin.

"You're looking . . . healthy, Velonne," said Felicia. "Considering your busy schedule."

"You're looking well preserved yourself, Felicia. What's your secret?"

"Celibacy. You might wish to try it."

Velonne turned to Sandy. "Why is she here?"

"Wyatt invited her," said Sandy.

"Should have guessed that." The well-dressed attorney glared at me. I said nothing. Demure. Contrite. I tried to focus my aura of maleness into an intense beam. Didn't work. Maybe a punch in the nose. Too primitive.

"What is it you want?" Velonne said.

"Mrs. York is aware of your relationship with her husband—"

"Which is by no means an exclusive relationship," said Felicia, interrupting. "You are one of many pathetic whores whom my husband, the hormonal bastard, is screwing."

"I don't know what you're talking about."

Felicia laughed and put a hand to her throat. "How delightful, your denials. It must amuse my husband to have sex with someone so delightful."

"What about you and Fred Merrill?" said Velonne, as if she had tossed down a card and said, "Bridge." Sandy glanced at me quickly to see if I caught the significance of her statement. I did. Velonne knew about Merrill and Felicia. Which meant Alec York knew. Which gave him a reason to wish Merrill dead.

"Yes. And he is wonderful. Perhaps you could attract more men if you would provide penicillin shots at each encounter, though that would probably tax the pharmaceutical industry."

"You bitch!" said Velonne.

"How common," said Felicia. "I would expect more from someone with a law degree. But you probably fucked your way through that, as well."

Velonne's nails were digging into the tablecloth. "I really don't have time to exchange words with some pitiful lush."

Felicia sipped her wine. "Yes, you probably need to rush off to some liaison at the bowling alley with a truck driver. If you had as many sticking out of you as you've had stuck in you, you would resemble a porcupine."

Velonne's shoulders shivered, and through her parted lips the white teeth were set together. I stifled an impulse to whistle lowly.

Velonne would need stitches after this conversation. I'd been fortunate to exchange barbs with Felicia York when she was sedated with Scotch.

"I ought to pull your hair out by its gray roots," hissed Velonne.

"I would enjoy it infinitely if you would try," said Felicia.

"Ladies," said Sandy. "This is unnecessary. You've already allowed a man to embarrass you; do you wish to compound it by embarrassing yourself in front of another?" Meaning me. "This is not what we wished to happen."

"What did you think would happen?" said Velonne, her ebony eyes still on her opponent.

"Francine Wilson was a client of yours, Mrs. Cavalerri. You met with her once before she was killed. What was the reason she came to you?"

"Probably to compare notes," said Felicia York, interrupting. "The little tramp was also fucking Alec."

Sandy looked at me.

I smiled.

Bridge.

"I've had enough of this," Velonne said, standing up quickly and nearly toppling her chair. She turned on her heel and left.

"Oh my," said Felicia, placing a hand to her chest, as if surprised. "I hope I didn't offend her. My apologies to both of you."

"No need," I said. "You were magnificent."

She turned her head to one side to consider me and said, "If one is not careful, one could begin to become fond of you."

"He is rather magic that way," said Sandy.

"Though it is rather like developing a fondness for a timber wolf."

Sandy nodded. "You'll get no argument here."

Sandy and I left at 10:45 to touch base with Chick back at the motel. Chick's information affirmed what we'd learned talking to

Mrs. York and Mrs. Cavalerri: that Francine Wilson was having an affair with Alec York. Sharon had withheld the information before. She was scared. "Besides," she had told Chick, "Francine made me promise not to tell—ever! But then she didn't know she was going to die." It was an important piece of the puzzle, but it caused a melancholy feeling to settle inside me, for I harbor certain old-fashioned, romantic attitudes about women and the chastity of schoolgirls. It was a patronizing attitude. Probably even a trifle chauvinistic, but the thought of that eel, Alec York, huffing and puffing away over the young Francine Wilson was an image washed in murky gray tones. Besides, they were my attitudes and not subject to fashion.

"Francine always met him at the Red Cedar," said Chick. "All that stuff Sharon told the boyfriend, Ken Mantle, was a smoke screen. Francine was a good girl who had a mixed-up, soap-opera view of her relationship with a married guy. She thought it made her a mysterious woman, a tragic figure of romance and intrigue. She was crazy about the creep. Hell, she wasn't old enough to vote in the last presidential election. She *was* a virgin before she started the affair with York." He shook his head. "I am depressed."

"Will you both spare me the tragic male remorse," said Sandy. "Francine was a big girl and knew what she was doing."

"I'm not sure I agree with that," I said. "Though that seems to be the prevailing wisdom. Kids have been exposed to more than we were, sure, and in that context, perhaps, they become more sophisticated. But they are less aware, less mature in their relationships. They watch a couple of Sharon Stone movies, and they think fulfillment and happiness will be theirs if they attract and pursue some secret or forbidden love."

"Men are not immune to that," said Sandy.

"No argument here," I said.

Chick said, "There's an island in the south Pacific where the natives used to sacrifice a virgin every five years. They thought it kept their island from sinking into the ocean."

"I'm sure I'll regret it, but I'll ask anyway," said Sandy. "Do they still sacrifice virgins?"

"Well, finally they got to the point where they had to settle for young ladies of limited experience."

"You're impossible," Sandy said. "Just where is this island?"

"Nobody knows," said Chick. "It sank into the ocean."

"I should have known better," Sandy said.

"Don't blame yourself," said Chick. "I am irresistible and non-fattening, though habit-forming."

35

There is no way to mask the institutional flavor of a jail. No amount of paint can change its stark gray ambience. No architectural design can disguise the constrictive texture of confinement. The walls are hard, the floors cold, the acoustics harsh and hard-edged, and the light casts pale shadows of rectangles and men bent by the weight of despair and loneliness.

At 2:00 the same afternoon, after an officer patted me down, and I'd removed my wallet, belt, and jacket, I was allowed into a cheerless square room with a Plexiglas window crisscrossed with a diamond pattern of tiny wires to prevent its shattering. On the other side stood Kenneth Mantle. The fretted window cast a spiderweb shadow across his face. His eyes were dark and worried, and the huge shoulders sagged in the faded denim shirt his jailers had issued him—another uniform for a different team, one he hadn't meant to try out for. He looked not so much the ferocious all-American lineman as he did a little boy caught out in a cold, driving rain.

"I didn't kill her, Mr. Storme," he said. It was the first thing out of his mouth, sheeplike, pleading me to believe. But denial is the prisoner's mantra, guilty or innocent.

"You okay?" I asked.

He nodded. "Yeah," he said. "I don't like it here. The other guys make fun of me. Call me 'fresh meat' and 'all-American lady-killer.' One guy keeps picking at me. Says he's the boss-con and the baddest man here. I want outta here. I didn't kill her. I . . . I loved her." His eyes watered, but no tears fell.

"You should have told me you left the team the night she was killed. I told you the police would get around to that."

"I was scared when I found out."

"Where did you go that night?"

He licked his lips and looked down at his hands. "Chief York told me not to talk to anybody. He said the police were still looking for another suspect."

"And you believe that?"

"I got to."

"Look, kid," I said. "They don't arrest one guy and continue to look for another. York has been blowing to the press how he has put you and Pethmore inside for killing Francine and Chastity. He's a big hero. He cuts you loose, and he looks bad for putting a local college football star in jail for a crime he didn't commit." I shook my head. "He needs you to take the fall. Otherwise, it's a political disaster."

He shook his head. "But my lawyer says I shouldn't talk to anyone else, either."

"Who's your lawyer?" I said, as if I couldn't guess.

"Velonne Cavalerri." He saw me shaking my head. "She's real sharp. She says she thinks she can get me off."

"You keep believing that, and you'll be playing for the prison team at Jeff City. Cavalerri is York's girlfriend. Francine went to visit her just before she was killed. Chastity, the call girl who was killed? She also used Cavalerri."

"No," he said, shaking his head. "No. That can't be. She's been real nice to me. She says she'll get me off."

"Yeah. And she'll be appropriately shocked and despondent when you're pronounced guilty. I'll bet she's already got her apology worked out." I let it sink in for a few seconds. "Tell me where you were the night Francine was killed."

"I went to a bar in Cape Girardeau to meet a guy. I was out of 'roids," he said. "Somebody must've stole them outta my bag before we left town. I called my connection, and he told me where I could get some more in Cape. I snuck out of my room and met the guy. He gave me some uppers, too."

"Who's your connection?"

"Guy named Robby Blue."

I tried to keep the disappointment out of my face. They had the kid in a tight trap. Robby Blue probably had somebody lift Mantle's steroids, knowing he would need some in a hurry. Then he conveniently hooked the kid up in Cape Girardeau. I'd bet my NFL pension check that when they went to find the dealer to provide an alibi, he would either be untraceable or never corroborate Mantle's story. But, for various reasons, including the complexity and convenience of the crime, I didn't believe Kenneth Mantle killed Francine Wilson.

"No drug dealer is going to admit he sold drugs to you," I said. "You need to know that. Robby Blue knew it." Who else knew it? "They've got you in a box unless you change your game plan."

He put his head in his hands, and I saw the anguish shiver electrically through his body. The sinewy cords on the thick neck purpled and stood out like vines on an oak tree. The shoulders began to tremble, and I could hear muffled sobbing behind the glass.

After several seconds he raised his head, and I saw the tears roll down his cheeks. "What'm I gonna . . . do?" he said. "Who's gonna help me?"

"I'll try," I said. "But you have to do what I say. And you have to promise to get off the needle."

"But . . . but I need it," he said. "I gotta have it if I'm going to get into the pros."

"That's crap. It's not that great a destination anyway. And it's irrelevant. You're not going to get into the pros if you're wearing a seven-digit number and living in the gray-bar dorm, are you?"

He shook his head, slowly. "What do you want me to do?"

"Fire Cavalerri."

"How can I do that? I gotta have a lawyer, and I don't know nobody else."

"What about your parents? Maybe they know somebody."

"My parents died when I was in junior high. Car wreck."

The back of my neck tingled. I said, "I can get you one. I know a guy in Kansas City who's one of the best in the country. George Fairchild's his name. He represents the Kansas City Chiefs, among others."

"How'm I going to afford him?"

"You can't. I'll take care of that part," I said. "You just do what I say and don't lie to me again."

He stared at me for a minute. "Why're you doing this for me?"

"Because," I said, "I was young once. And there wasn't anyone to help."

After I retrieved my jacket, belt, and wallet, I walked out of the lockup into the fresh air. The kid was inside. Just a kid who wanted to play football. I understood that. But sometimes dreams get tangled with complexities. Even if he was able to overcome the drugs and get drafted and make the team, there would be other problems, other entanglements. And for every Derrick Thomas there were thousands of Kenneth Mantles. And each year there would be more. Chasing the dream and finding the nightmare. I'd been lucky. I came along at a time when the Cowboys had a guy with Olympic speed and needed a second receiver to go across the middle and catch the ball and go deep when necessary. I made the team and got out just ahead of the erosion that years of pounding and playing injured exacted. And, unlike many others, I had hung on to my money, resisting the temptation to mortgage my future to live in the great, omnipresent Now. So I had been able to retire at an early age and on my own terms.

But, in one sense, Mantle was right. He probably couldn't make the pros without the steroids. He was big enough for small college football, but too small for an NFL lineman and probably too slow to be a linebacker. But he had bought into the dream, and there would always be someone around to sell him sleeping pills. More Robby Blues. I couldn't kill them all.

I shrugged my shoulders and rolled my neck, hearing the small crunching noises of bone against bone, one of my souvenirs of catching the ball in the NFL's rush hour traffic.

A police car roared by within a few feet of me, its lights dancing. I felt a whoosh of air as it passed. I walked across the street to where the Bronco was parked. On the windshield, pinned under the wiper blade, was a parking ticket.

Oh well.

36

Tomorrow morning," said Sandy Collingsworth, poised and resplendent in a business outfit, her elegant legs crossed, her hands in her lap. "We go public with what we have."

It was two days after the shooting in the parking lot of the Bull Ship Lounge. Fred Merrill had recovered, and Sandy and Dave Snipes had uncovered more particulars of the shady land deal involving So-Mo Holding Company and the principals of North Branson. Merrill and Snipes thought they had enough to proceed with their investigation. George Fairchild had come to town, and Mantle had fired Velonne Cavalerri, so she had one more reason to dislike me.

Mylon Taylor had provided some names for Sandy, and coupled with what we had learned in the last few days we were ready to go to war. We were sitting in Alec York's office in the early afternoon—Sandy, Chick, and myself. Chick was half slouched in his chair, a bemused smile on his face. York leaned back in his executive chair, elbow on the chair arm, his hand over his mouth in a thoughtful pose. He removed the hand from his mouth and said, "And what do you think you have, Miss Collingsworth?"

"Comparing testimony from different sources, I believe there was an undisclosed relationship between you and Francine Wilson that altered the focus of the investigation into her murder. That you took over the forensic investigation of Francine Wilson's murder in order to falsify the lab report and—"

"That's a fabrication!" said York, interrupting.

"—that Kenneth Mantle is being framed for her murder."

"That's preposterous. The kind of thing that only a television personality could conceive of as feasible."

"Mantle is presently being defended by George Fairchild, one of the top attorneys in the Midwest. He is well known. This case is now high-profile, and I don't think your investigatory tactics will bear much scrutiny. I've also learned there is a land deal cooking with the Disney people that is being kept under wraps. A land deal that involves extortion, phony death certificates, and the seizure of land under dubious legal machinations." The color in York's face rose like a thermometer placed on a radiator. Sandy continued.

"You used your office to get dirt on the landowners and bought the land at bargain-basement prices in exchange for dropped charges and assurances of discretion. One of the former landowners molested a ten-year-old boy, and you let him off in exchange for the land."

"This is ridiculous," said York. "You are acting irresponsibly."

"I am giving you an opportunity to respond before we air this story. I will push to have an independent forensic expert examine Francine Wilson's body. One who will not conveniently find traces of steroids in the semen sample."

"You are delusionary."

"I don't think so. You were involved with Francine Wilson and should have recused yourself. Instead you took the lead in the investigation. Tell me, Chief York, is it standard for the chief of police to personally conduct an autopsy?"

"It is an important case, and I felt motivated to take an active part."

"I think a more personal motivation was involved, and I believe my story will reveal that."

"This will ruin you," he said.

"I think you have your pronouns confused. You're in this too deep."

"You run any of this unsubstantiated tripe, and I'll begin the litigation process."

I watched them back and forth like I was watching a tennis match. Sandy was hitting winners, and her outfit wasn't even wrinkled. "Do what you think is right," she said. "But you must be aware that we wouldn't run this unless our information was good."

"I'm afraid I'll have to ask you to leave," he said. "Right now."

"I take it you are not making a statement?"

He stood and walked around his desk, the whites of his eyes showing around the pupils.

"I will make you sorry you ever came to North Branson," he said.

"I already am," said Sandy.

Back at the motel, there was a message for me. I called the number I was given, and Swope Archibald answered. "Mr. Conrad would like to meet with you and Miss Collingsworth."

"When?" I asked.

"As soon as possible."

"Where?"

"Five miles south of Point Lookout there is a road that leads to an abandoned quarry. Can you be there in an hour?"

I didn't like the idea of them choosing a place they were familiar with and I wasn't. Meeting at an abandoned quarry suggested impure thoughts. "No good," I said. "We meet, I name the place."

"That is unacceptable."

"Then adios, partner."

"Wait! Can you hold a moment?"

"Haven't got all day."

There was a pause, and the only noise was the hiss of fiber

optics. Thirty seconds passed before he came back on the phone. "All right," he said. "It will be as you wish, Mr. Storme." The way he said *Mister* sounded like *Mistah*. "Name the place, and we will be there."

I thought of the resort construction site Sandy and I had run through. It was open, it was on high ground, it was neutral, and I had been there and maybe they hadn't. I described its location for him.

"All right," he said. "One hour, then?"

"Need longer," I said. I didn't want them to know Sandy was leaving town, but I wanted to find out what was on their minds. "Make it four o'clock."

"We'll be there."

I hung up.

Sandy looked at me quizzically.

"Travis Conrad wants to see me," I said.

"How nice," she said.

"You also."

"Hmmm," she said. "You didn't tell them I wouldn't be able to be there."

"Must've slipped my mind."

"Be careful, Wyatt."

"My middle name."

"Okay," said Chick. "Before you go to the airport, tell me again what was going on with the land deal. I want to know what mistakes to avoid if I ever run a scam like this."

Sandy smiled. "Some small bits of the land were bought in the names of transient indigents," she said, "who were given a pittance and then phony death certificates arranged. Some of the land, of course, was purchased legally, but there were small patches needed to ensure that the group would control the entire area. Some of the landholders were threatened with prosecution, like the child molester. In addition, I learned there is a group lobbying the state legislature to open up riverboat gambling in counties where sixty percent of the revenue is from tourism."

"Which explains the dock," said Chick.

"Exactly," said Sandy. "If either deal goes through, they become multimillionaires overnight."

Chick smiled and shook his head. "Pretty sharp for a media cupcake."

"Thank you."

"So why do you hang out with Storme?"

"When will I see you again?" asked Sandy after Chick had left.

"I've got to talk to you," I said.

"I don't have much time now," she said. "I've got to start packing." She held my face between her hands and kissed me. When she opened her eyes and looked into my face, she said, "It's serious, isn't it?"

"Yeah." We sat together on the side of the bed. I searched for the words. The right ones. "Sandy, I love you. You know that."

Her lips were slightly parted, and the corners of her mouth turned down. "What is it, Wyatt?"

"Something happened that night at the football stadium. More than what the police told you. I've been debating whether to tell you or not because I can't stand to see you hurt."

She reached up and touched the hair on the side of my face with her hand. "It's okay, Wyatt," she said. "Go ahead."

"I can't think of a pretty way to say this." I felt a burning sensation behind my eyes. "The person who rendered you unconscious used a drug, scopolomine. Takes away your memory. Makes you compliant. Then, he—he raped you."

She put a hand to her eyebrow, then with both hands smoothed her skirt. Her eyes focused on the floor. She took a deep breath. She lifted her face to look at me and tried to smile, but it broke and fell from her face like withered leaves and her lower lip began to tremble. The sensation of her pain was sharp, as if my heart was being squeezed by a giant hand with talons like knives.

"Hold me," she said.

I moved closer and held her against my chest, felt her body

shudder against me. A low whimper escaped her lips, and waves of emotion rolled over her. I kissed her hair and cupped the back of her delicate neck with my hand. After a while she sat up. She held my face between childlike hands and looked into my eyes.

"That was hard for you, wasn't it?" she said.

"Yes."

"You would rather I didn't know about it?"

"Yeah."

"But you knew I would rather know than not, so I could deal with it on my own terms?"

"The violation was personal," I said. "Yours. I can't understand how you must feel, how you will feel, but I'll be with you to help you through it."

She was quiet, then said, "I suspected it. Was afraid that's what had happened. It is better to know than to wonder. It's a cheap love that is afraid to share the difficult."

"Why don't I feel better, then?" I said.

"I love you, Wyatt."

I pulled her to me and kissed her. Tenderly. She put her forehead against mine, lightly, like the touch of an angel.

"I told Mylon Taylor about Heather and Aubrey."

"I know," she said. "Chick told me. I think it was a bit of a shock for him." She searched my eyes briefly. "We've had quite a week, haven't we?"

"It was hard to talk about." I leaned away from her. "It's part of why I need you."

"I know. It's also part of why you can't let things rest sometimes."

We were quiet for a moment, resting from the emotions.

"He shouldn't have touched you," I said.

"You want revenge, don't you?" she asked.

"It's tough to think about," I said. "What he did."

"You can't change what happened."

"I realize that."

"But there is no use asking you"—she hesitated as she searched for the words—"not to do anything that would . . . there is no use, I guess, in asking you to promise not to avenge it physically, is there?"

"I can't promise that, Sandy." I shrugged. "Selfish, maybe."

"Just remember, like you, I would be unable to cope if something were to happen to you."

"Nothing's going to happen to me," I said.

"I thought that, too," she said.

37

Remember," said Dave Snipes, "it's critical that they say something incriminating. An admission they were cheating people out of their land or that Travis Conrad sent Tad Bodrine to shoot Fred."

"Gee," said Chick. "That should be easy. You hold them down, Wyatt, while I tickle them." Before Sandy left for the airport, I had called Snipes and told him of the call from Swope Archibald. He had called a judge and received permission to wire me for sound.

"Hold still," said Snipes as he taped the wire to my body. "It's hard enough to get this thing on right."

"Well," I said. "Your hands are cold. I'd think you'd have the decency to microwave them beforehand."

"There," said Snipes. "Got it." I put my shirt back on. "Now, be natural. Don't get yourself in trouble. If they want to talk about it, okay. Don't try to lead them into it. That's entrapment."

"That mean we can't, like, hold them under water until they confess?" said Chick.

"There can be no duress," said the detective.

"You mean we'll have to unduress them to get them to talk?" Snipes looked at me.

"All the time," I said. "He's like that all the time."

"This won't be funny if you screw up," said Snipes. "We'll only get one shot. The judge wasn't happy about any of this. Fortunately, he's less happy about somebody busting a cap on a police detective. Also, he likes Fred and wants somebody to burn for it. But this thing doesn't go down right, there'll be one less black detective on the force."

"Which will leave how many?"

"None."

Chick and I were thirty minutes late for our appointment with Travis Conrad. Good for them to wait. It would teach them patience. I drove up the hill leading to the resort, the tires of the Bronco crunching on the gravel. Behind us the Branson–North Branson skyline stretched out like a Christmas tree, a tableau of green trimmed with pastel buildings and strung with a thousand neon lights. A neon country skyline. Once it had been raw and green, inhabited by hillbillies and wildlife and songbirds that whispered across the sky.

Call someplace paradise, and man will pour concrete to preserve it.

Swope Archibald was sitting in a charcoal gray Lexus sedan at the entrance. Sleepy Joe Shaunessy was in the passenger seat. As we pulled close to them, the driver's window of the Lexus slid down silently.

"Where is Miss Collingsworth?" Archibald asked.

"She had to go to Wal-Mart," I said. "She wanted to get the latest Travis Conrad CD."

He seemed confused. As if he didn't know if I was serious or not. He started the car and led us through the resort. They were waiting for us in the main quadrant of the unfinished project. They got out of two cars when we pulled up—Travis Conrad, Alec

York, and a man I didn't know but suspected was Justin York. He looked like an older version of his brother. Same dark hair, though flecked with gray at the temples. Same nose and jawline, though the tissue had broken down around the jowls and throat.

The construction site was abandoned except for loose lumber and the residual flotsam of the carpenters, including the mechanical tree shredder.

"Welcome, boys," said Conrad. Expansive. Jovial. "Can we get you somethin' to drink? We brought our own. Got beer, whiskey, Scotch. What'll it be?"

Sleepy Joe got out of the Lexus and eyed us from the other side of it, his arms folded across his chest. Alec York was swirling ice in a small circle in a plastic cup.

"Wild Turkey," said Chick, smiling at Joe. "On the rocks with a splash of air."

"Nothing for me," I said.

Conrad reached inside a Mercedes and poured Chick's drink from a pint bottle of bourbon and handed it to him. The personal touch. Quite a departure from our previous encounter when Archibald fixed the drinks and we were asked to leave. What a difference the day makes.

"Where's the reporter?" asked Lieutenant Governor Justin York. As yet, no one had bothered with introductions.

"Yeah," said Conrad. "Where is that good-lookin' filly of yours?"

"Nobody said she was mine," I said. I looked at both Yorks, then at Conrad.

"We do our homework," said Archibald.

"Storme here's real touchy about women," said Conrad.

"Let's get to it," I said.

"All right, then," said Travis Conrad. "Seems we have us a little public relations problem." He looked at me as if I was supposed to say something. I didn't. A light breeze blew a little cloud of dust across the raw parking lot.

"We are prepared to make a deal with you all. Something that'll keep you happy. Make us happy, too."

"What's the deal?" I asked.

"Let's wait until the girl gets here," said Alec York.

"She's not a girl," I said.

"Where is she?"

"Right about now she's getting on a plane for Denver."

"Swope," said Conrad. "Call the airport." The business manager reached into the Lexus and brought out a cellular phone.

"Put it down, Archibald," I said.

"We just want to talk with her," said Conrad.

"Nobody here has any contact with her. Not now. Not ever."

"Why's that?" asked Alec York.

"Because I'll kill you if you try."

"That's brave talk," said Sleepy Joe from behind the Lexus. Nothing moved but his lips when he said it. His eyes were looking sidelong at Chick.

"That's what Toad thought," said Chick. "See him anywhere?"

"My God!" said Justin York. "What is going on here?"

"No reason to get hostile, Storme," said Conrad. He pronounced *hostile* as if it was two words. "I take it you speak for her, then?"

"Nobody needs to speak for her."

"I don't understand this at all," said the politician, his heavy face reddening. "Why are you here, then?"

"We were invited. What's the deal?"

"Can you stop Miss Collingsworth from damaging our enterprise?" asked Conrad.

"What's it worth to you?"

"We'll give you fifty thousand."

"You'll make that a thousand times over."

"Make it one hundred thousand, then."

"One hundred thousand dollars?" I said.

Conrad smiled. "That's right."

"In exchange for what?"

"You leave town, and the gir—I mean, Miss Collingsworth keeps quiet."

"Keeps quiet about which thing? She has copious information."

Conrad sipped his whiskey. He and Alec York looked at each other. Conrad said, "About those things she talked with Chief York about."

"You mean about Cavalerri?"

"No," said Chief York. "About Francine Wilson. She doesn't mention the affair we were having."

"That too," said Conrad. "But mostly we don't want her to go public with the land deal."

I pretended to be confused. "Land deal?" I said. "I thought you were worried about Chief York taking a fall for interfering with the murder investigation. And about Conrad's bodyguard trying to murder a police detective. What difference will it make to the Disney people if you came by the land in creative ways? I don't see how that hurts you."

"They'll shy away from us if there is any suggestion of impropriety," said Justin York. "Alec became somewhat heavy-handed dealing with some of the locals. However, it was necessary to the enterprise." He sat up, put an arm on his brother's shoulder, and patted it. "This will be a good thing for North Branson. For all of Missouri, for that matter. We need you to persuade Miss Collingsworth to temper her report so that it does not touch on those acquisitions that might be considered, uh, sensitive."

"All Sandy has to do, then," I said, "is leave out the information about coercion, extortion, and any cover-up of investigations in progress? That right?"

York nodded. Something a wire wouldn't pick up on. I didn't know if I had enough. Nobody had really said specifically that they'd done anything illegal, though they had connected Alec York to some questionable manueverings.

"Sounds fair," I said. "Okay then, one hundred thousand dollars."

"Swope, take care of this man, will you?" said Conrad. With an electronic button, Archibald popped open the trunk of the Lexus, which yawned open like a coffin lid.

"That's one hundred large for Chastity Yablonski."

"What?"

"I figure one million for Francine Wilson and another million for Fred Merrill. What are we up to now, Chick?"

"Never was any good at math, but I'd guess two million, one hundred thousand." As he spoke, Chick's eyes took inventory of our situation. "I'd like a case of Dom Perignon, too."

"Well, you pig," I said.

"Don't want to feel left out."

"This is ludicrous," said the lieutenant governor.

"Two million dollars is a shitload of scratch," said Conrad.

"I'm not done," I said. "I want something for myself."

Alec York and Conrad looked at each other, then at me. Conrad said, "What would that be?"

"I want the man who raped Sandy Collingsworth imprisoned."

"We can't give you that."

"You're not listening. You have no choice. I want him castrated, his head on a pole, or his worthless carcass in prison. Your choice."

"I have had enough of this," Lieutenant Governor York said. "This whole conversation is offensive."

"Shut up, York," I said. "You don't have the capacity to be offended."

Justin York drummed his fingers on the hood of the Mercedes. Swope Archibald looked as if he'd just swallowed a cotton ball. Conrad lit a cigarette. Chick sipped whiskey and amused himself with some private thought. Sleepy Joe did his imitation of a statue. In the distance I could hear the low hum of traffic.

Conrad took a good belt from his whiskey glass, swallowed, and said, "There is no reason to be contrary. You come here swole up as a penned rooster and ask for impossible shit."

"Man has a way with a simile," said Chick.

"That's why he's a star," I said.

" 'Swole up as a penned rooster.' It sings, doesn't it?"

"I'm gettin' awful goddamned sick and tired of trying to be nice to you boys. You interested in our offer or not?"

"Not," I said.

"Then, why'd you come by?"

"Because you're crowding the plate, and I wanted to sail one under your chin. You're involved in a fraudulent land deal and a pair of murders, and someone assaulted Sandy, and when I find out who I'm going to dislocate his life."

"If we can't deal," said Conrad, "then we'll have to lean the other way."

"You want to clarify that?"

"I might have to have Joe kick the shit out of you."

"Boy, southern hospitality ain't what it used to be," said Chick.

"There's no reverence for tradition anymore," I said.

"That Chuck Norris shit won't do you no good against a professional boxer," said Conrad, smiling. "Joe, throw out the trash."

Joe wasn't moving.

"Joe!" said Conrad, more sharply now. "Did you hear me, boy? Get over here."

"I heard you," the boxer said. "I'm a bodyguard, not a boy, not a hood. I didn't sign on to beat people up. Or to protect guys who abuse women." He looked at Alec York. "And I especially don't like guys with short eyes."

"Goddam it, Joe," said Conrad. "You do what I say, or you're fired."

He laughed a silent laugh that caused his shoulder to raise along with his crossed arms on his chest. "I quit."

"Doesn't look good, Trav," said Chick. "The only guy we were worried about just switched uniforms."

Conrad smiled and leaned against the Mercedes. "Y'all too cocky. My old daddy was a gambler. He always said win if you can, lose if you must, but always cheat." He swiveled his head back a quarter turn and said, "You back there, Jerry?"

"Sure," said a voice, stepping from behind the tree shredder, gun in hand. Jerry was a blond man with an eye patch. "Hello, asshole," he said, pointing the gun at my midsection. "Good to see you again. Told you to get the fuck out of town, didn't I?"

38

Nice gun, Jerry," I said. I hoped Dave Snipes was listening closely. "What kind is it? Glock?"

"Sig-Sauer," said the one-eyed man. "Difference it make?"

"Hate to get shot by some cheap piece of iron. Want to go out with style."

"Always got something to say, don'tcha?" said Jerry. "But not for much longer." He smiled.

"Not here," said Justin York, running a hand through his hair. "Damn! How did I allow myself to become a part of this?"

"Same as me," said Conrad. "Power. And money. And plenty of both. So quit your bellyaching. Unbecoming in a man about to become a governor and a millionaire." He turned his attention to Chick and me. "Y'all can just relax. Nobody's gonna shoot you. No need. Not yet, anyway."

He walked forward, pushed back his jacket, and placed both hands on his lower back, elbows out. "Got one more card to play before I upset the table," he said. "We already knew the Collingsworth woman was headed out. We been watching the airports.

Cecil's waiting for her in Denver. We give the word, she don't make it home tonight. You already got a pretty good idea who we got Cecil and Jerry from. Their employers want to see gambling get legalized in this area. They got some interesting ideas about doing business, if you know what I mean." He smiled. "So here's the deal. You take the fifty grand, get the hell out of Dodge, and your little heifer don't come up lame. And, so you or her don't get any grand ideas about journalistic integrity and such, you need to know that if she airs any of this, somebody'll be by to split her like a ripe watermelon."

"Anything happens to her," I said, feeling the emotion ride up my back like a jagged fingernail, "there won't be anyplace you can hide I won't find you and square things."

He laughed. "May not be necessary, son. You're way too excitable. Take the fifty, walk out of here, and everything will be as fine as country wine. We'll proceed, and the assistant governor here and his brother will clean things up. You'll have some nice pocket money, and your woman is safe. Otherwise, well, you know how it is. Business decision."

I looked at Chick. He shrugged, then said, "What the hell, Wyatt. Let's deal and ride out of here." He was buying us some time.

I made a show of considering it. "It has some merit," I said. "But we've got a lot of time invested in this. Maybe I'd feel better about it if I knew exactly what has been going down. Tell you what. You fill in a couple of blanks, and I'll take the money and talk to Sandy. How's that sound?"

"Keep talking," said Conrad.

"Who killed Chastity?"

"The hooker? They got the right guy locked up for it. The cop, Pethmore. He was into kinky sex, isn't that right, Alec?" York nodded. "He was into S and M stuff, choking her to increase the force of climax. He went too far and strangled her to death."

"If that's true, then who took a shot at me at the marina?"

"That was Tad."

"You send him?"

He smiled. "I wouldn't do that. Hell, I'm the friendly type. He just didn't like you and your friend."

"Now he's off the board, too. How does Chastity figure, then? Somebody talked her into calling me and Sandy."

"Y'all were getting too close," Conrad said. "Robby Blue said it was just a matter of time before the hooker started yakking to you and the woman. She knew about Alec and the Wilson girl at the Red Cedar. She had a john in another room the night the college girl died. Saw York leav—"

"That's enough," said Alec York, rising. He pulled a Glock auto pistol from under his jacket. "There's no reason to tell him any of this."

"Relax, Alec," said Conrad. "This all's just hearsay now the hooker's passed on."

"It was you, wasn't it?" I said to York. "You killed Francine. Then you raped Sandy."

He pointed the Glock at me. "Don't get overwrought about it. I didn't kill the girl. Didn't do the other thing, either. Goddammit, Travis, you talk too much."

"Way I've got it figured, Tad and Robby Blue or someone else were out at the marina," I said. "I doubt Conrad would let his sweet country self get personally involved. He hires things done. Shaunessy's a puncher; not his style to shoot someone from cover. Jerry and Cecil were in the motel parking lot all night. That leaves you, Chief. Or Bredwell. I choose you.

"What you didn't figure on was Pethmore killing Chastity, then trying to frame me," I said. "Yeah, I like it. Then you found out about your wife and Merrill, so you told Conrad that Merrill's investigation was getting too close so Travis sends Tad and Robby Blue to pop Merrill."

"You've got an active imagination," he said.

"You were in a big hurry to talk to Sandy when she woke up at the hospital. I think you were checking to see if she remembered anything. You had access to scopolamine. You put it in her water. Yeah." I nodded my head, settling on it. "It makes sense that way. You had to make sure she didn't remember anything."

"Guess we'll never know," he said.

I looked at him. Felt something cooking inside me, popping and bubbling over. The dragon was loose, beating leathery wings against my skull. I wondered if I could reach York and break his jaw before his gun could end my life. York saw it in my eyes. "Get it out of your head, Storme," he said. "There's no way you'll get to me before I shoot you. I didn't do it, anyway."

"Better shoot now," I said. "One way or another, I'm going to burn you down."

"This isn't going to work," said the police chief. "I've met the Collingsworth woman. She is too full of herself and her mission to be bought off. We are reaching a point where we have little choice but to simplify the equation."

"Let's get out of here first," said Justin York. "None of us can afford to be a part of this. That's what we've got Jerry for."

"Maybe Jerry ain't enough to take both of us," said Chick.

How far off was Snipes? "You kill us, and it'll call too much attention to what's going on. That'd be stupid, and I don't think you're stupid."

I heard a car nearing the resort and turn in. Snipes?

The group looked expectantly in the direction of the noise. The cooling evening air had caused the breeze to lie down. Everything was more pronounced. Sounds carried, and objects seemed to possess more clarity, as if someone had adjusted the knob on a huge television set.

"Besides," I said, "we've got company. Hard to whack somebody if you got witnesses."

The car came into view, a nondescript blue Chevy. There were two people inside. The driver was Officer Bredwell. The passenger was female.

Sharon Keltner.

Maybe it just wasn't my day.

Bredwell got out of the car, dragging Sharon by the arm along the front seat behind him. He pulled her out of the car, and she stumbled onto the ground. He jerked her to her feet, and one of her shoes came off. As she reached down to pick it up, he pulled on the arm again, and her hair snapped like a flag in the wind. She began crying.

"Found her, Chief," said Bredwell.

"Please," said Sharon. Her face was stained with trails of mascara, and there was a bruise on one cheek. "I don't know anything. Just . . . let me go . . . p-please!"

"Shut up!" said Bredwell.

"You're a real tough guy, aren't you, Bredwell," I said. "Beating up on college girls."

Bredwell's eyes had the look of a man who had been inside a dark hole for too long. The pupils were dilated and stark against the whites. I'd seen it before. In Vietnam. PCP. Angel dust. An animal tranquilizer that raged through your system like a lightning-spooked horse, wild-eyed and crazed.

"Fuck you, Storme."

"Jerry," said Conrad. "Get the girl." Jerry put away his gun and took Sharon from Bredwell. Bredwell relinquished her and glared at me with glazed eyes.

"Please," said Sharon, her eyes pleading. "Help me."

"Hang on, Sharon," I said. "It's going to be all right. Just a bunch of guys with wires loose in their heads."

"Take her over to the shredder," said Alec York. "And turn it on."

"What've you got in mind?" asked Conrad.

"Maybe there's a way to still salvage something from this. If they are too noble to deal for money, maybe they'll do so for the girl's life."

Jerry pulled the girl to the shredder. He started it, and it whirred to life.

"What is he . . . ," said Sharon as she looked from the shredder to York. Jerry pulled her up onto the lip of the machine and held her arm over the feeding chute. "Noooo!" she wailed. The cry was plaintive and haunting, sweeping through the quadrant like a icy winter wind.

"You bastards," said Chick. "He hurts her, and you guys have bought the fucking whirlwind." There was fury in his face, a mirror of the bitter anger burning inside me.

"What is it you want from us, York?" I said.

"A guarantee that your bitch won't blow this project."

I felt my teeth setting on edge. I exhaled. "What else?"

"There's no way we can trust these boys," said Conrad.

"Sure we can," said Alec York. "They don't have anything on us yet. Storme doesn't want to see the girl mutilated. Do you, Storme? I'm asking you a question. Better answer."

"No," I said. "Let her go. We'll give you what you want."

"Not yet," said York. "He also doesn't want his lady to run into Cecil." He was enjoying himself now. He liked control. "Isn't that right, Storme?"

I nodded.

While we were talking, Bredwell had moved closer to me and was looking into my face with unfocused eyes.

"I don't fucking like you," said the cop.

"You ought to lay off the dust, Bredwell. You're not coping with it very well."

"I've had about enough of your mouth, buddy." He pulled his nunchaku from its sheath and began to twirl it beside him.

"Getta hold of yourself, boy," said Conrad.

Bredwell was weaving the nunchaku in a figure-eight pattern close to my face. "Whatta you think of this, punk?" said Bredwell.

I held one hand up, and with my other hand I began to loosen my belt buckle. The others were watching Bredwell with the fascination of monkeys. "Take it easy," I said. "We're about to get this resolved."

I heard the sound of several car engines, coming fast now. "You're fucked, guys," said Chick. "That's the cavalry. We're wired for sound."

"Bredwell," said York, panic on his face. "Sheath that damn thing."

"I had it with him," said Bredwell, his words mushy. "Tired of him fucking with me." The arc of the nunchaku was close enough now I could feeling it pushing the air past my face. I took a step back and quickly pulled on my belt. It slithered from the loops, and I snapped it into the fulcrum of the nunchaku. The nunchaku folded itself around the belt, ceasing its gyrations like a toy whose batteries had run down. I reached out, grabbed the oriental weapon, pulled Bredwell to me, and punched him in the face with my free hand.

Then everything went to hell in a hurry.

As Bredwell's head snapped back, Jerry started to push Sharon's arm down into the shredder. Chick freed his Walther and shot Jerry through the upper body, and the thug released Sharon, who fell to the ground in a heap. Justin York opened the door of the Mercedes and jumped inside, covering his head with his arms. Travis Conrad pulled up a big Colt auto, and Chick shot him through the shoulder. Conrad dropped the gun and fell to his knees in agony.

Swope Archibald started to jump into the car, but Shaunessy grabbed him by the collar, pulled him out, and held him.

Bredwell recovered and tried to grab me just as Alec York took a shot in my direction. There was a sound like a baseball bat striking a bag of feed, and Bredwell fell forward on me.

I threw him aside as Alec York fired two errant shots at Chick before York ran between the condominiums. Jerry, though wounded, had managed to pull his gun and was spraying bullets in our direction. I kneeled, trying to free my Browning as Chick took aim and placed two shots dead center through the body of the patch-eyed shooter. Jerry stopped shooting.

Three police cars roared into the quadrant in a cloud of dust. Dave Snipes jumped out of the passenger side of his unit with his gun drawn and his badge out.

"North Branson Police!" he said. "Everybody freeze! Get your hands where we can see them. Now!"

Chick and I both laid our guns on the ground as Police Chief Alec York disappeared between the buildings and down the slope of the hill.

Justin York had gotten back out of the car. "Officer," he said, "arrest these men."

"You too, sir," said Snipes. "Put your hands on your head and step away from the vehicle."

"Why, this is preposterous," said the lieutenant governor. "Do you have any idea who I am?"

"Sure do," said Snipes. "You're the guy I'm placing under arrest. Kind of makes you want to rethink your position on affirmative action, doesn't it?"

39

We didn't find Alec York. He had vanished like the tourists who disappeared from North Branson after a hard freeze.

Justin York, Swope Archibald, and a wounded Travis Conrad were taken into custody by Snipes and his officers. Bredwell died instantly after being accidentally shot by his boss. Jerry, the patch-eyed hood, died of his wounds the next day. He never regained consciousness. Joe Shaunessy was arrested with Justin York and Conrad, and later released in view of the testimony of Chick and myself.

Alec York, in absentia, was charged with fraud, manslaughter, and attempted murder, and a warrant was issued for his arrest, thus clearing the boyfriend, Kenneth Mantle. Further investigation of York's activities revealed drugs and several thousand dollars missing from that which had been seized in the recent publicized drug raid.

York was not charged with the rape of Sandra Collingsworth.

Cecil, also known as Rude Dog Chaney, was arrested by the FBI at the Denver airport. He was carrying an unregistered concealed weapon. He also had an outstanding warrant in connection with the murder of a mob boss who had been killed in the desert outside Las Vegas in May of the year.

Sandy was the first to break the story on national television on *Morning Coffee Break* and followed that with an article she wrote for the *Los Angeles Times*. Jill Maxwell's account and byline appeared in several national newspapers. Both she and Sandy were careful to leave out the name of a certain ex–NFL star.

After Sandy turned in her story, we spent a few days recuperating at my Colorado cabin. The emotions she had been dealing with hit Sandy with the force of a wrecking ball. We slept late, and I fixed breakfast for her, and we hiked the surrounding mountains. She spent many hours sitting on my deck or at the huge bay window, looking out over the Little Silver River, her eyes fixed on some faraway object I couldn't see. I didn't interrupt at those times.

Sometimes, her eyes would fill and she would wipe them, absently, with the backs of her hands. We had little physical contact and then only when she initiated it. I was careful with her pain. I had no solutions and no magic twelve-step program; only my presence to offer her. She struggled with her knowledge, and I watched her. It was hard to watch.

Conversations were tentative, as if we had forgotten each other and were becoming reacquainted. My attempts to lighten the atmosphere with humor were met with wan smiles and blue eyes that apologized.

At night, sleep, which often was, at best, fitful for me, became elusive. On the second night, I sat on the dark deck, the mountain air frigid on my face, and smoked cigars. And I thought about Alec York and what he had robbed from us.

On the third day it snowed. The snow fell in large, gentle flakes, floating and sparkling and covering the mountains where it glistened in the sunlight. She watched, and the light of its whiteness reflected in her eyes.

"I want to go skiing," she said.

"Okay," I said. "Let's go."

We packed up and spent four days at Winterpark, and she taught me to ski.

"It's odd you never learned to ski after living this many years in the mountains." she said one evening while we were eating dinner at the resort restaurant. The color had returned to her face, and her eyes had regained the childlike sparkle I loved.

"I haven't had time to indulge in the bourgeois pursuits of the elitist class. My life is too chock-full of significance for trivial pursuits," I said. It was good to have a lighthearted conversation again. "Are you going to finish your steak, or just worry it to death?"

She ignored me. "I called the TV station in Springfield this morning. The police officially dropped the charges against Kenneth Mantle today. He was already out on bond. Tell me something, Wyatt. How was Kenneth Mantle able to afford George Fairchild?"

"You know George," I said, eyeing her steak. "He's a nice guy. Maybe he was in a philanthropic mood."

"Yes, I know George. And I like him. But he's a lawyer, and lawyers get paid. And few are paid as well as George Fairchild."

"Probably some booster club member. Lot of money around the lake."

"Uh-huh," she said. "There's no chance it was some softhearted former pro with more money than brains who provided the funds, then?"

"I hate to see you waste food," I said. "Do you know that what's on your plate would feed a family of five in Beverly Hills?"

"You're so transparent," she said. "I can see right through you."

"I'd known you could do that, I would have worn underwear."

She smiled, and then that faraway look came back into her eyes. "Have you heard from Chick?" she asked, looking down at her plate.

"Yeah," I said. "Today."

"Has he turned up anything?"

"No. He hasn't. Don't worry, hon, he will."

She picked up her fork and stabbed at her meat. Her hand was shaking, almost imperceptibly, but shaking nonetheless. She put down the fork and placed her hands in her lap. "I just don't know what to think," she said. "Or how to feel about things. There's nothing I can do. I've never felt so helpless in my life. I don't like hating someone so much, and I don't like myself for wishing . . . for wishing, well, you can imagine what I'm wishing."

"It's natural. I feel the same. Chick will find York," I said. "When he does, he will turn him over to the authorities."

"But," she said, "that won't end the memory of what . . . of what he did."

"No," I said. "No, it probably won't."

"What are we going to do?"

I looked at her, into the face of the woman I loved more than I loved my own life, and said, "I don't know."

But I had other thoughts. Somehow I would make Alec York pay. I had the hunter's advantage. I could bait the trail. I could build a fire. I could wait.

Then I would be ready.

40

~~~

He was ready in case this happened," Chick said in one late night phone conversation. He was calling from Missouri. "He is a contingency guy. It's why he was a good police chief. Besides the drug money he lifted, he must've had money squirreled away and a place to go to ground if things went sour."

"Yeah," I said.

"Still want him, don't you?"

"He'll come to me."

"I'd say you're right. You'll be hard to find in Colorado."

"I'd be easier to find in Missouri."

There was a pause at his end. "I know what you're thinking, Storme. Yeah, you could draw him in if you came back to Missouri. But you be ready if he comes."

"I'm looking forward to it."

"Your desires are becoming a little twisted, partner. Don't take him lightly," said Chick. "He's a freak, man. Not your normal sicko. He's smart and knows how the police work. He'll know what things to avoid. Besides, there's nothing inside him. No

compassion, no humor, no remorse. He's wounded and dangerous, and you're the guy wounded him. He's got nothing to lose.
Stay ready. Everywhere and always. And have a backup plan if
things go bad."

Sandy began to have trouble sleeping again. On more than one
occasion I held her in my arms until she could sleep while I
thought about Alec York.

I wanted to hurt him. Drive a stake through his heart and make
him twist in the wind. Revenge was driving my thoughts. It had
been a long time, but I was starting to think about long, burning
swallows of Jack Daniel's whiskey. But that was from another
time. And I had made myself a deal. If I lied to myself, then I was
not who I thought I was. Besides, it would slow me down when I
did what I wanted to do.

What I had to do.

Alec York's whereabouts were unknown.

He was at large.

Sandy's recovery at Winterpark had been brief, and the demons
were back. Without warning she would become morose and depressed and given to crying jags when fatigued. During these
times I would remain quiet and ride them out, comforting her
when I could. After three weeks, they became less frequent and of
shorter duration.

"I'm getting better," she said one afternoon after we had hiked
the mountains near my cabin. Her face was flushed, and the
musky scent of her exertion was exhilarating. It is a very hard
thing to love someone the way I love Sandra Collingsworth. Even
harder to watch that person hurt. But the catharsis of the injury
brought us closer. She learned to deal with her wound, a wound
no man, try as he might, could understand.

And the knowledge of her injury and the extent of it caused the bitterness inside me to callous over. As it toughened, it gave way to discernment and resolve.

I stayed with her until the network sent her to California to interview Governor Pete Wilson. She wanted to go back to work and prevailed upon me to take a few days to myself and do some hunting.

"I'm much better, Wyatt," she said. "Sooner or later I have to do this myself. I know you will stay beside me forever if I ask you. Despite your overprotective tendencies, you are a comfort. And if you were less protective, you would not be who you are. And who you are, I never want to change. You are uncontrollable and are two generations behind, but I love you, you hardheaded, high-testosterone Jeremiah Johnson."

"Wait a minute," I said. "You mean you don't think I'm a progressive, sensitive nineties guy?"

"No," she said. "You are the *Tyrannosaurus rex* of American males."

"Thank God," I said.

"Besides, we can't allow him to rule our lives," said Sandy.

I agreed with that in theory but knew the reality of the shadow that had lived inside me since Vietnam. I could not close the book on Alec York until I wrote his last chapter.

Intuitively, I knew it was the same with him.

I knew he would come. He was coming.

It was time to make it easier for him to find me.

Sandy left and went to California, and I returned to my Missouri cabin to do some bow hunting for white-tailed deer. And to assuage my anxieties, I sent Chick to shadow her. Whether she liked it or not.

There would be no repeat performances of the disaster in North Branson.

The Missouri autumn had peaked, and the days were growing shorter. The trees began to resemble multiarmed, kaleidoscope-fingered scarecrows, and the moon hung in the late autumn sky like a pumpkin.

Uncharacteristically, I made myself visible while I was at my cabin. I granted, solicited actually, an interview with a *Kansas City Star* reporter, telling all of Missouri that I would be hunting at my cabin, alone, for the next two weeks.

The trail was baited.

Then I waited.

I hunted whitetail deer every day while Sandy was in California. I called her daily.

I filled my tag on a Wednesday in early November, taking a nice eight-pointer as he pawed the ground, sniffing at a scrape. He wasn't the deer I wanted but was too nice to pass up. It was two weeks before gun season started, leaving me with little to do until quail season opened. Each day I cut wood.

Each day I carried the Browning nine on my hip. Each day I practiced shooting it—drawing and firing from several positions. I went through several boxes of shells while I waited.

At night, with the Browning under my pillow and a loaded shotgun under the bed, I dreamed of the rice paddies and the insects and the searing heat and the sudden pouring rains and the sucking mud of Vietnam. During the day I cut wood, hauled it in a bruised 1973 Ford pickup I had bought for three hundred dollars, unloaded the wood, and ricked it up against the back of my cabin until I had enough to last through the winter.

And I thought of Sandy. And Francine Wilson.

And the bitterness of what Alec York had done burned inside me like the first ember in a forest fire.

Then he finally came.

It was mid-November. It had been raining for two days. A cold, soul-drenching rain that hissed against the windows and dripped off the limbs of the barren trees in a cascade of heavy drops, which slapped against my hat and clothes like water balloons.

I kept a fire burning in the fireplace.

The day he came I had been out in the woods, checking to see if the buck I'd tried to take during bow season was still haunting the same stretch of woods. I wore a hooded camouflage rain poncho. Before entering the cabin, I lifted a flap of the canvas that covered the pile of wood and selected a few logs.

He was waiting under the deck, concealed in the shadows from the boards of the deck. I had no idea how long he had been waiting.

"Hello, Storme," he said, stepping from underneath the deck. He had the Glock in his hand. "Remember me?"

I considered him dully over the load of firewood in my arms. His face was covered with a scraggly beard, and his eyes were glazed with fatigue and hate.

"I'll have to remember to put mothballs under my deck," I said. "Keep the snakes away."

"Excellent," he said. "I was hoping you'd have something to say. Makes what I came to do more satisfying."

"Might as well come in out of the rain," I said, looking back into his eyes. "I'd as soon kill you inside as out here."

He laughed. "You are delightful, though delusionary. I'm the one with the gun."

I felt a dullness behind my eyes, and my voice echoed in my ears. "Won't be enough," I said.

He laughed, then gestured toward the cabin with the gun. "After you, then."

41

He stood there, his gun trained on my heart. I turned away from the fire and faced him. Rainwater dripped from my poncho. He smiled and said, "Well, Storme. You probably weren't expecting to see me again, were you?"

"Cancer's hard to get rid of," I said. I felt a dullness inside. "Usually have to cut it out."

"Well, that's not a friendly attitude, is it? And after I've come all this way to see you. It would seem you would be a more gracious host. Oh, yes. Please give me the gun you probably are carrying. I'll not make that mistake twice."

I reached under the poncho and pulled Robby Blue's .25 Beretta from my jacket pocket, placed it on the floor, and kicked it across the room toward him. "Why'd you kill Francine Wilson?" I asked.

His mouth formed a bow, and there was a strange light in his bloody eyes. He looked as if he was deciding something.

"It's very complicated," he said. "I'm not sure you'd understand. She crossed the line."

I nodded my head to keep him talking. "How?"

"She thought we were in love, which, of course, was ridiculous. She was merely a form of recreation. Then she found out about Velonne."

"That's why she went to see Cavalerri?"

"The first time. Velonne explained to her that it didn't change anything. Velonne had a more progressive attitude concerning our relationship."

"That's because she's more of a prostitute than Chastity."

"My, my. How judgmental. I'd forgotten how prudish you were for a man who played professional sports. You, better than anyone, should understand whoredom. Anyway, that's when the naïve bitch decided to try to make me jealous." His mouth pursed, and he shook his head. "Never screw college girls. They're far too unsophisticated."

I thought about it. "She tried to make you jealous with Travis Conrad."

He nodded. "But that country imbecile was drunk and forced himself on her and started bragging about the land deal we were involved with. Then she went and told Velonne about it as if to threaten us. She was a foolish girl."

"You used scopolamine to get her in the bathtub."

"Allows you complete control." He smiled, showing his capped teeth in a set line like a row of bullets. "I like that."

"You killed Chastity, didn't you? She could put you at the Red Cedar before Francine was killed. Then you framed Pethmore, who was trying to frame me."

"Pethmore is a cretin," he said. "I had him for a scapegoat regardless of how things played out. He picked up Francine one night and tried to molest her. He had a history of that."

"And you kept him on the force."

"Assured his loyalty."

"Chief York and his devoted moral cripples."

"Everything was fine until you and Easton began stirring things. I have plans for him after I'm finished with you."

"Getting to me is a lot easier than getting to Chick. Go after him, he'll kill you."

"That will make it more interesting, then, won't it?"

I didn't say anything. The giant was squeezing my heart again. I laid the firewood by the fireplace and took a hand and wiped rainwater from my face, felt the scratch of my beard. I put my hands back under the poncho.

He was oblivious to me, lost in the moment. "You certainly live out in the boondocks, don't you?" he said. "You could do anything you wanted out here, and no one would ever know. Shoot off a bazooka out here. Even kill someone." He was enjoying himself now. "Yes. You certainly could kill someone, bury them, and no one would ever know." His smile was malevolent. I had been clenching my teeth and with some effort, unclenched them. The fire behind me popped and sizzled. It was hot on the back of my legs, yet I felt it only intermittently, and then only on the periphery of my awareness.

"You're uncharacteristically closemouthed," he said. "Why is that? You're not still upset with me over the Collingsworth woman, are you?"

"Don't say her name," I said. The words hissed between my teeth.

"What?" he said. My words amused him. "Don't say her *name*? That's so . . . *provincial.* I've done more than say her name. You know that. Is that why your reception is so cold? She and I have been *intimate.*" My teeth clenched again. "But forgive me. This is difficult for you, isn't it?

"She was the best, you know," he said. "The apex. She struggled and fought. Even under the effects of the drug. Sluggishly, of course." He smiled now, amusing himself. "A woman of beauty. And unique substance. You chose well, my friend. She will be difficult, no, impossible to top. However, after I dispose of you and Easton, I'm considering a reunion visit to her. To console her, of course."

I continued to stare at him. A sensation like rabid spiders gnawed at the back of my neck.

"Why are you so reticent?" he said. "This is a reunion of sorts. Almost a celebration. I'm so happy to see you. What have you been doing?"

"Waiting for you," I said and shot him twice high in the chest.

My poncho shivered as the nine-millimeter roared. The force of the slugs spun him away from me, and he fell to the floor. His gun flew from his hand and bounded across the hardwood floor.

The echo of the Browning rang in the confines of the room.

There were two smoking black rings in my poncho. The stink of cordite reminded me of the Fourth of July.

Independence Day.

The front door burst open, slamming back against the wall, and I felt my breath catch in my chest. It was Chick, the Walther PPK held out in front of him, its dark eye searching. He was drenched with rain and his boots were covered with mud. He relaxed when he saw York lying on the floor. He looked at me. "You're shot."

I shook my head. Stuck a finger through one of the holes in the poncho. "I put them there," I said. "From the inside out."

"I followed him here," Chick said. "Got the car stuck in this damn Missouri mud. Figured he was headed here. I heard the shots. Looks like you didn't need my help."

York lay on the floor, twitching, his breath rattling in his chest. I walked across the room and stood over him. I felt a calm sweep over me, as if a fire had been extinguished. His eyes looked toward his gun six feet away.

"Funny, isn't it," I said to York, "how in the movies a guy can get shot and still function. But this is real life, and the shock power of a nine-millimeter nullifies everything else." I uncocked my pistol.

"What—" began York. He coughed for several seconds and winced each time he did.

I knelt beside him. "That cough sounds pretty bad. You ought to wear a hat in this weather." I scratched the side of my head with the barrel of the Browning. Folksy. I pulled a Buck knife from its sheath and held it up where he could see it. He wasn't dead yet. His eyes widened.

"What . . . are you . . . going to do with . . . with that?"

"When you're dead"—I could smell his blood. His fear. It smelled good.—"I'm going to cut your head off and skin you out like a skunk. There's an old well back in the woods. I'm going to toss your body in it and let the worms and the cockroaches have it. No obituary, no three-cornered flag, no twenty-one-gun salute."

"What . . . till then?"

"I'm going to watch you die," I said. My breath felt hot in my throat. "And enjoy every minute of it."

His eyes squeezed tight, and he began to whimper. "It . . . h-h-hurts."

"I'll bet it does."

"Sh-sh-shoot . . . finish it."

I clicked back the hammer on the Browning. "You should never have touched her."

He coughed again and turned his head away from me.

"Not your style, Storme," said Chick. His voice sounded disembodied, as if it were floating around inside my head. "Need a little reflection here, partner. Turn the burner down some."

"I want to watch him die," I said.

"There are worse things than dying. But do what you want. Your pain, not mine."

I thought about Kenneth Mantle. About how miserable he'd been in the county lockup.

"Cops do hard time, Wyatt," said Chick. "Let the prosecuting attorney throw him inside with the bull queers and the child molesters."

"I won't get to see it," I said.

"And Sandy don't get to see this. What's she get out of it?"

My pulse throbbed in my neck. I took a deep breath. Let it out. Slowly.

"I want to whack him as bad as you do," said Chick. "But him dying won't change the way you feel. For Sandy either. It'll just change what you are. You want to exchange that for this piece of shit? He worth it?" He stood looking at me, his gun straight down at his side. "Either way, you still gotta deal with what happened to Sandy. You don't need any residual regrets."

I dropped the gun to my side and watched the rain pound against the window. I let out a deep breath. Nodded my head. "Okay," I said. "Call the sheriff."

"You hear that, York?" Chick said. "You're going inside for all day." He picked up the phone and punched in the numbers. He explained the situation and told them they would need an ambulance.

Chick hung up the phone. "They're coming."

"Hooray," I said. I looked at Chick's boots. "Get off the floor. You're getting mud everywhere."

Chick looked at me, shook his head. "Well, that's great," he said. "You get on me but you don't say nothing to the guy bleeding all over the place."

I looked at York. The nine millimeter had broken his clavicle. Jagged white bone protruded through a hole in his shirt. The other wound was four inches lower and may have nicked a lung. He was bleeding and in pain. Still, unless he bled to death, he would live. York would live. But his life wouldn't include lunch at the club and nights in Velonne Cavalerri's bed. It was something, anyway.

I dressed York's wounds. Then we waited for the sheriff to come and arrest him.

It wasn't much. Wasn't enough, in fact.

Sorry, Sandy. It was all I could get.